Littlest Pet Shop

OPEN FOR BUSINESS

COVER BY
Nicanor Peña

COVER COLORS BY
Victoria Robado

HC ISBN: 978-1-63140-087-2
SC ISBN: 978-1-63140-257-9

17 16 15 14   1 2 3 4

® Licensed By: Hasbro

Ted Adams, CEO & Publisher
Greg Goldstein, President & COO
Robbie Robbins, EVP/Sr. Graphic Artist
Chris Ryall, Chief Creative Officer/Editor-in-Chief
Matthew Ruzicka, CPA, Chief Financial Officer
Alan Payne, VP of Sales
Dirk Wood, VP of Marketing
Lorelei Bunjes, VP of Digital Services
Jeff Webber, VP of Digital Publishing & Business Development

www.IDWPUBLISHING.com
IDW founded by Ted Adams, Alex Garner, Kris Oprisko, and Robbie Robbins

Facebook: **facebook.com/idwpublishing**
Twitter: **@idwpublishing**
YouTube: **youtube.com/idwpublishing**
Instagram: **instagram.com/idwpublishing**
deviantART: **idwpublishing.deviantart.com**
Pinterest: **pinterest.com/idwpublishing/idw-staff-faves**

Originally published in LITTLEST PET SHOP issues #1–5.

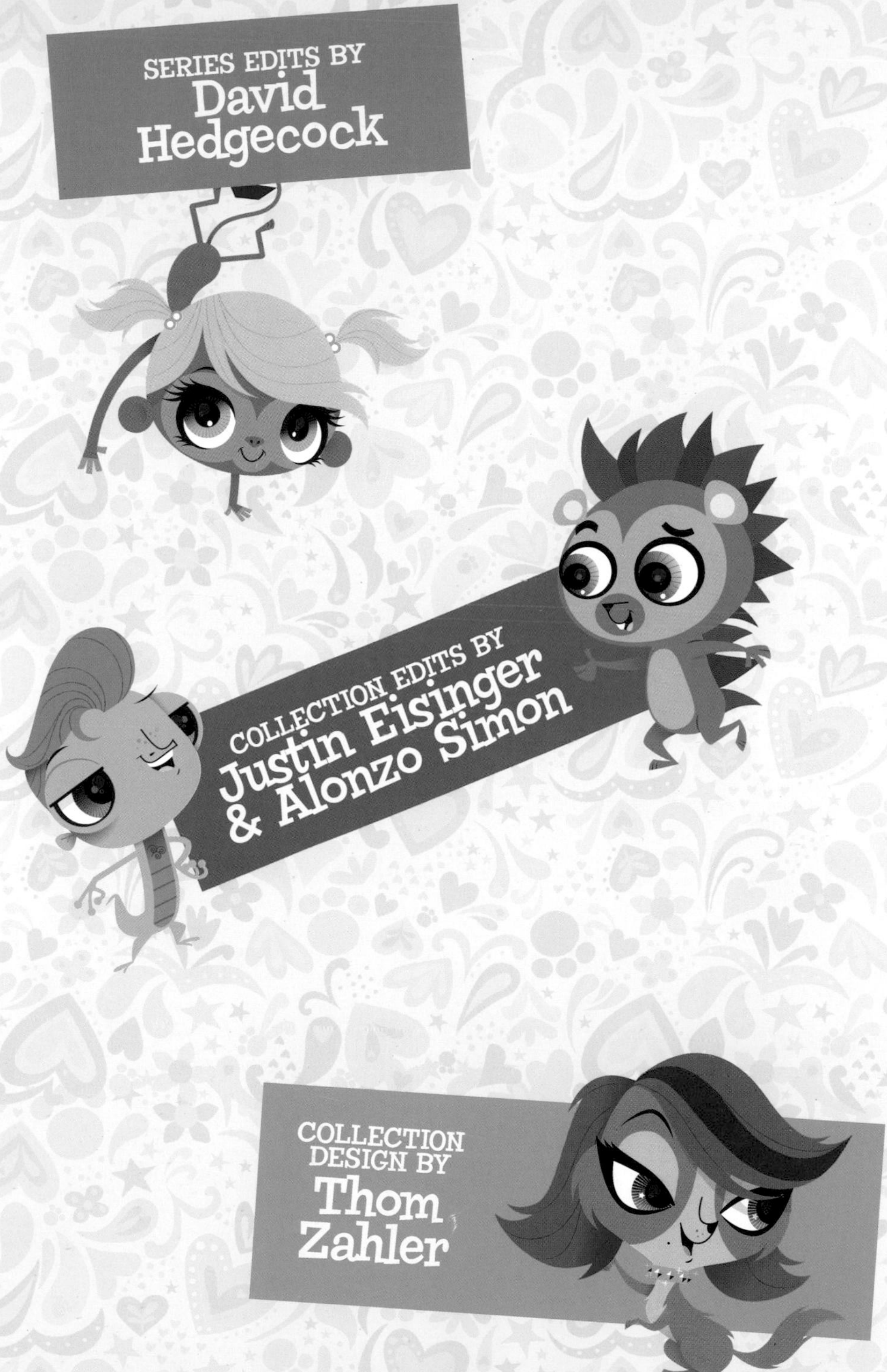
SERIES EDITS BY
David Hedgecock
COLLECTION EDITS BY
Justin Eisinger & Alonzo Simon
COLLECTION DESIGN BY
Thom Zahler

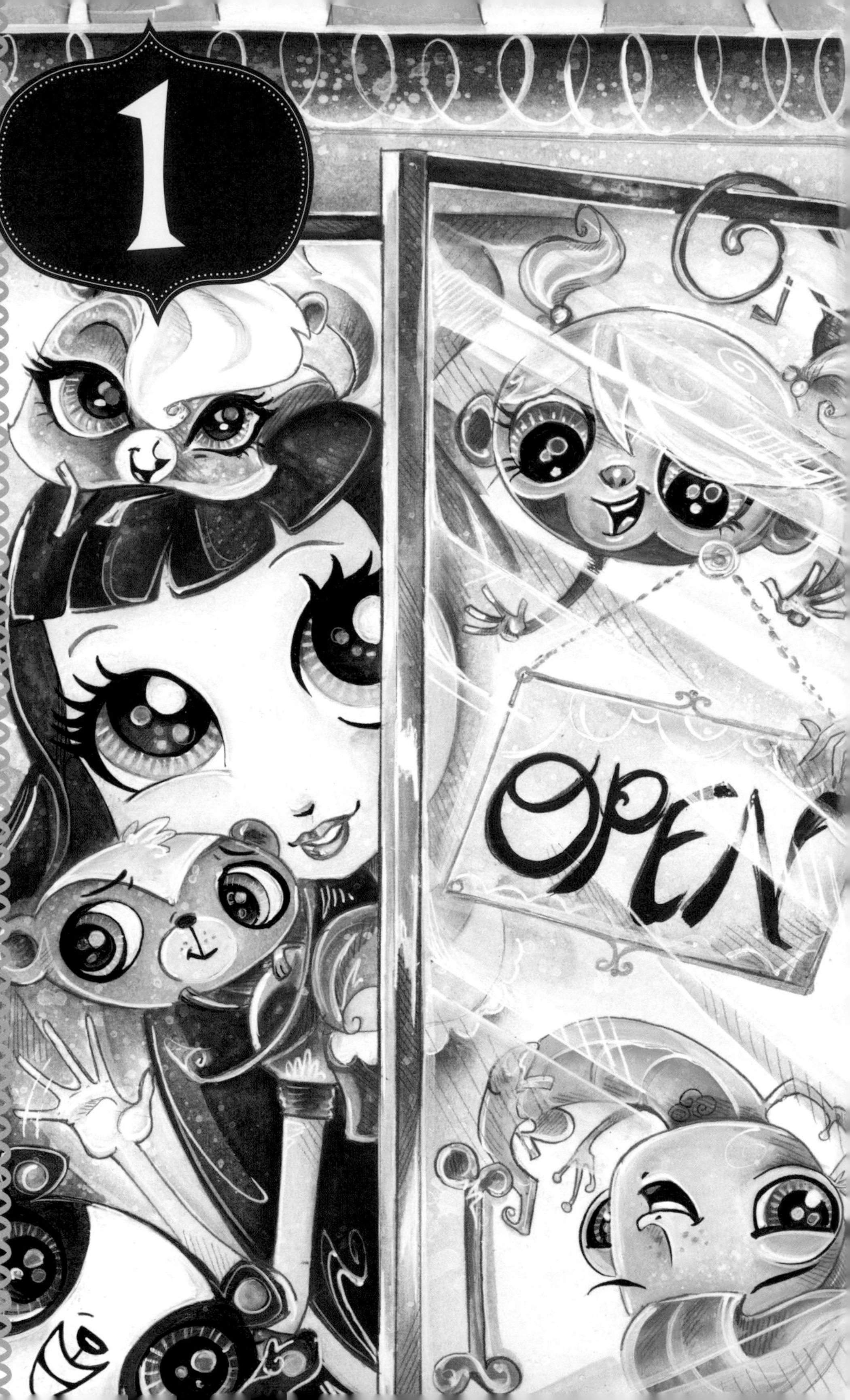
1
OPEN
art by: Sara Richard

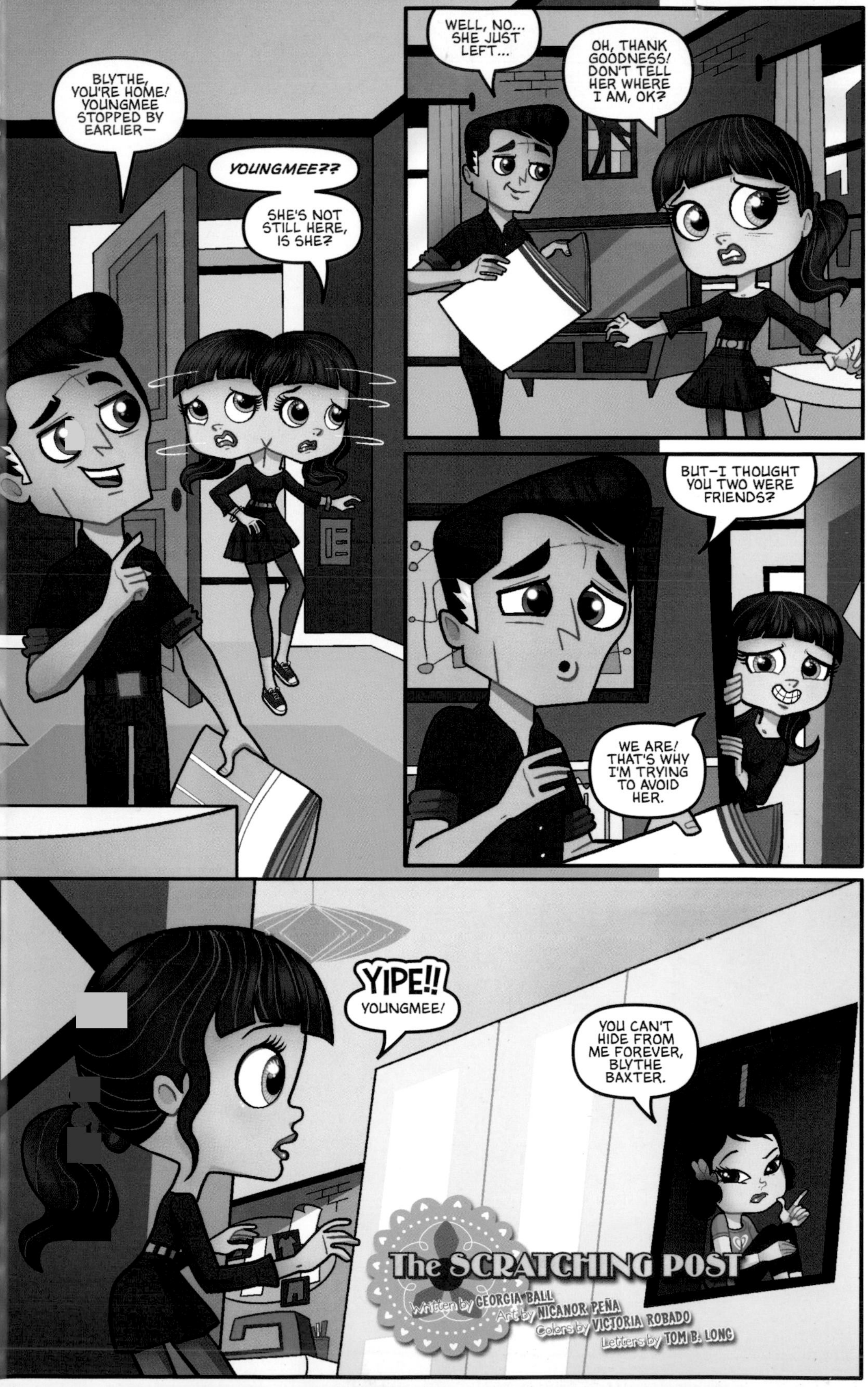
BLYTHE, YOU'RE HOME! YOUNGMEE STOPPED BY EARLIER—
YOUNGMEE??
SHE'S NOT STILL HERE, IS SHE?
WELL, NO... SHE JUST LEFT...
OH, THANK GOODNESS! DON'T TELL HER WHERE I AM, OK?
BUT–I THOUGHT YOU TWO WERE FRIENDS?
WE ARE! THAT'S WHY I'M TRYING TO AVOID HER.
YIPE!! YOUNGMEE!
YOU CAN'T HIDE FROM ME FOREVER, BLYTHE BAXTER.
The SCRATCHING POST
Written by GEORGIA BALL
Art by NICANOR PEÑA
Colors by VICTORIA ROBADO
Letters by TOM B. LONG

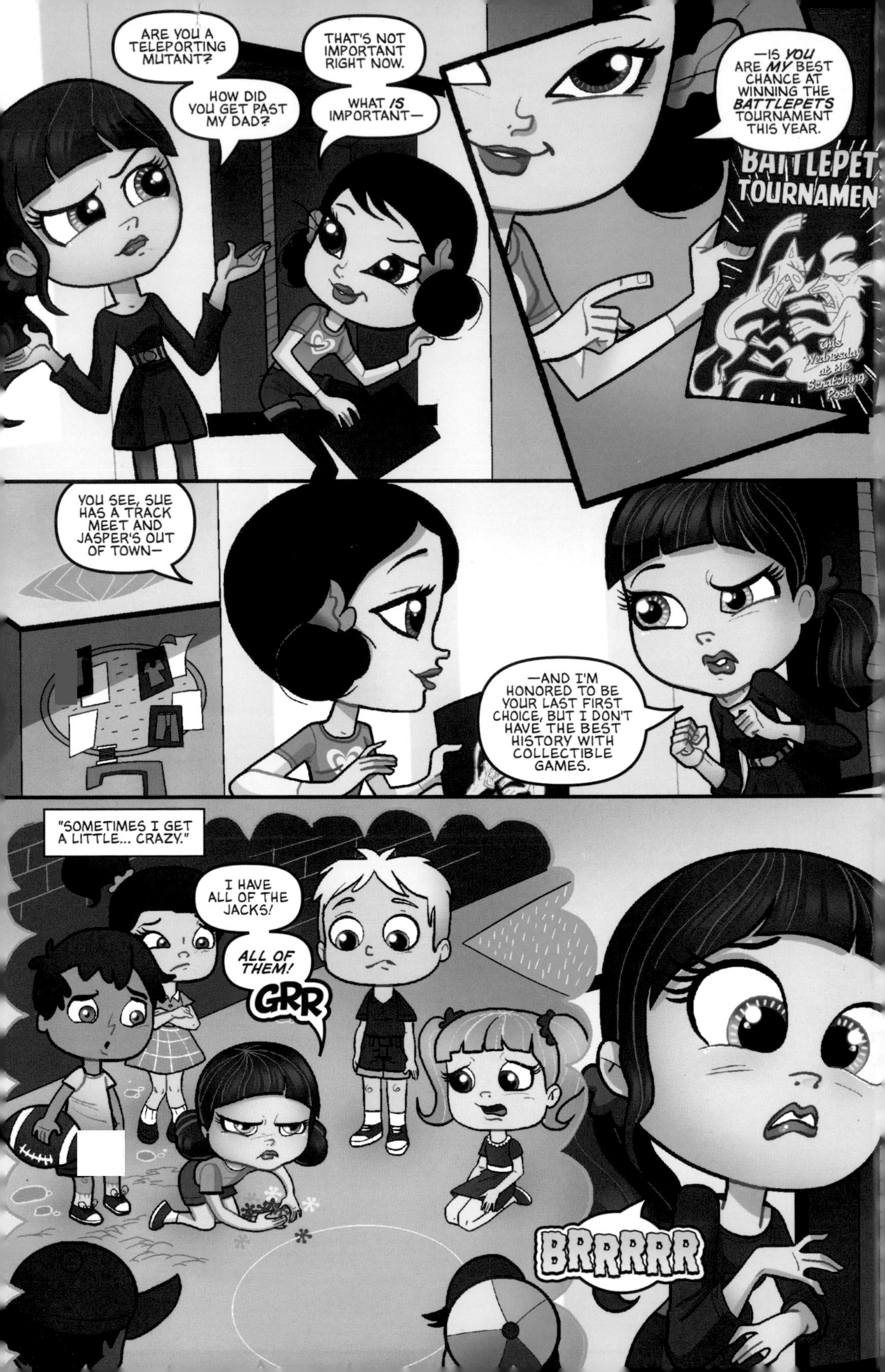
ARE YOU A TELEPORTING MUTANT?
HOW DID YOU GET PAST MY DAD?
THAT'S NOT IMPORTANT RIGHT NOW.
WHAT *IS* IMPORTANT—
—IS *YOU* ARE *MY* BEST CHANCE AT WINNING THE *BATTLEPETS* TOURNAMENT THIS YEAR.
BATTLEPET TOURNAMEN
This Wednesday at the Scratching Post!
YOU SEE, SUE HAS A TRACK MEET AND JASPER'S OUT OF TOWN—
—AND I'M HONORED TO BE YOUR LAST FIRST CHOICE, BUT I DON'T HAVE THE BEST HISTORY WITH COLLECTIBLE GAMES.
"SOMETIMES I GET A LITTLE... CRAZY."
I HAVE ALL OF THE JACKS!
ALL OF THEM!
GRR
BRRRRR

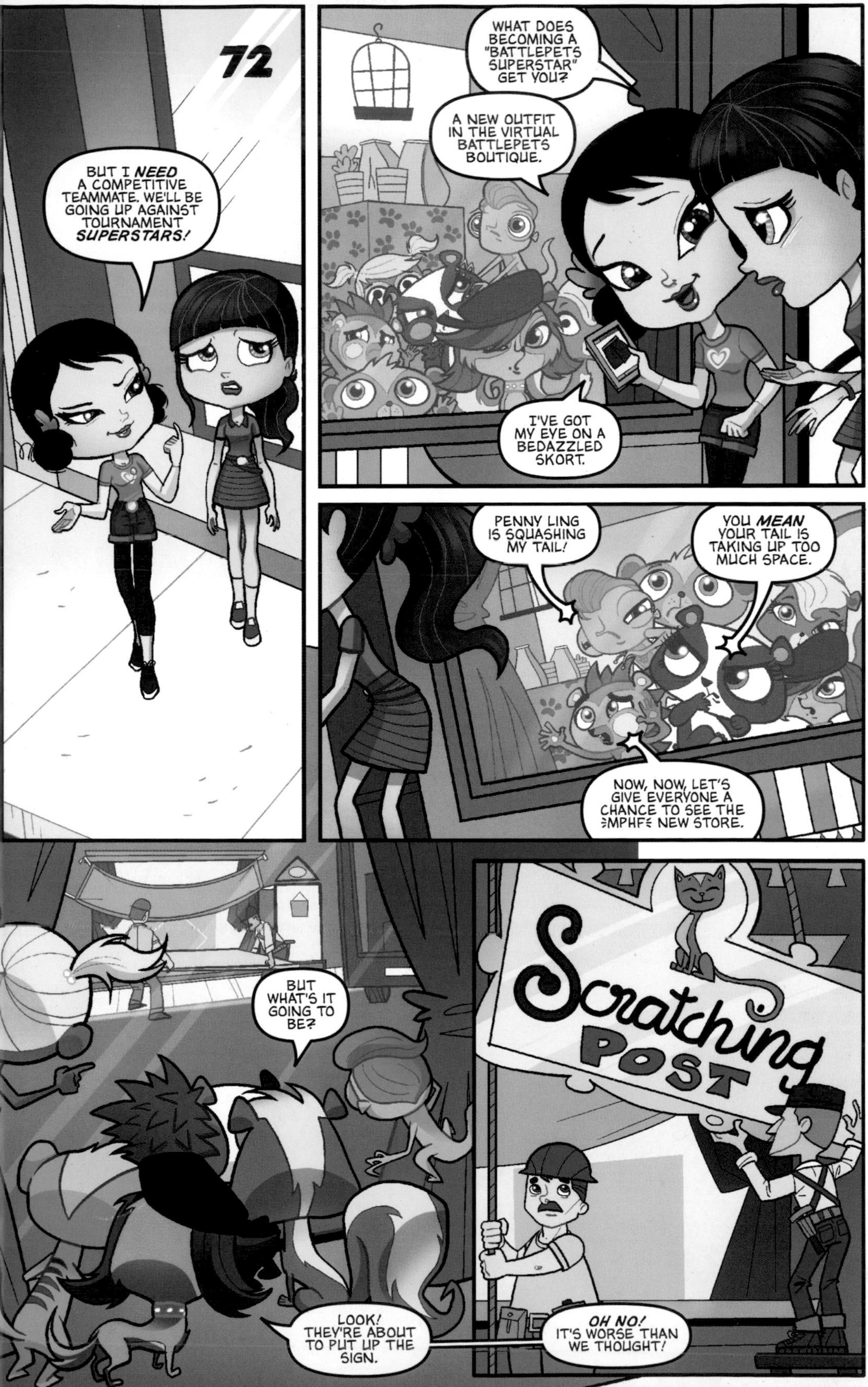
72
BUT I *NEED* A COMPETITIVE TEAMMATE. WE'LL BE GOING UP AGAINST TOURNAMENT ***SUPERSTARS!***
WHAT DOES BECOMING A "BATTLEPETS SUPERSTAR" GET YOU?
A NEW OUTFIT IN THE VIRTUAL BATTLEPETS BOUTIQUE.
I'VE GOT MY EYE ON A BEDAZZLED SKORT.
PENNY LING IS SQUASHING MY TAIL!
YOU *MEAN* YOUR TAIL IS TAKING UP TOO MUCH SPACE.
NOW, NOW, LET'S GIVE EVERYONE A CHANCE TO SEE THE *MPHF* NEW STORE.
BUT WHAT'S IT GOING TO BE?
Scratching POST
LOOK! THEY'RE ABOUT TO PUT UP THE SIGN.
OH NO! IT'S WORSE THAN WE THOUGHT!

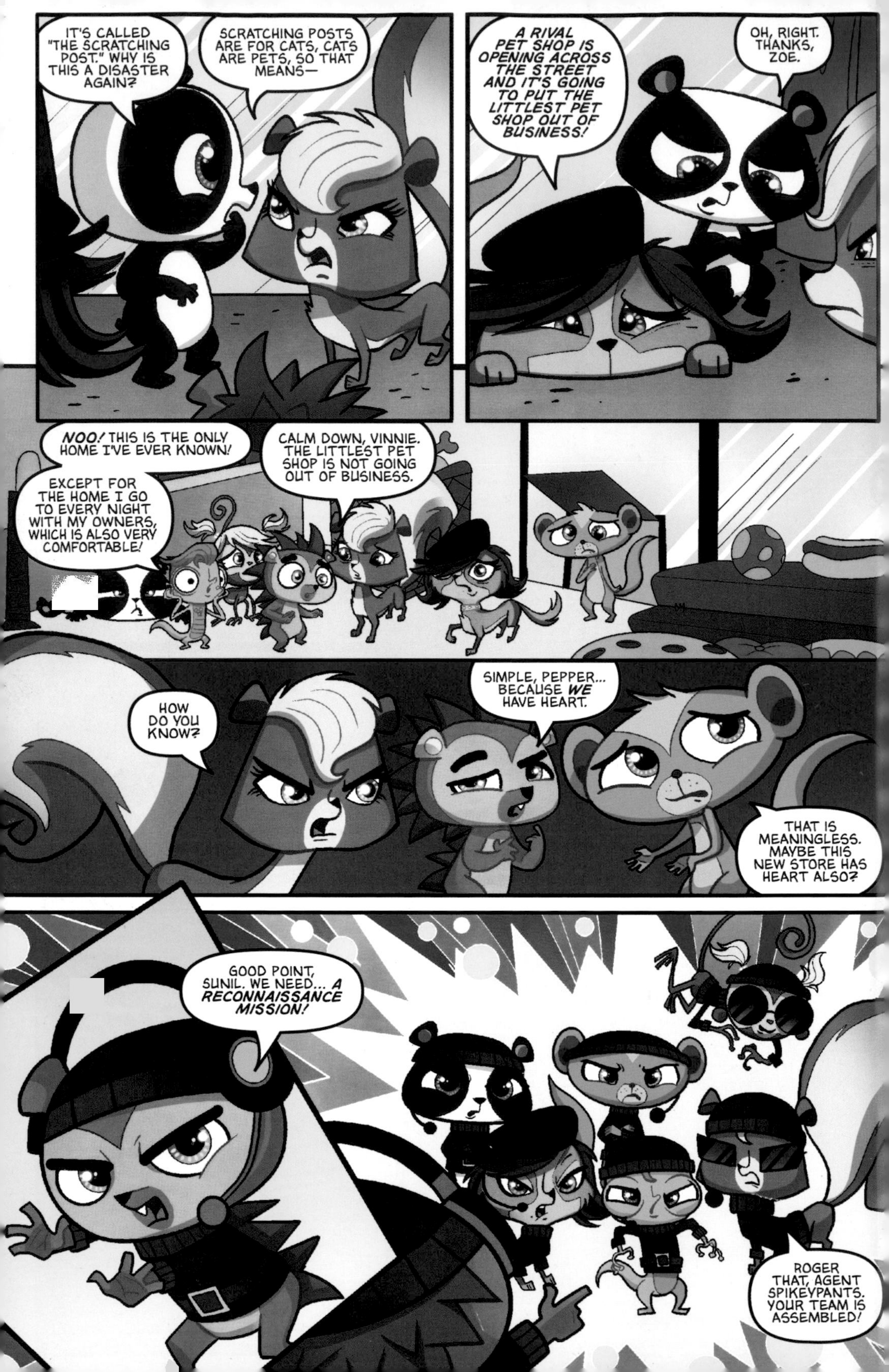
IT'S CALLED "THE SCRATCHING POST." WHY IS THIS A DISASTER AGAIN?
SCRATCHING POSTS ARE FOR CATS, CATS ARE PETS, SO THAT MEANS—
A RIVAL PET SHOP IS OPENING ACROSS THE STREET AND IT'S GOING TO PUT THE LITTLEST PET SHOP OUT OF BUSINESS!
OH, RIGHT. THANKS, ZOE.
NOO! THIS IS THE ONLY HOME I'VE EVER KNOWN!
EXCEPT FOR THE HOME I GO TO EVERY NIGHT WITH MY OWNERS, WHICH IS ALSO VERY COMFORTABLE!
CALM DOWN, VINNIE. THE LITTLEST PET SHOP IS NOT GOING OUT OF BUSINESS.
HOW DO YOU KNOW?
SIMPLE, PEPPER... BECAUSE WE HAVE HEART.
THAT IS MEANINGLESS. MAYBE THIS NEW STORE HAS HEART ALSO?
GOOD POINT, SUNIL. WE NEED... A RECONNAISSANCE MISSION!
ROGER THAT, AGENT SPIKEYPANTS. YOUR TEAM IS ASSEMBLED!

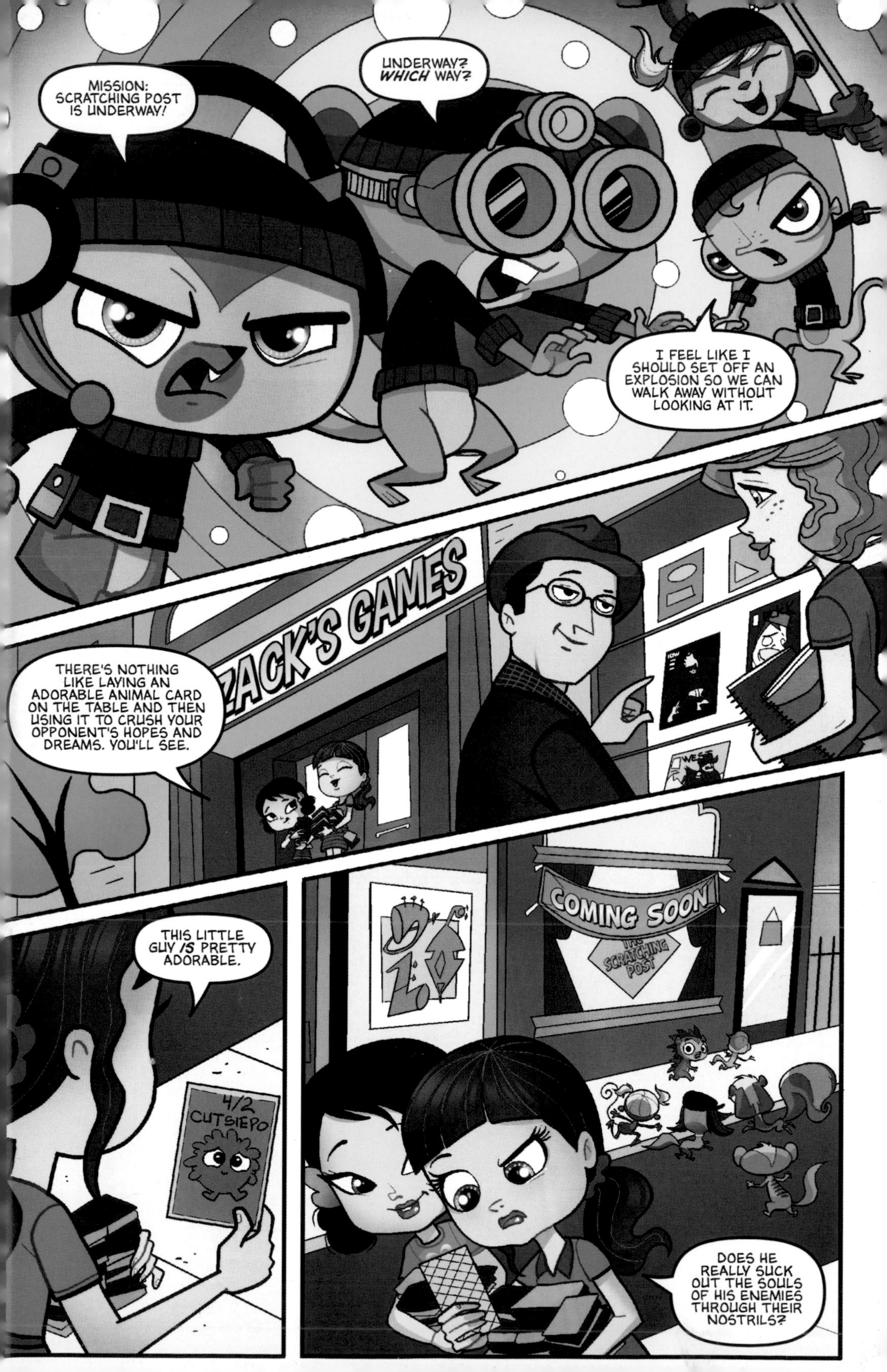
MISSION: SCRATCHING POST IS UNDERWAY!
UNDERWAY? *WHICH* WAY?
I FEEL LIKE I SHOULD SET OFF AN EXPLOSION SO WE CAN WALK AWAY WITHOUT LOOKING AT IT.
ZACK'S GAMES
THERE'S NOTHING LIKE LAYING AN ADORABLE ANIMAL CARD ON THE TABLE AND THEN USING IT TO CRUSH YOUR OPPONENT'S HOPES AND DREAMS. YOU'LL SEE.
COMING SOON
THE SCRATCHING POST
THIS LITTLE GUY *IS* PRETTY ADORABLE.
4/2
CUTSIEPO
DOES HE REALLY SUCK OUT THE SOULS OF HIS ENEMIES THROUGH THEIR NOSTRILS?

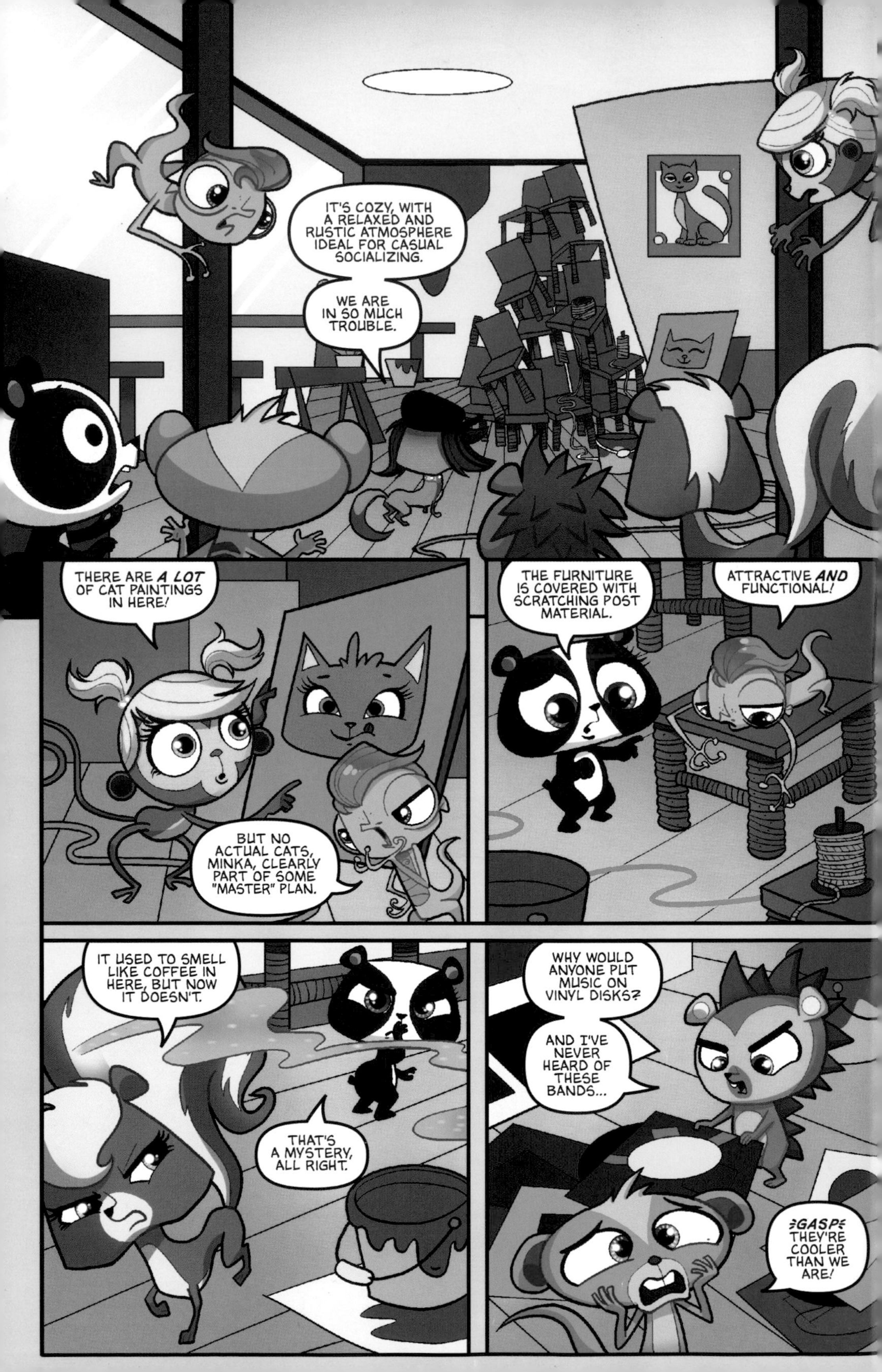
IT'S COZY, WITH A RELAXED AND RUSTIC ATMOSPHERE IDEAL FOR CASUAL SOCIALIZING.
WE ARE IN SO MUCH TROUBLE.
THERE ARE *A LOT* OF CAT PAINTINGS IN HERE!
BUT NO ACTUAL CATS, MINKA, CLEARLY PART OF SOME "MASTER" PLAN.
THE FURNITURE IS COVERED WITH SCRATCHING POST MATERIAL.
ATTRACTIVE *AND* FUNCTIONAL!
IT USED TO SMELL LIKE COFFEE IN HERE, BUT NOW IT DOESN'T.
THAT'S A MYSTERY, ALL RIGHT.
WHY WOULD ANYONE PUT MUSIC ON VINYL DISKS?
AND I'VE NEVER HEARD OF THESE BANDS...
GASP THEY'RE COOLER THAN WE ARE!

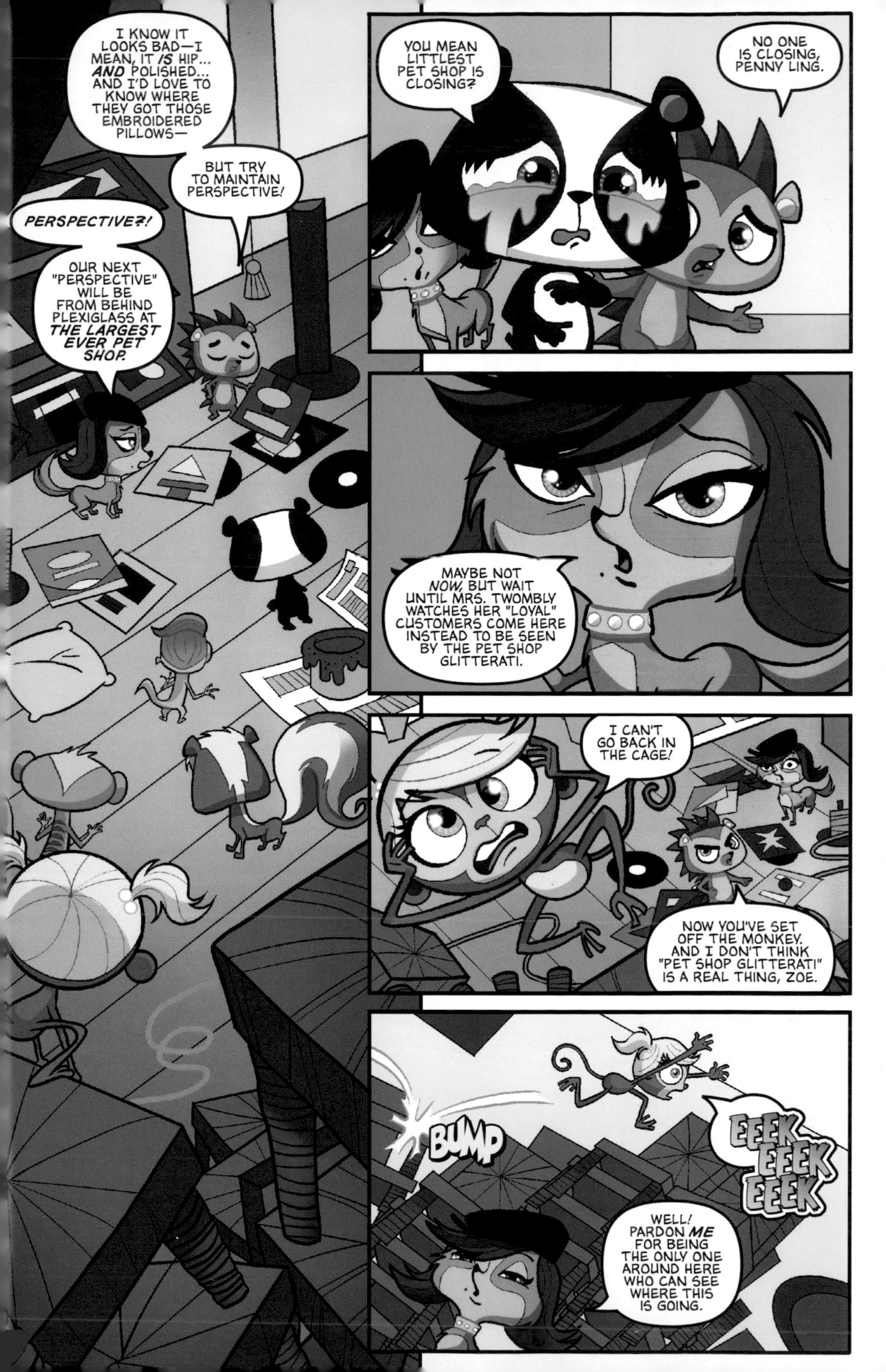
I KNOW IT LOOKS BAD—I MEAN, IT *IS* HIP... ***AND*** POLISHED... AND I'D LOVE TO KNOW WHERE THEY GOT THOSE EMBROIDERED PILLOWS—
BUT TRY TO MAINTAIN PERSPECTIVE!
PERSPECTIVE?!
OUR NEXT "PERSPECTIVE" WILL BE FROM BEHIND PLEXIGLASS AT ***THE LARGEST EVER PET SHOP.***
YOU MEAN LITTLEST PET SHOP IS CLOSING?
NO ONE IS CLOSING, PENNY LING.
MAYBE NOT *NOW*, BUT WAIT UNTIL MRS. TWOMBLY WATCHES HER "LOYAL" CUSTOMERS COME HERE INSTEAD TO BE SEEN BY THE PET SHOP GLITTERATI.
I CAN'T GO BACK IN THE CAGE!
NOW YOU'VE SET OFF THE MONKEY. AND I DON'T THINK "PET SHOP GLITTERATI" IS A REAL THING, ZOE.
BUMP
EEEK EEEK EEEK
WELL! PARDON ***ME*** FOR BEING THE ONLY ONE AROUND HERE WHO CAN SEE WHERE THIS IS GOING.

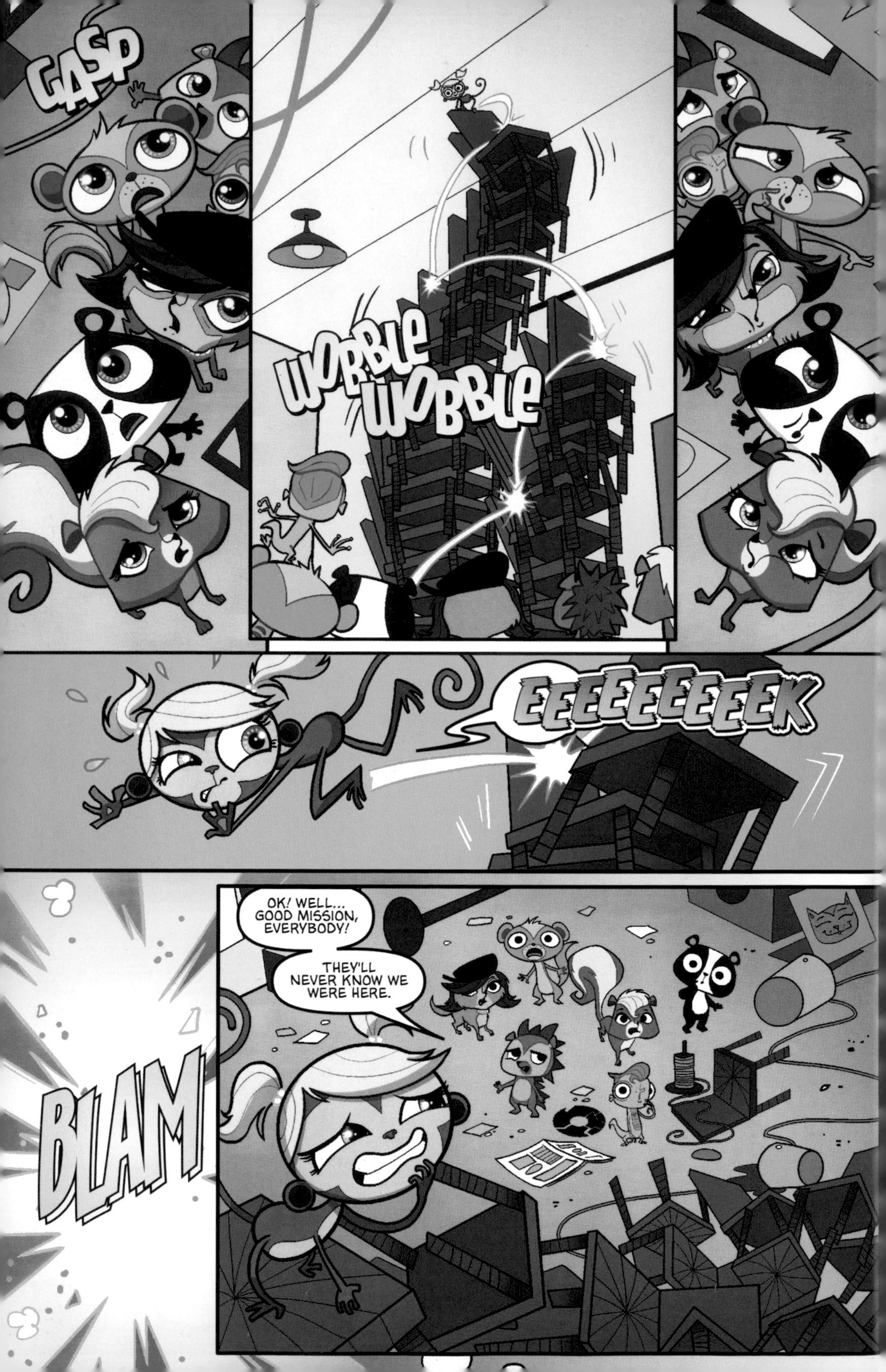
GASP
WOBBLE WOBBLE
EEEEEEEEEK
BLAM
OK! WELL... GOOD MISSION, EVERYBODY!
THEY'LL NEVER KNOW WE WERE HERE.

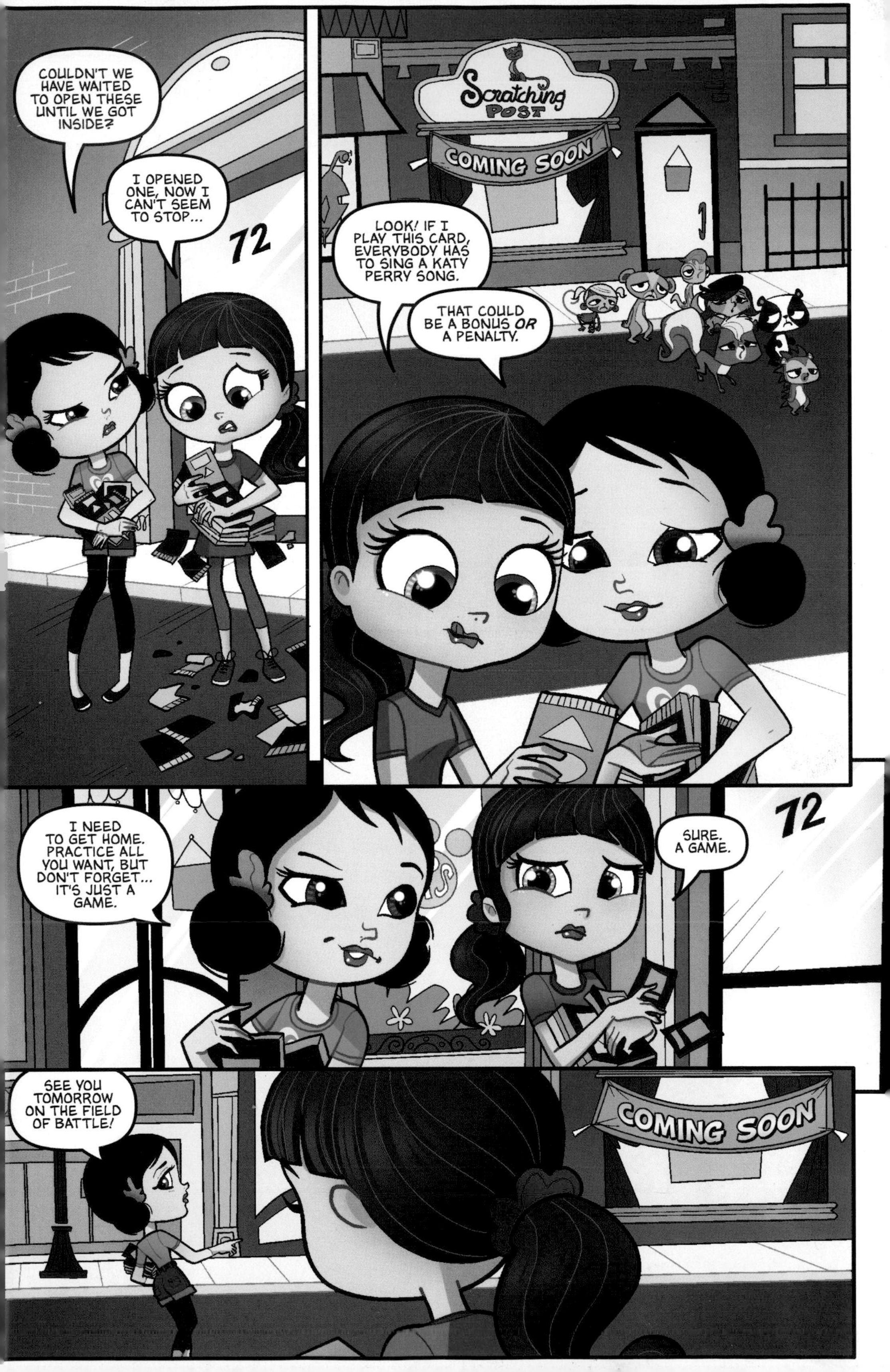
COULDN'T WE HAVE WAITED TO OPEN THESE UNTIL WE GOT INSIDE?
I OPENED ONE, NOW I CAN'T SEEM TO STOP...
72
Scratching POST
COMING SOON
LOOK! IF I PLAY THIS CARD, EVERYBODY HAS TO SING A KATY PERRY SONG.
THAT COULD BE A BONUS *OR* A PENALTY.
I NEED TO GET HOME. PRACTICE ALL YOU WANT, BUT DON'T FORGET... IT'S JUST A GAME.
72
SURE. A GAME.
SEE YOU TOMORROW ON THE FIELD OF BATTLE!
COMING SOON

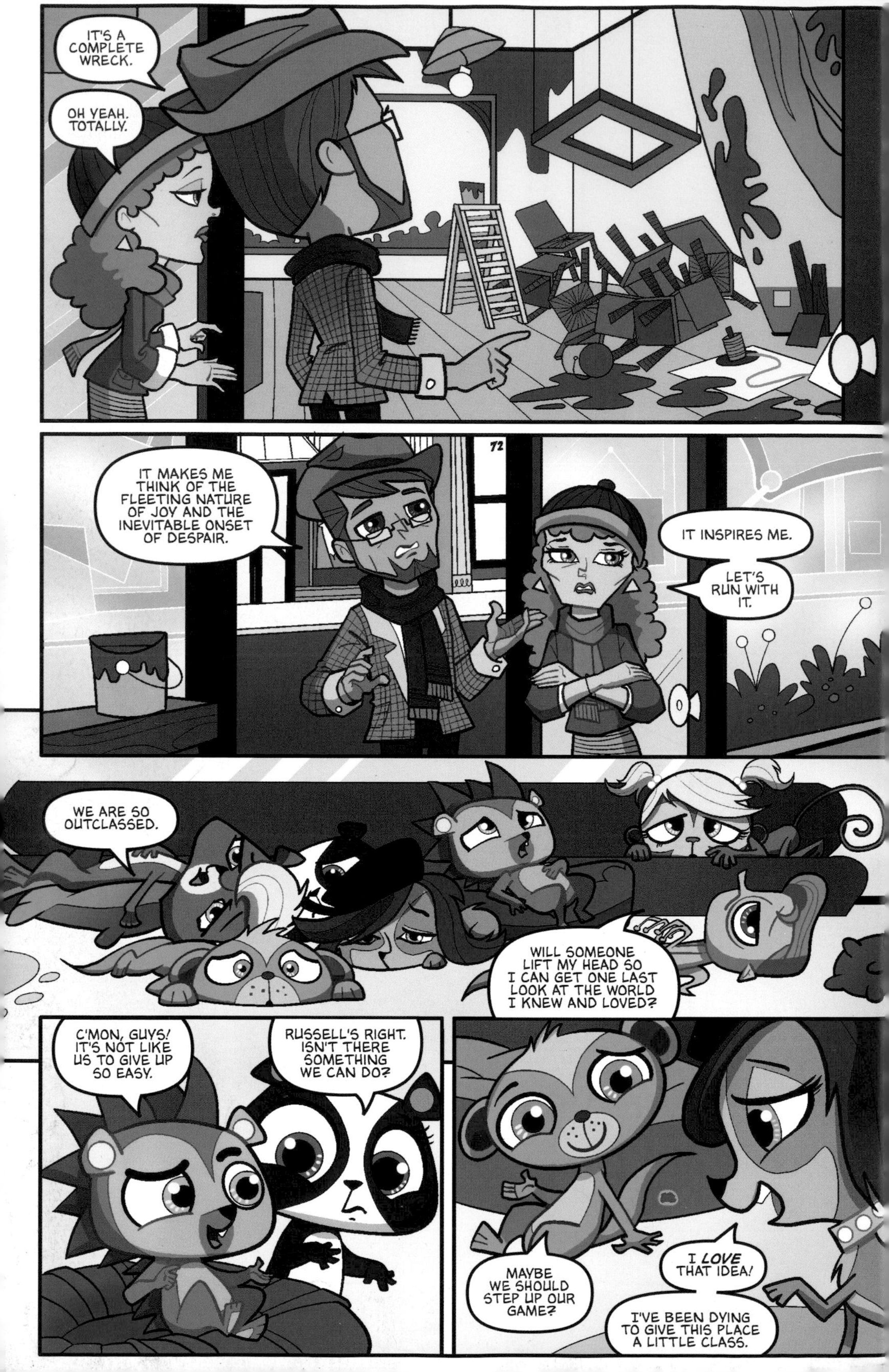
IT'S A COMPLETE WRECK.
OH YEAH. TOTALLY.
72
IT MAKES ME THINK OF THE FLEETING NATURE OF JOY AND THE INEVITABLE ONSET OF DESPAIR.
IT INSPIRES ME.
LET'S RUN WITH IT.
WE ARE SO OUTCLASSED.
WILL SOMEONE LIFT MY HEAD SO I CAN GET ONE LAST LOOK AT THE WORLD I KNEW AND LOVED?
C'MON, GUYS! IT'S NOT LIKE US TO GIVE UP SO EASY.
RUSSELL'S RIGHT. ISN'T THERE SOMETHING WE CAN DO?
MAYBE WE SHOULD STEP UP OUR GAME?
I *LOVE* THAT IDEA!
I'VE BEEN DYING TO GIVE THIS PLACE A LITTLE CLASS.

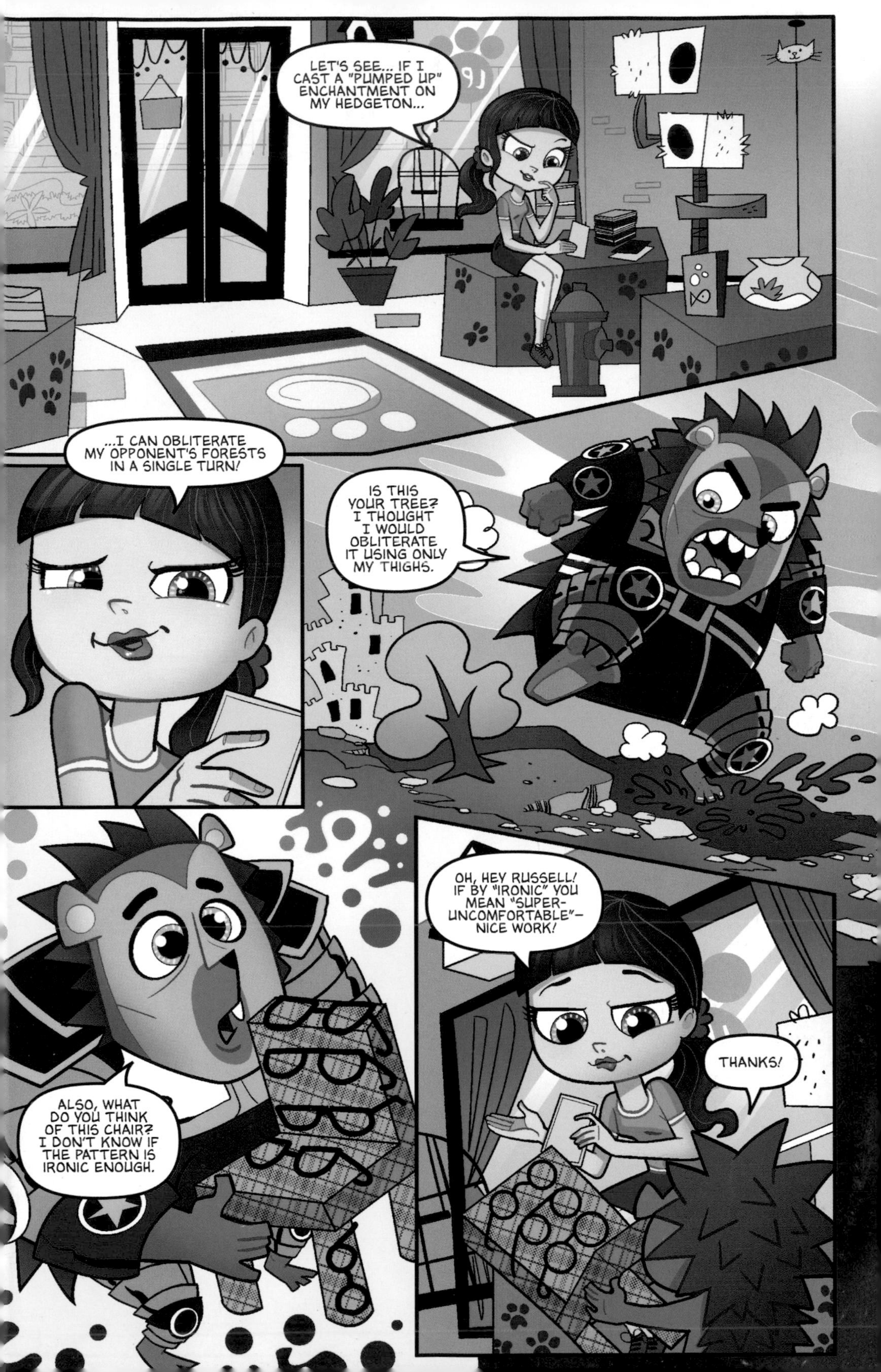
LET'S SEE... IF I CAST A "PUMPED UP" ENCHANTMENT ON MY HEDGETON...
...I CAN OBLITERATE MY OPPONENT'S FORESTS IN A SINGLE TURN!
IS THIS YOUR TREE? I THOUGHT I WOULD OBLITERATE IT USING ONLY MY THIGHS.
ALSO, WHAT DO YOU THINK OF THIS CHAIR? I DON'T KNOW IF THE PATTERN IS IRONIC ENOUGH.
OH, HEY RUSSELL! IF BY "IRONIC" YOU MEAN "SUPER-UNCOMFORTABLE"—NICE WORK!
THANKS!

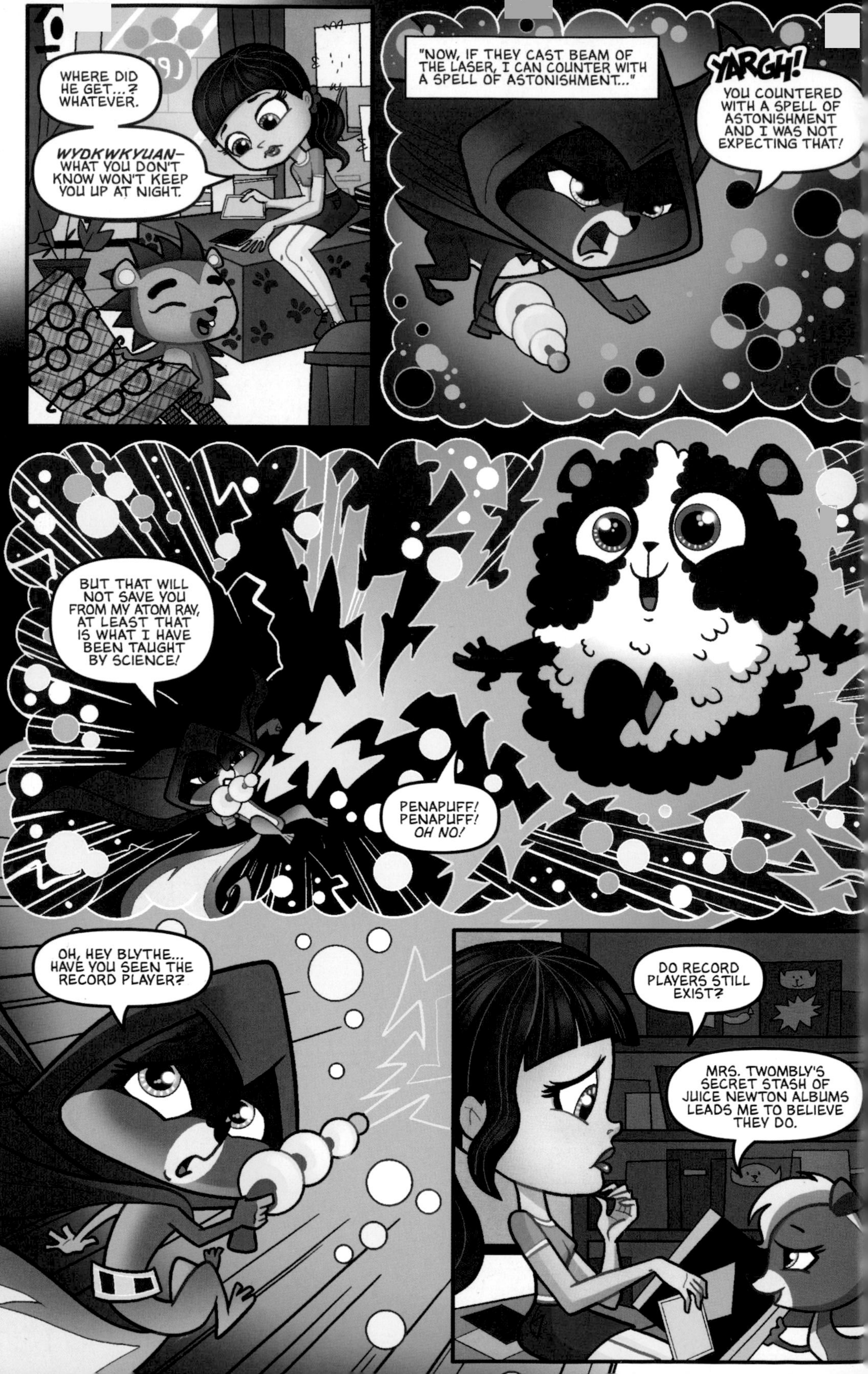
WHERE DID HE GET...? WHATEVER.
WYDKWKYUAN– WHAT YOU DON'T KNOW WON'T KEEP YOU UP AT NIGHT.
"NOW, IF THEY CAST BEAM OF THE LASER, I CAN COUNTER WITH A SPELL OF ASTONISHMENT..."
YARGH!
YOU COUNTERED WITH A SPELL OF ASTONISHMENT AND I WAS NOT EXPECTING THAT!
BUT THAT WILL NOT SAVE YOU FROM MY ATOM RAY, AT LEAST THAT IS WHAT I HAVE BEEN TAUGHT BY SCIENCE!
PENAPUFF! PENAPUFF! OH NO!
OH, HEY BLYTHE... HAVE YOU SEEN THE RECORD PLAYER?
DO RECORD PLAYERS STILL EXIST?
MRS. TWOMBLY'S SECRET STASH OF JUICE NEWTON ALBUMS LEADS ME TO BELIEVE THEY DO.

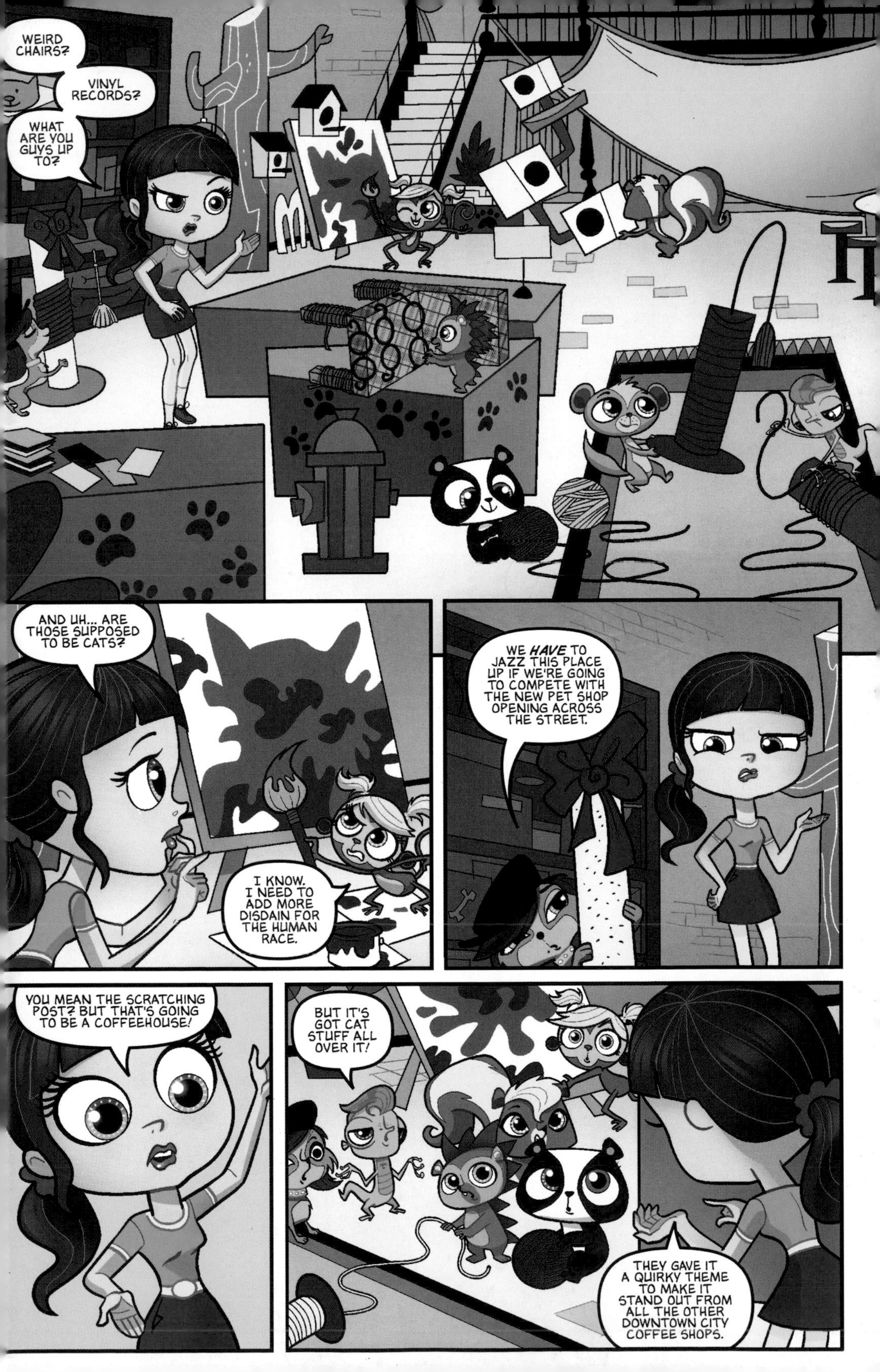
WEIRD CHAIRS?
VINYL RECORDS?
WHAT ARE YOU GUYS UP TO?
AND UH... ARE THOSE SUPPOSED TO BE CATS?
I KNOW. I NEED TO ADD MORE DISDAIN FOR THE HUMAN RACE.
WE *HAVE* TO JAZZ THIS PLACE UP IF WE'RE GOING TO COMPETE WITH THE NEW PET SHOP OPENING ACROSS THE STREET.
YOU MEAN THE SCRATCHING POST? BUT THAT'S GOING TO BE A COFFEEHOUSE!
BUT IT'S GOT CAT STUFF ALL OVER IT!
THEY GAVE IT A QUIRKY THEME TO MAKE IT STAND OUT FROM ALL THE OTHER DOWNTOWN CITY COFFEE SHOPS.

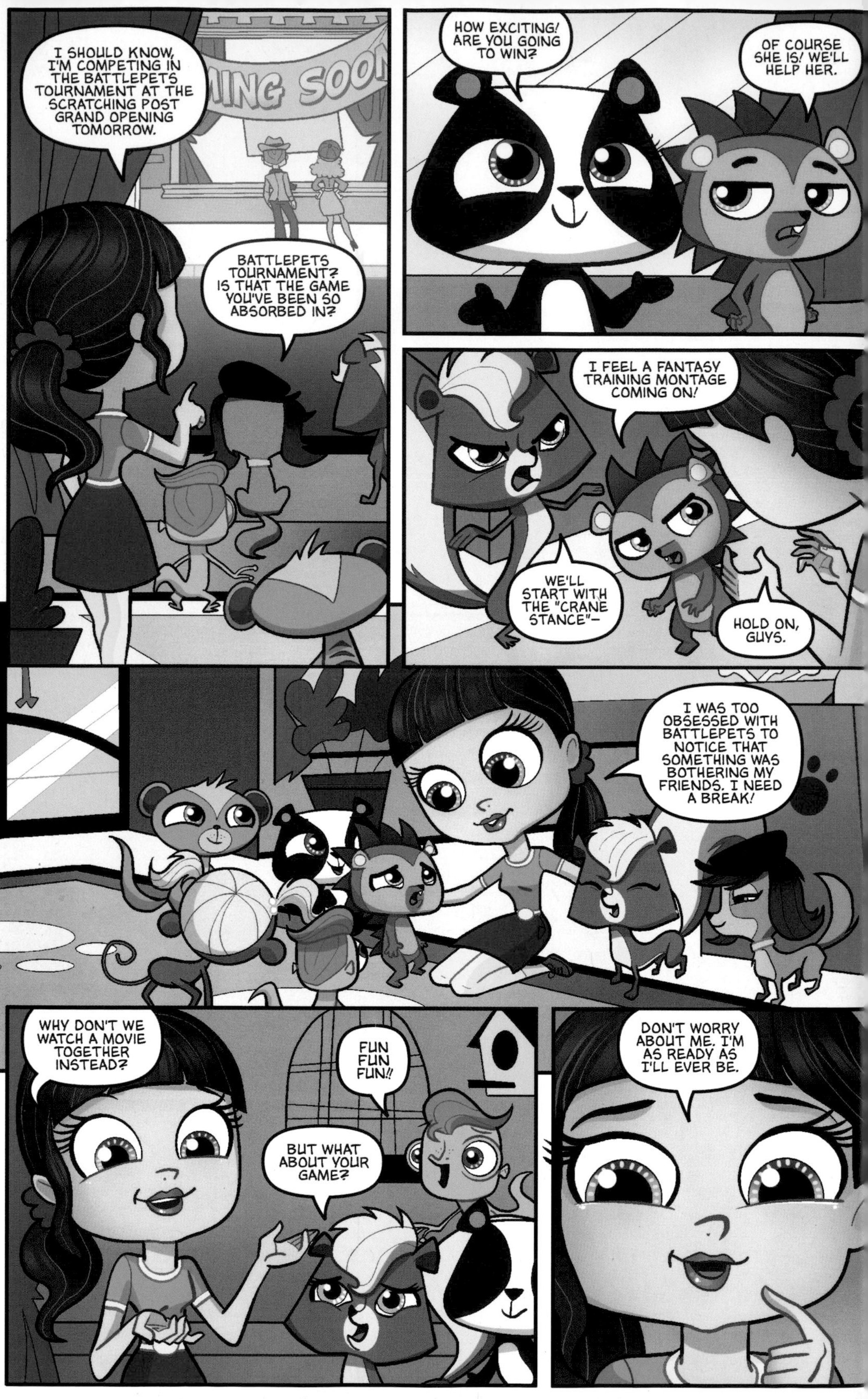
I SHOULD KNOW, I'M COMPETING IN THE BATTLEPETS TOURNAMENT AT THE SCRATCHING POST GRAND OPENING TOMORROW.
BATTLEPETS TOURNAMENT? IS THAT THE GAME YOU'VE BEEN SO ABSORBED IN?
HOW EXCITING! ARE YOU GOING TO WIN?
OF COURSE SHE IS! WE'LL HELP HER.
I FEEL A FANTASY TRAINING MONTAGE COMING ON!
WE'LL START WITH THE "CRANE STANCE"–
HOLD ON, GUYS.
I WAS TOO OBSESSED WITH BATTLEPETS TO NOTICE THAT SOMETHING WAS BOTHERING MY FRIENDS. I NEED A BREAK!
WHY DON'T WE WATCH A MOVIE TOGETHER INSTEAD?
FUN FUN FUN!!
BUT WHAT ABOUT YOUR GAME?
DON'T WORRY ABOUT ME. I'M AS READY AS I'LL EVER BE.

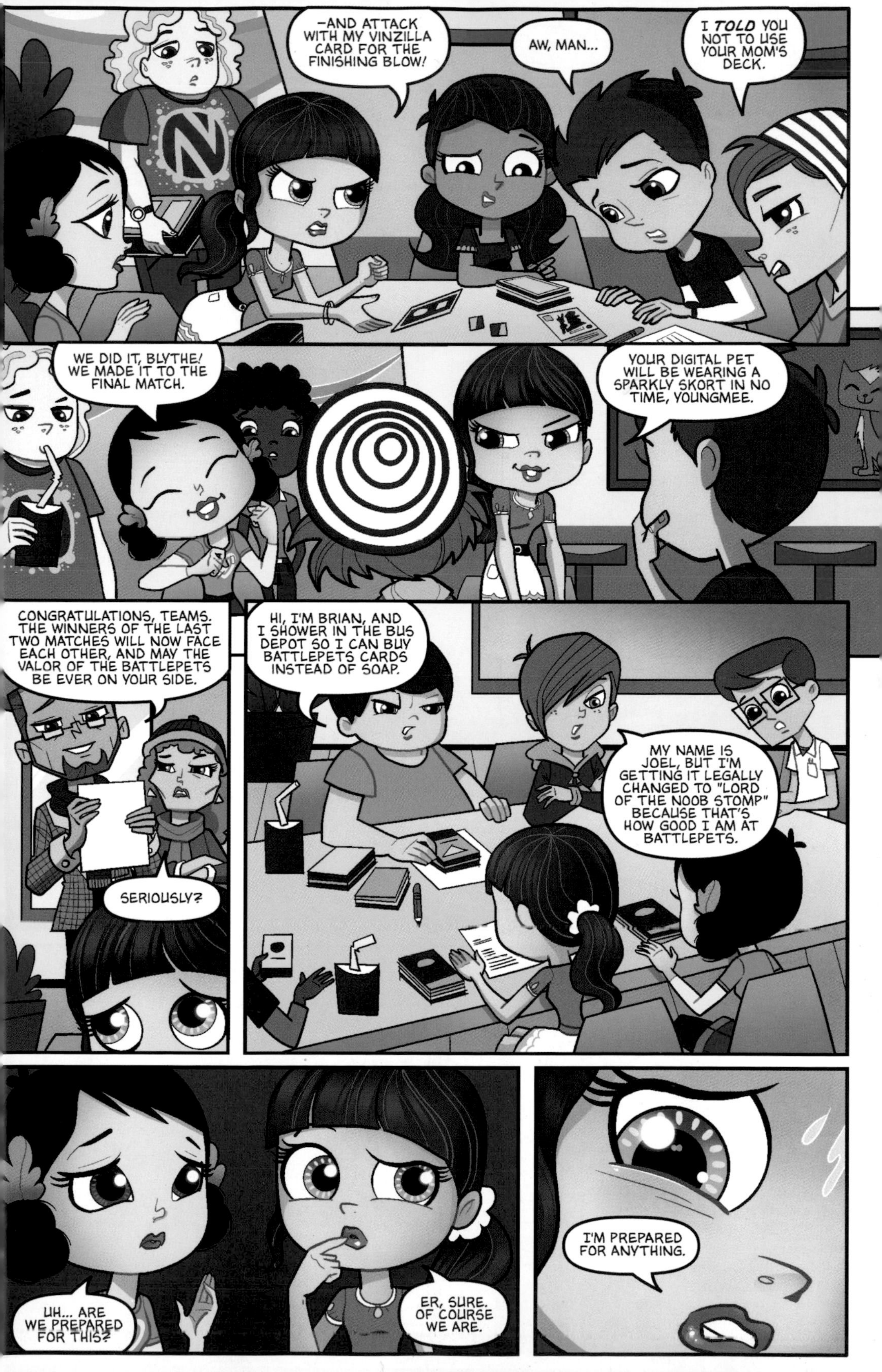

–AND ATTACK WITH MY VINZILLA CARD FOR THE FINISHING BLOW!
AW, MAN...
I *TOLD* YOU NOT TO USE YOUR MOM'S DECK.
WE DID IT, BLYTHE! WE MADE IT TO THE FINAL MATCH.
YOUR DIGITAL PET WILL BE WEARING A SPARKLY SKORT IN NO TIME, YOUNGMEE.
CONGRATULATIONS, TEAMS. THE WINNERS OF THE LAST TWO MATCHES WILL NOW FACE EACH OTHER, AND MAY THE VALOR OF THE BATTLEPETS BE EVER ON YOUR SIDE.
SERIOUSLY?
HI, I'M BRIAN, AND I SHOWER IN THE BUS DEPOT SO I CAN BUY BATTLEPETS CARDS INSTEAD OF SOAP.
MY NAME IS JOEL, BUT I'M GETTING IT LEGALLY CHANGED TO "LORD OF THE NOOB STOMP" BECAUSE THAT'S HOW GOOD I AM AT BATTLEPETS.
UH... ARE WE PREPARED FOR THIS?
ER, SURE. OF COURSE WE ARE.
I'M PREPARED FOR ANYTHING.

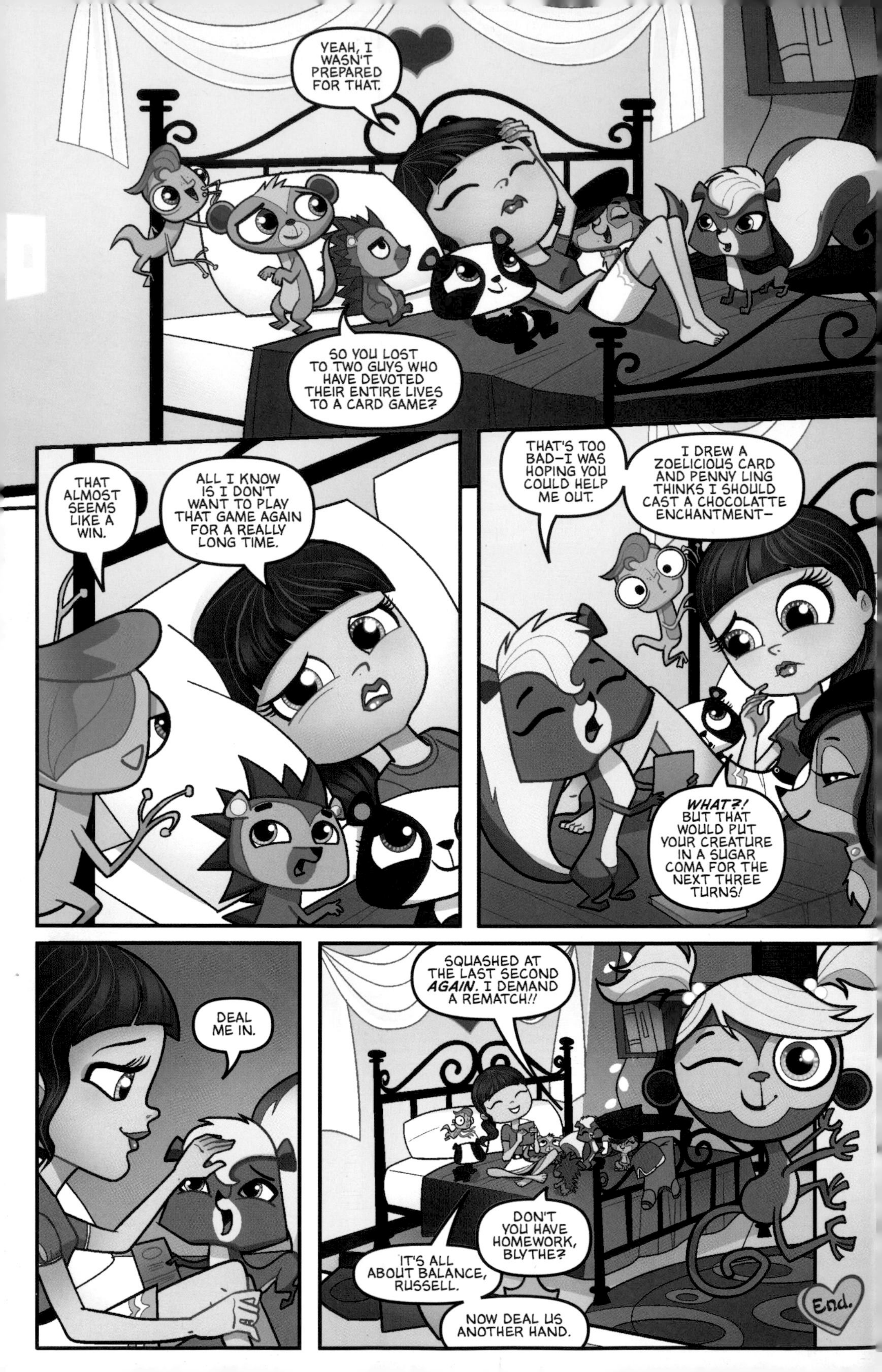
YEAH, I WASN'T PREPARED FOR THAT.
SO YOU LOST TO TWO GUYS WHO HAVE DEVOTED THEIR ENTIRE LIVES TO A CARD GAME?
THAT ALMOST SEEMS LIKE A WIN.
ALL I KNOW IS I DON'T WANT TO PLAY THAT GAME AGAIN FOR A REALLY LONG TIME.
THAT'S TOO BAD—I WAS HOPING YOU COULD HELP ME OUT.
I DREW A ZOELICIOUS CARD AND PENNY LING THINKS I SHOULD CAST A CHOCOLATTE ENCHANTMENT—
WHAT?! BUT THAT WOULD PUT YOUR CREATURE IN A SUGAR COMA FOR THE NEXT THREE TURNS!
DEAL ME IN.
SQUASHED AT THE LAST SECOND AGAIN. I DEMAND A REMATCH!!
DON'T YOU HAVE HOMEWORK, BLYTHE?
IT'S ALL ABOUT BALANCE, RUSSELL.
NOW DEAL US ANOTHER HAND.
End.

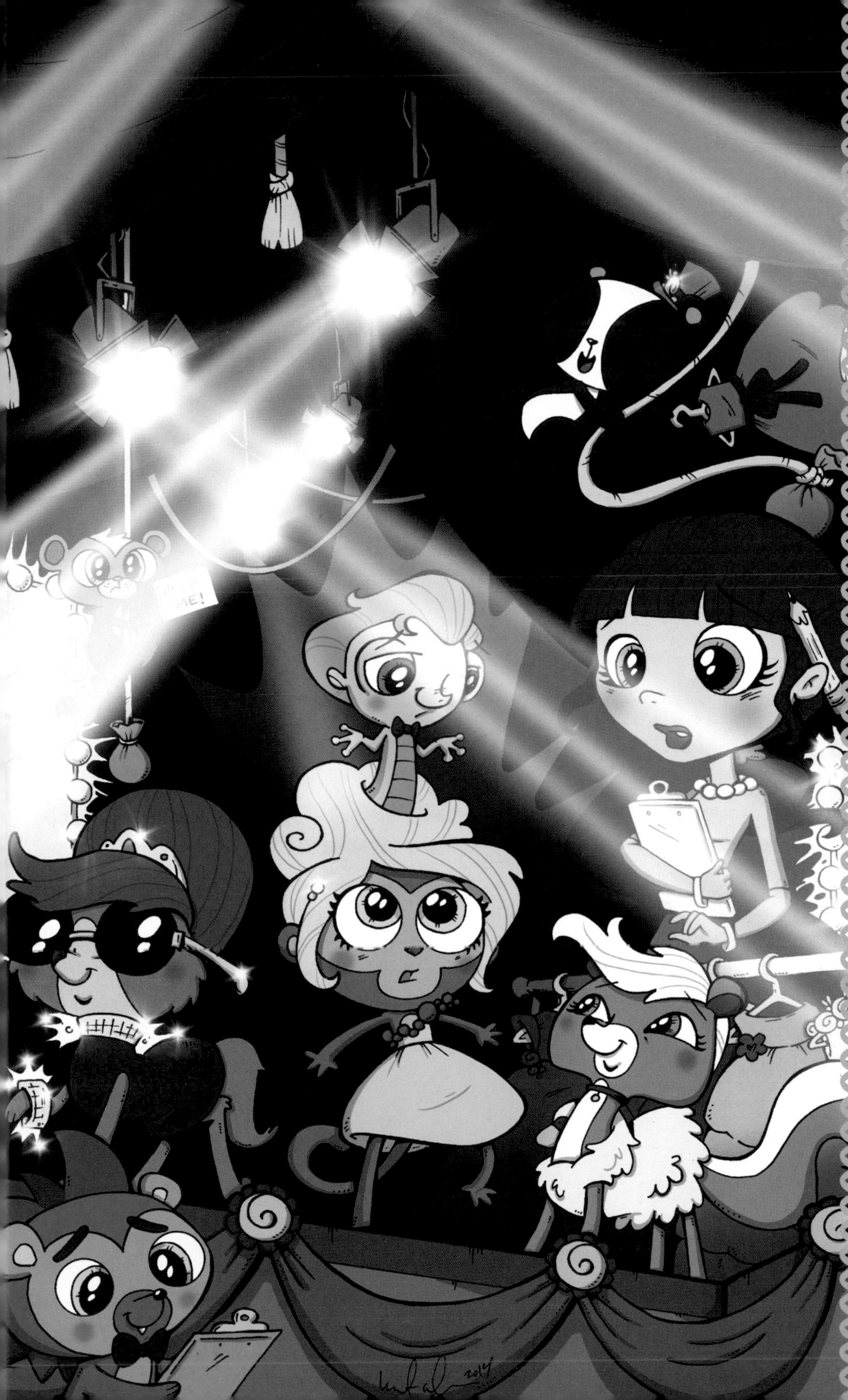
HELP ME!

art by: Katie Cook

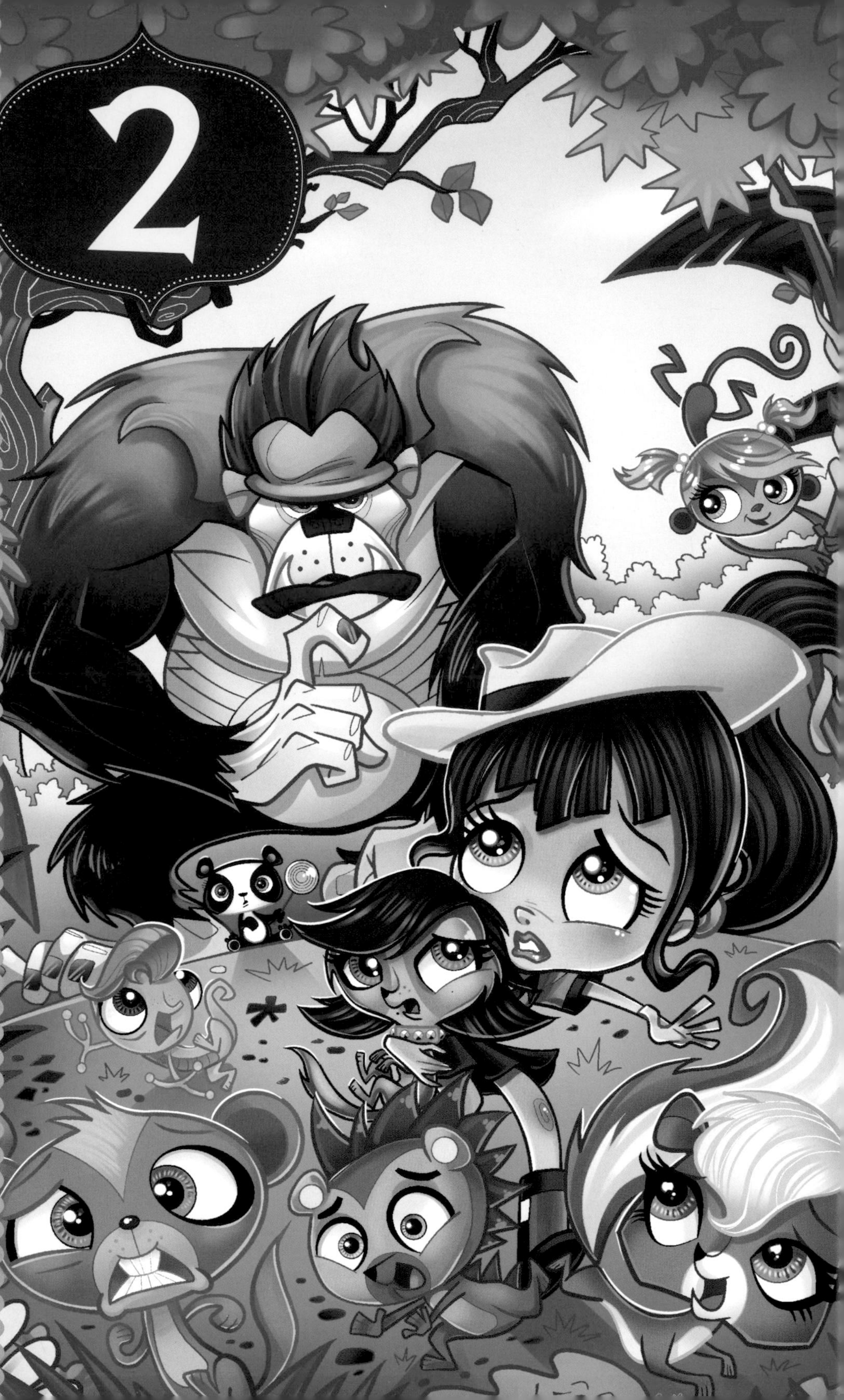
2

art by: Nicanor Peña • colors by: Victoria Robado

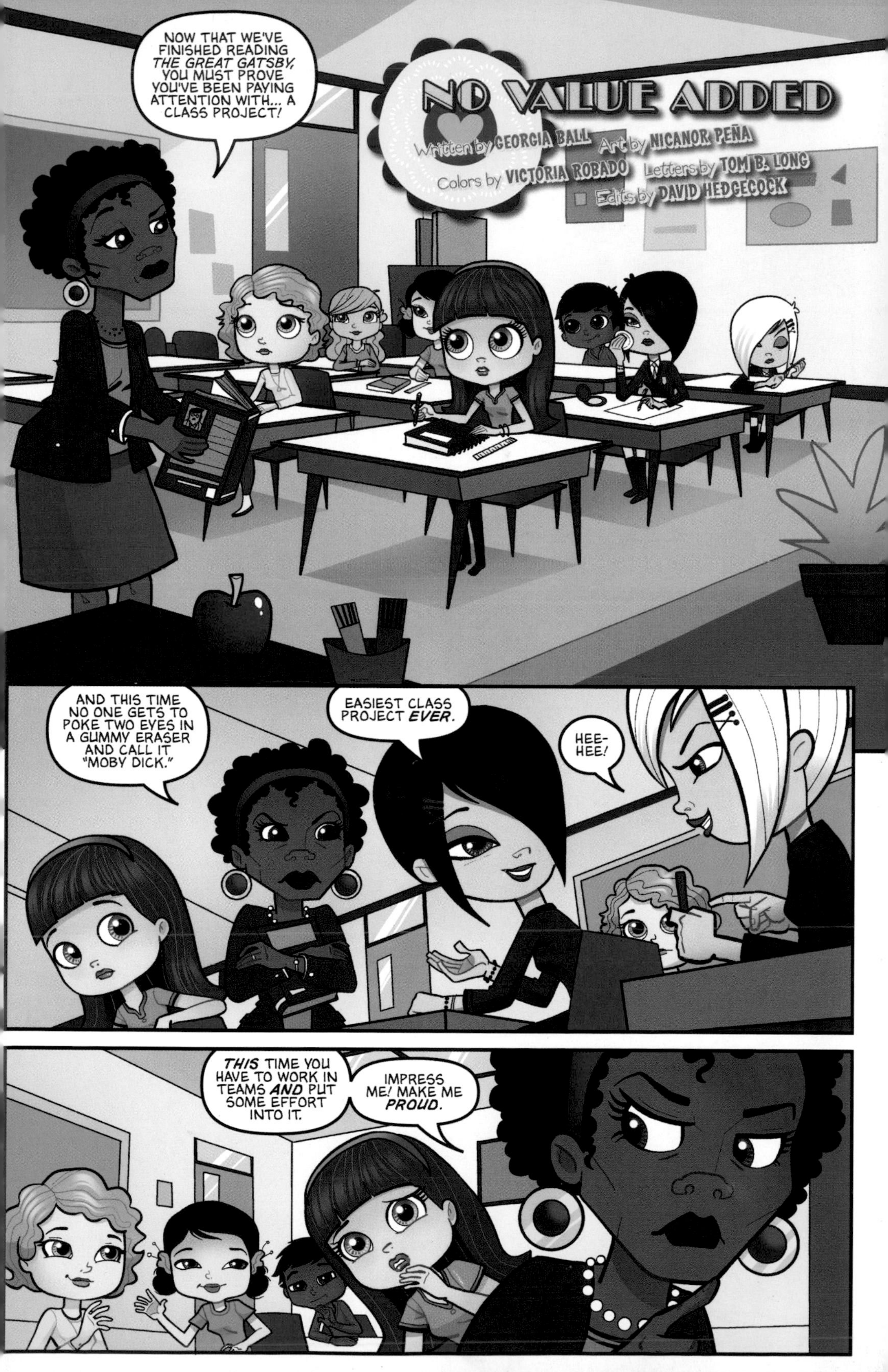
NOW THAT WE'VE FINISHED READING *THE GREAT GATSBY,* YOU MUST PROVE YOU'VE BEEN PAYING ATTENTION WITH... A CLASS PROJECT!
NO VALUE ADDED
Written by GEORGIA BALL
Art by NICANOR PEÑA
Colors by VICTORIA ROBADO
Letters by TOM B. LONG
Edits by DAVID HEDGECOCK
AND THIS TIME NO ONE GETS TO POKE TWO EYES IN A GUMMY ERASER AND CALL IT "MOBY DICK."
EASIEST CLASS PROJECT ***EVER.***
HEE-HEE!
THIS TIME YOU HAVE TO WORK IN TEAMS ***AND*** PUT SOME EFFORT INTO IT.
IMPRESS ME! MAKE ME ***PROUD.***

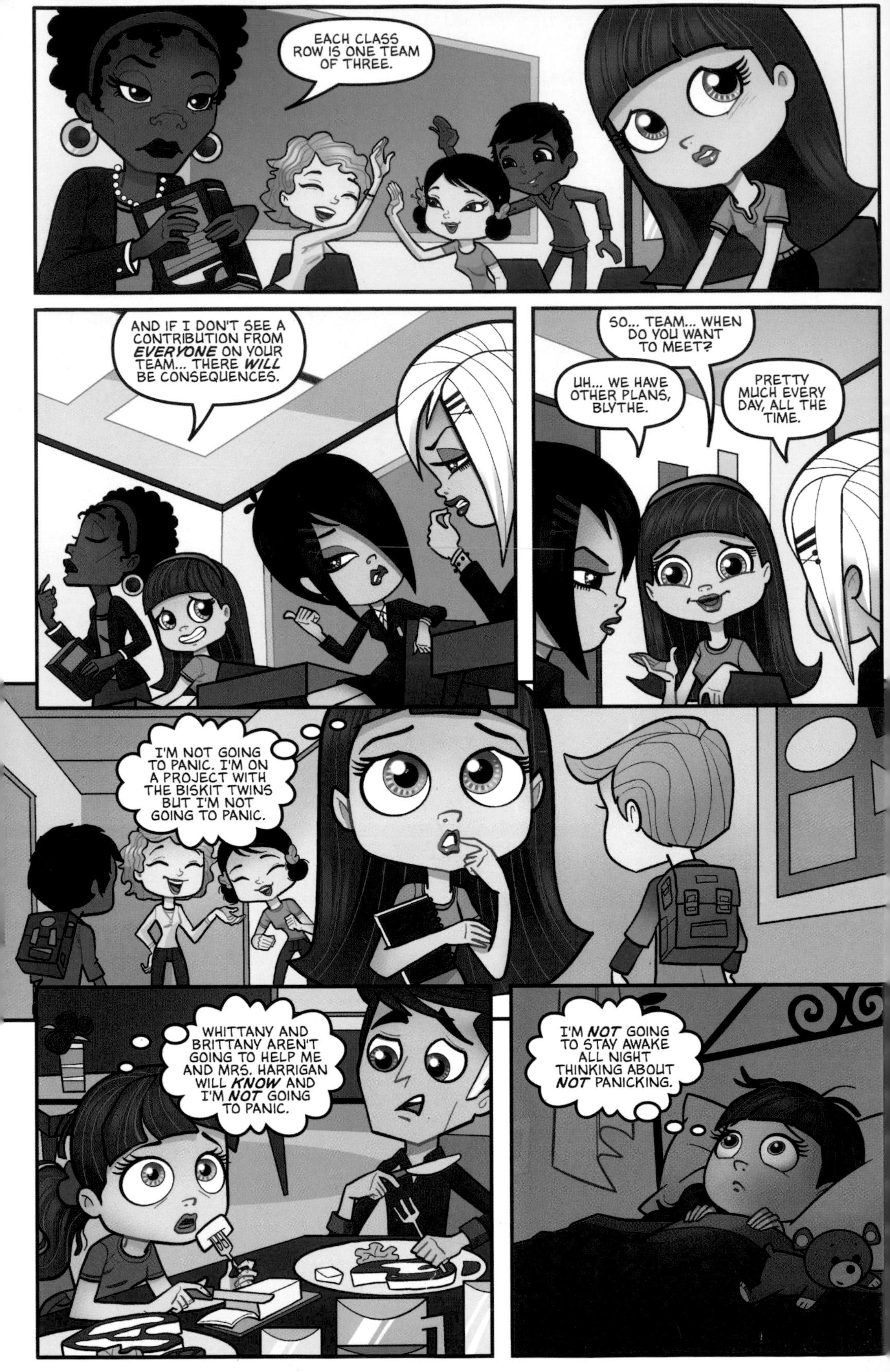
EACH CLASS ROW IS ONE TEAM OF THREE.
AND IF I DON'T SEE A CONTRIBUTION FROM ***EVERYONE*** ON YOUR TEAM... THERE ***WILL*** BE CONSEQUENCES.
SO... TEAM... WHEN DO YOU WANT TO MEET?
UH... WE HAVE OTHER PLANS, BLYTHE.
PRETTY MUCH EVERY DAY, ALL THE TIME.
I'M NOT GOING TO PANIC. I'M ON A PROJECT WITH THE BISKIT TWINS BUT I'M NOT GOING TO PANIC.
WHITTANY AND BRITTANY AREN'T GOING TO HELP ME AND MRS. HARRIGAN WILL ***KNOW*** AND I'M ***NOT*** GOING TO PANIC.
I'M ***NOT*** GOING TO STAY AWAKE ALL NIGHT THINKING ABOUT ***NOT*** PANICKING.

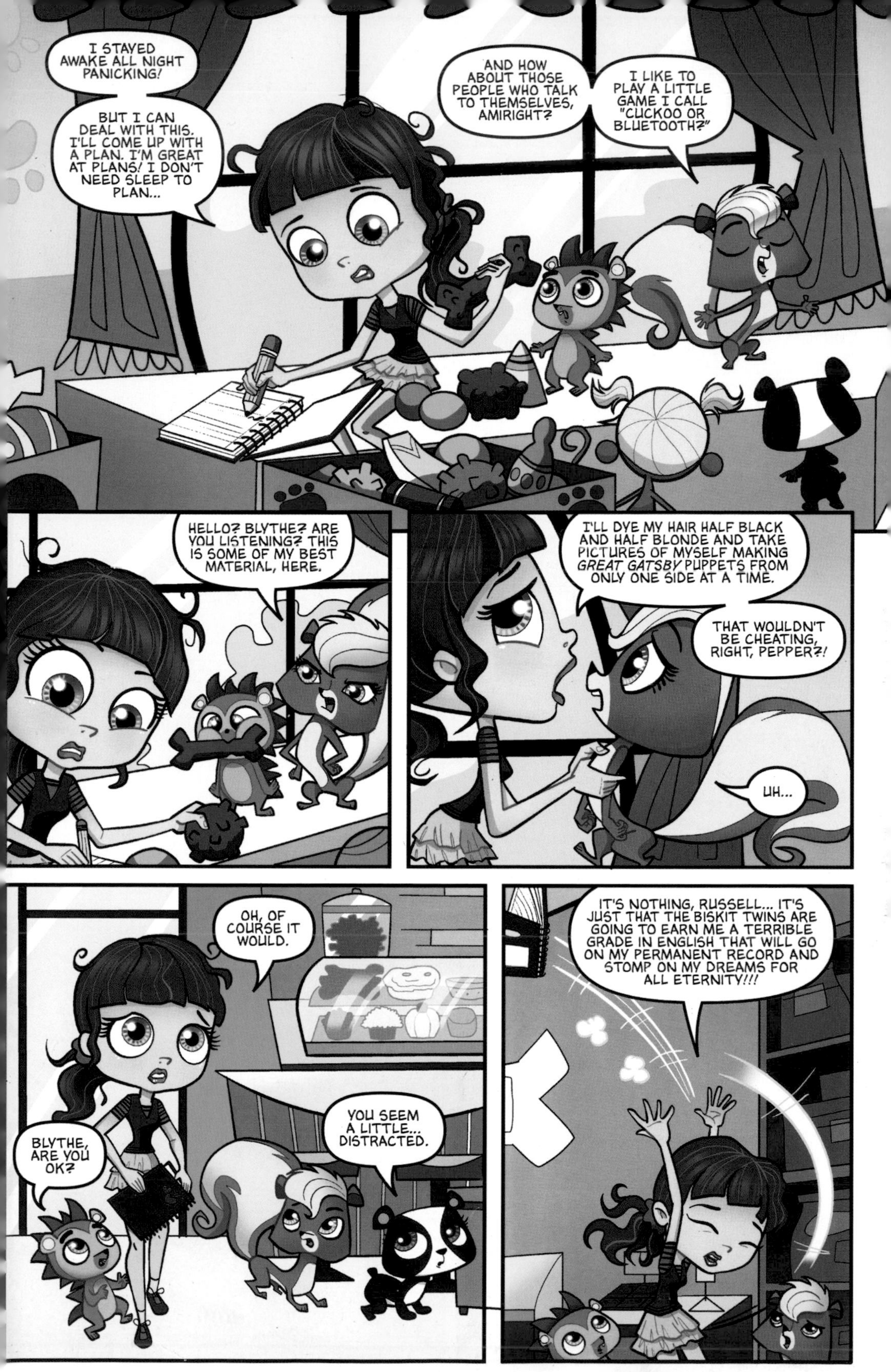
I STAYED AWAKE ALL NIGHT PANICKING!
BUT I CAN DEAL WITH THIS. I'LL COME UP WITH A PLAN. I'M GREAT AT PLANS! I DON'T NEED SLEEP TO PLAN...
AND HOW ABOUT THOSE PEOPLE WHO TALK TO THEMSELVES, AMIRIGHT?
I LIKE TO PLAY A LITTLE GAME I CALL "CUCKOO OR BLUETOOTH?"
HELLO? BLYTHE? ARE YOU LISTENING? THIS IS SOME OF MY BEST MATERIAL, HERE.
I'LL DYE MY HAIR HALF BLACK AND HALF BLONDE AND TAKE PICTURES OF MYSELF MAKING GREAT GATSBY PUPPETS FROM ONLY ONE SIDE AT A TIME.
THAT WOULDN'T BE CHEATING, RIGHT, PEPPER?!
UH...
OH, OF COURSE IT WOULD.
BLYTHE, ARE YOU OK?
YOU SEEM A LITTLE... DISTRACTED.
IT'S NOTHING, RUSSELL... IT'S JUST THAT THE BISKIT TWINS ARE GOING TO EARN ME A TERRIBLE GRADE IN ENGLISH THAT WILL GO ON MY PERMANENT RECORD AND STOMP ON MY DREAMS FOR ALL ETERNITY!!!

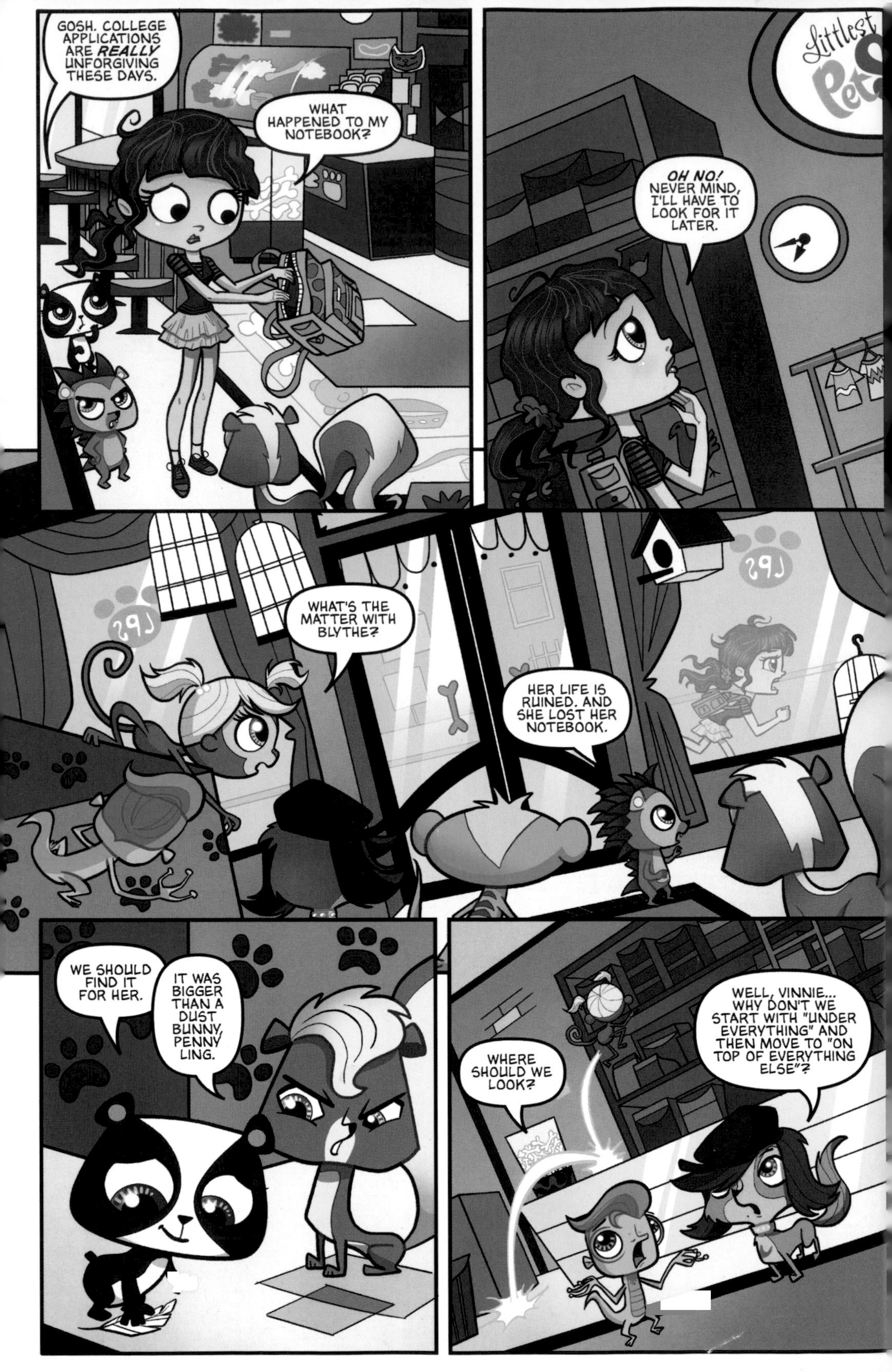
GOSH. COLLEGE APPLICATIONS ARE *REALLY* UNFORGIVING THESE DAYS.
WHAT HAPPENED TO MY NOTEBOOK?
OH NO! NEVER MIND, I'LL HAVE TO LOOK FOR IT LATER.
WHAT'S THE MATTER WITH BLYTHE?
HER LIFE IS RUINED. AND SHE LOST HER NOTEBOOK.
WE SHOULD FIND IT FOR HER.
IT WAS BIGGER THAN A DUST BUNNY, PENNY LING.
WHERE SHOULD WE LOOK?
WELL, VINNIE... WHY DON'T WE START WITH "UNDER EVERYTHING" AND THEN MOVE TO "ON TOP OF EVERYTHING ELSE"?

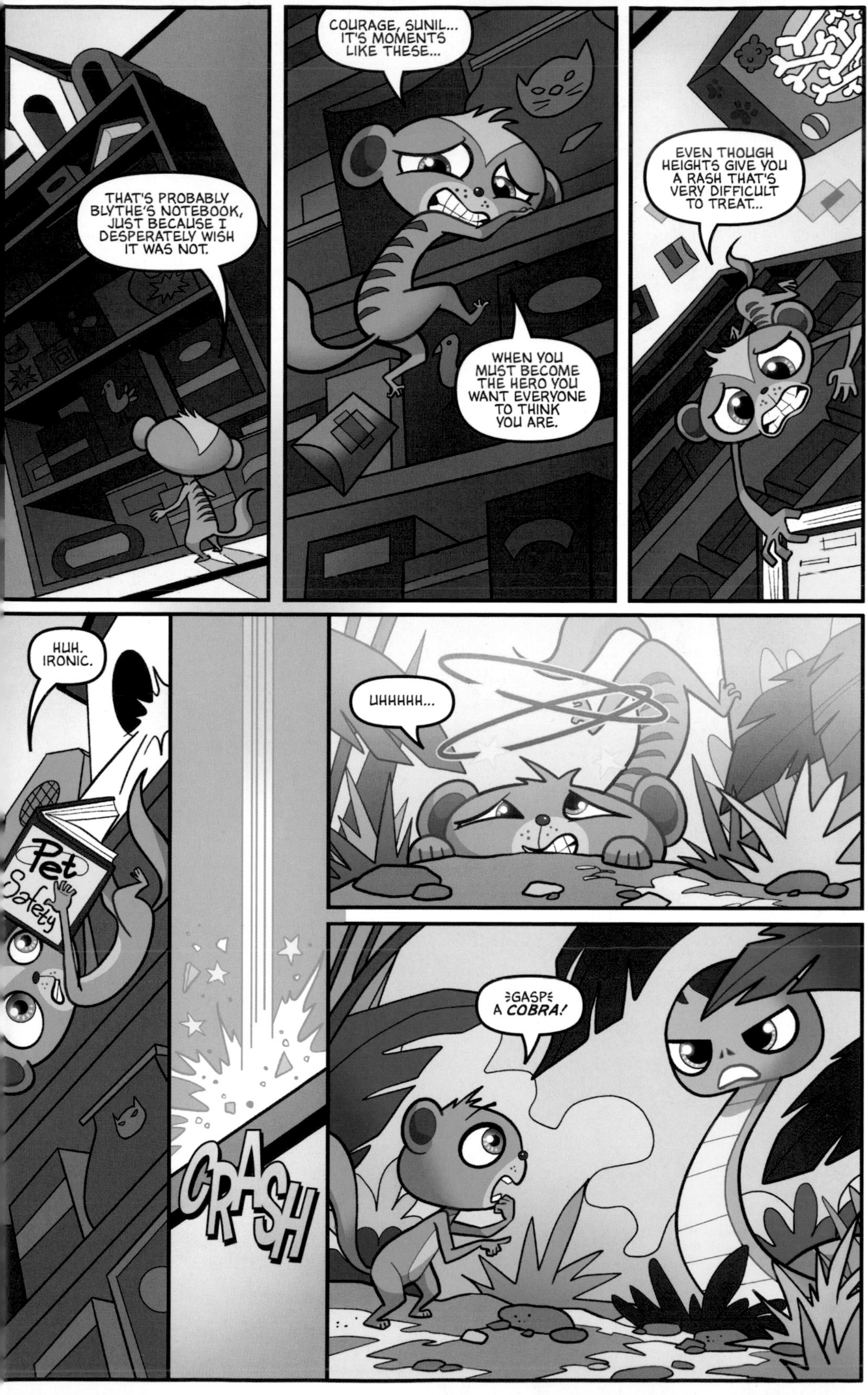
THAT'S PROBABLY BLYTHE'S NOTEBOOK, JUST BECAUSE I DESPERATELY WISH IT WAS NOT.
COURAGE, SUNIL... IT'S MOMENTS LIKE THESE...
WHEN YOU MUST BECOME THE HERO YOU WANT EVERYONE TO THINK YOU ARE.
EVEN THOUGH HEIGHTS GIVE YOU A RASH THAT'S VERY DIFFICULT TO TREAT...
HUH. IRONIC.
Pet Safety
CRASH
UHHHHH...
GASP A COBRA!

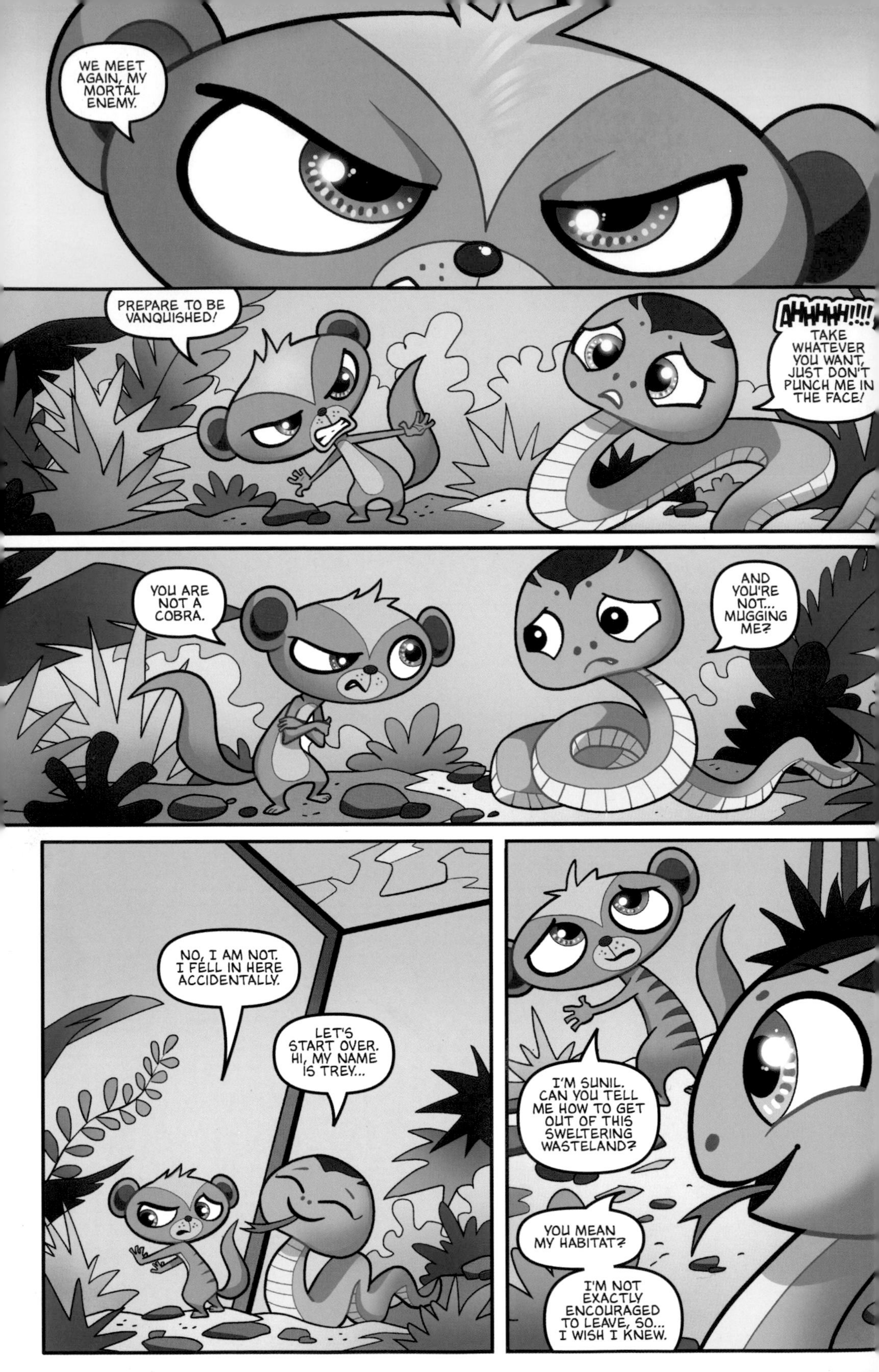
WE MEET AGAIN, MY MORTAL ENEMY.
PREPARE TO BE VANQUISHED!
AHHHHH!!!!
TAKE WHATEVER YOU WANT, JUST DON'T PUNCH ME IN THE FACE!
YOU ARE NOT A COBRA.
AND YOU'RE NOT... MUGGING ME?
NO, I AM NOT. I FELL IN HERE ACCIDENTALLY.
LET'S START OVER. HI, MY NAME IS TREY...
I'M SUNIL. CAN YOU TELL ME HOW TO GET OUT OF THIS SWELTERING WASTELAND?
YOU MEAN MY HABITAT?
I'M NOT EXACTLY ENCOURAGED TO LEAVE, SO... I WISH I KNEW.

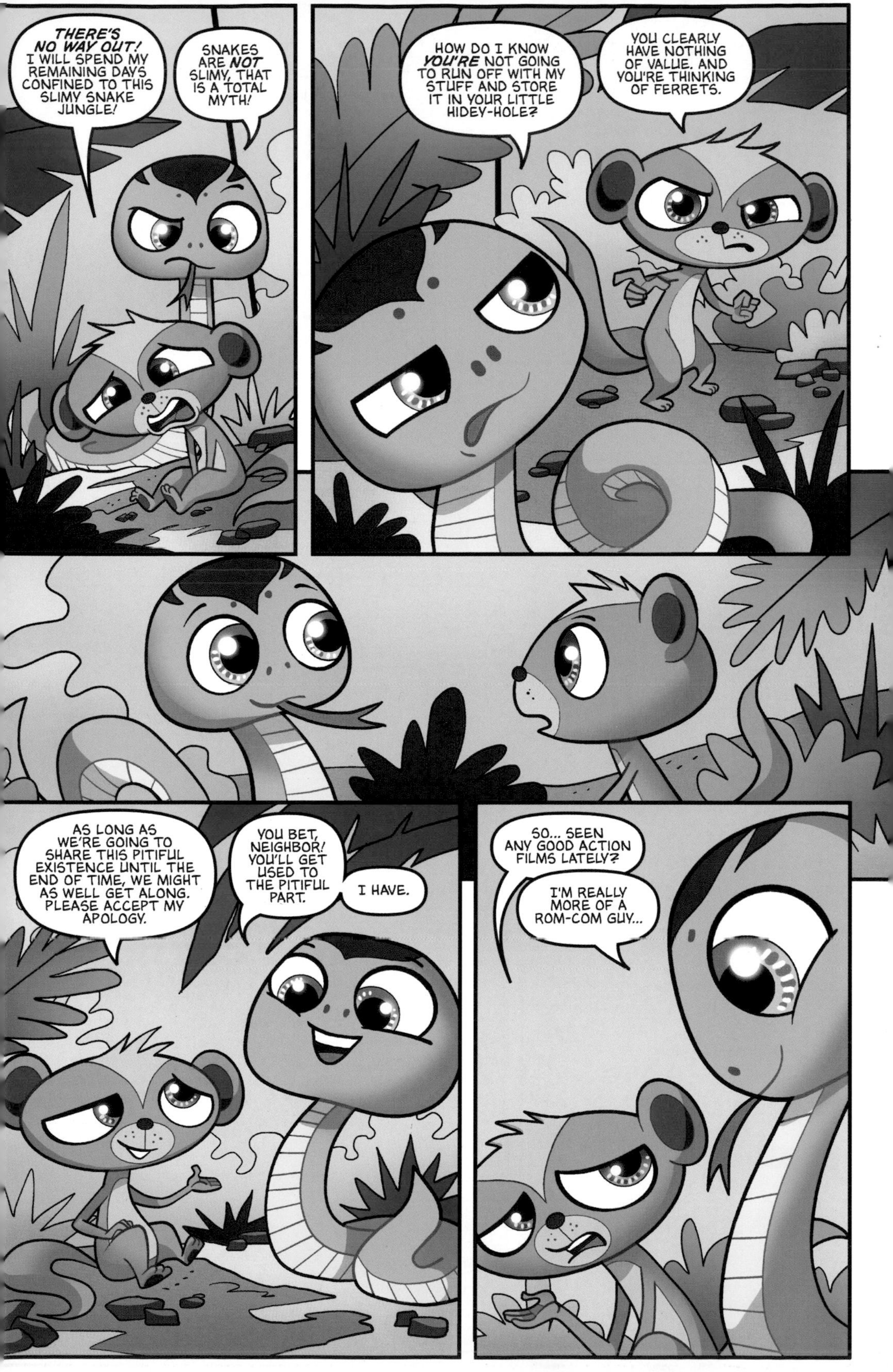
THERE'S NO WAY OUT! I WILL SPEND MY REMAINING DAYS CONFINED TO THIS SLIMY SNAKE JUNGLE!
SNAKES ARE NOT SLIMY, THAT IS A TOTAL MYTH!
HOW DO I KNOW YOU'RE NOT GOING TO RUN OFF WITH MY STUFF AND STORE IT IN YOUR LITTLE HIDEY-HOLE?
YOU CLEARLY HAVE NOTHING OF VALUE. AND YOU'RE THINKING OF FERRETS.
AS LONG AS WE'RE GOING TO SHARE THIS PITIFUL EXISTENCE UNTIL THE END OF TIME, WE MIGHT AS WELL GET ALONG. PLEASE ACCEPT MY APOLOGY.
YOU BET, NEIGHBOR! YOU'LL GET USED TO THE PITIFUL PART.
I HAVE.
SO... SEEN ANY GOOD ACTION FILMS LATELY?
I'M REALLY MORE OF A ROM-COM GUY...

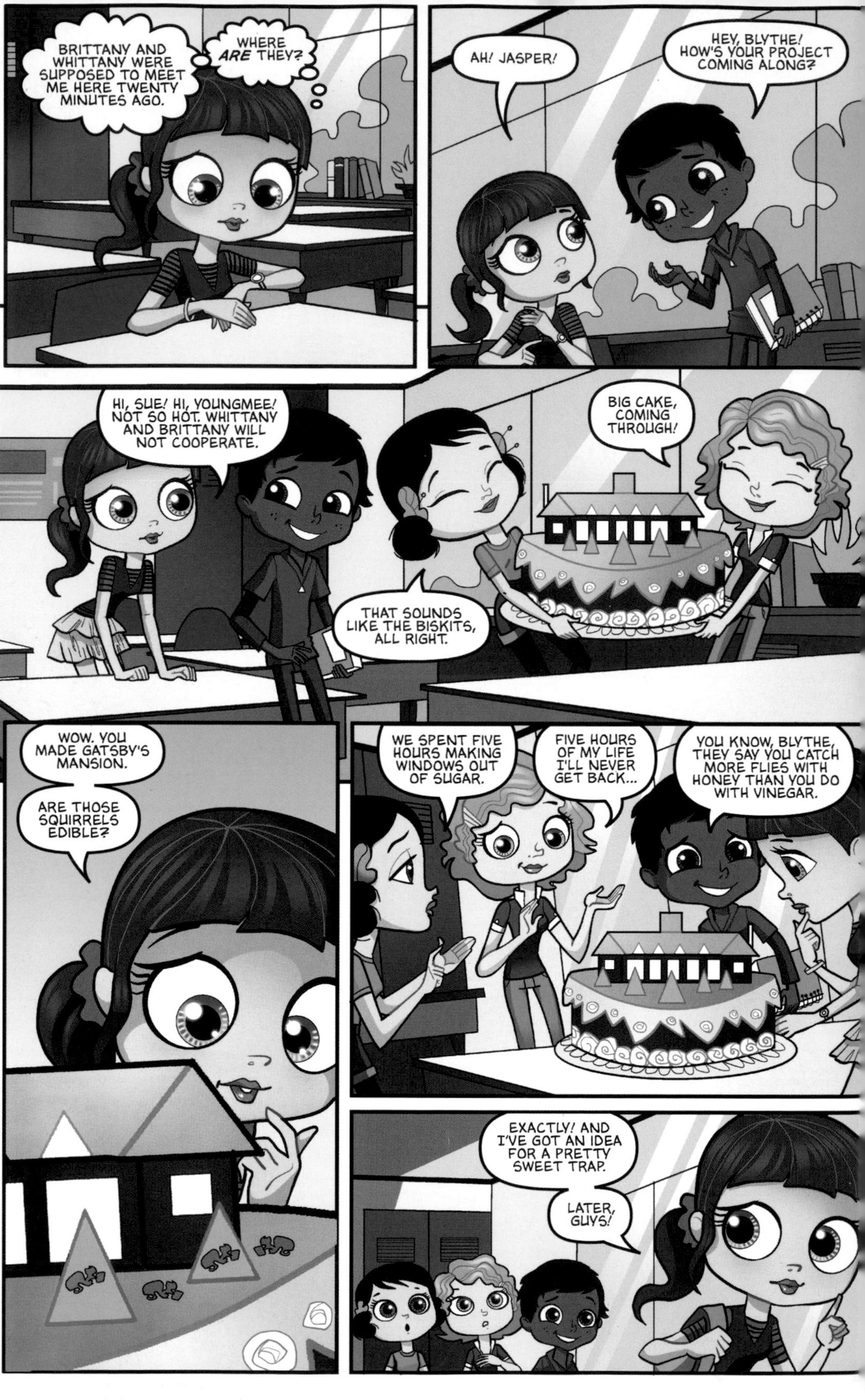
BRITTANY AND WHITTANY WERE SUPPOSED TO MEET ME HERE TWENTY MINUTES AGO.
WHERE *ARE* THEY?
AH! JASPER!
HEY, BLYTHE! HOW'S YOUR PROJECT COMING ALONG?
HI, SUE! HI, YOUNGMEE! NOT SO HOT. WHITTANY AND BRITTANY WILL NOT COOPERATE.
BIG CAKE, COMING THROUGH!
THAT SOUNDS LIKE THE BISKITS, ALL RIGHT.
WOW. YOU MADE GATSBY'S MANSION.
ARE THOSE SQUIRRELS EDIBLE?
WE SPENT FIVE HOURS MAKING WINDOWS OUT OF SUGAR.
FIVE HOURS OF MY LIFE I'LL NEVER GET BACK...
YOU KNOW, BLYTHE, THEY SAY YOU CATCH MORE FLIES WITH HONEY THAN YOU DO WITH VINEGAR.
EXACTLY! AND I'VE GOT AN IDEA FOR A PRETTY SWEET TRAP.
LATER, GUYS!

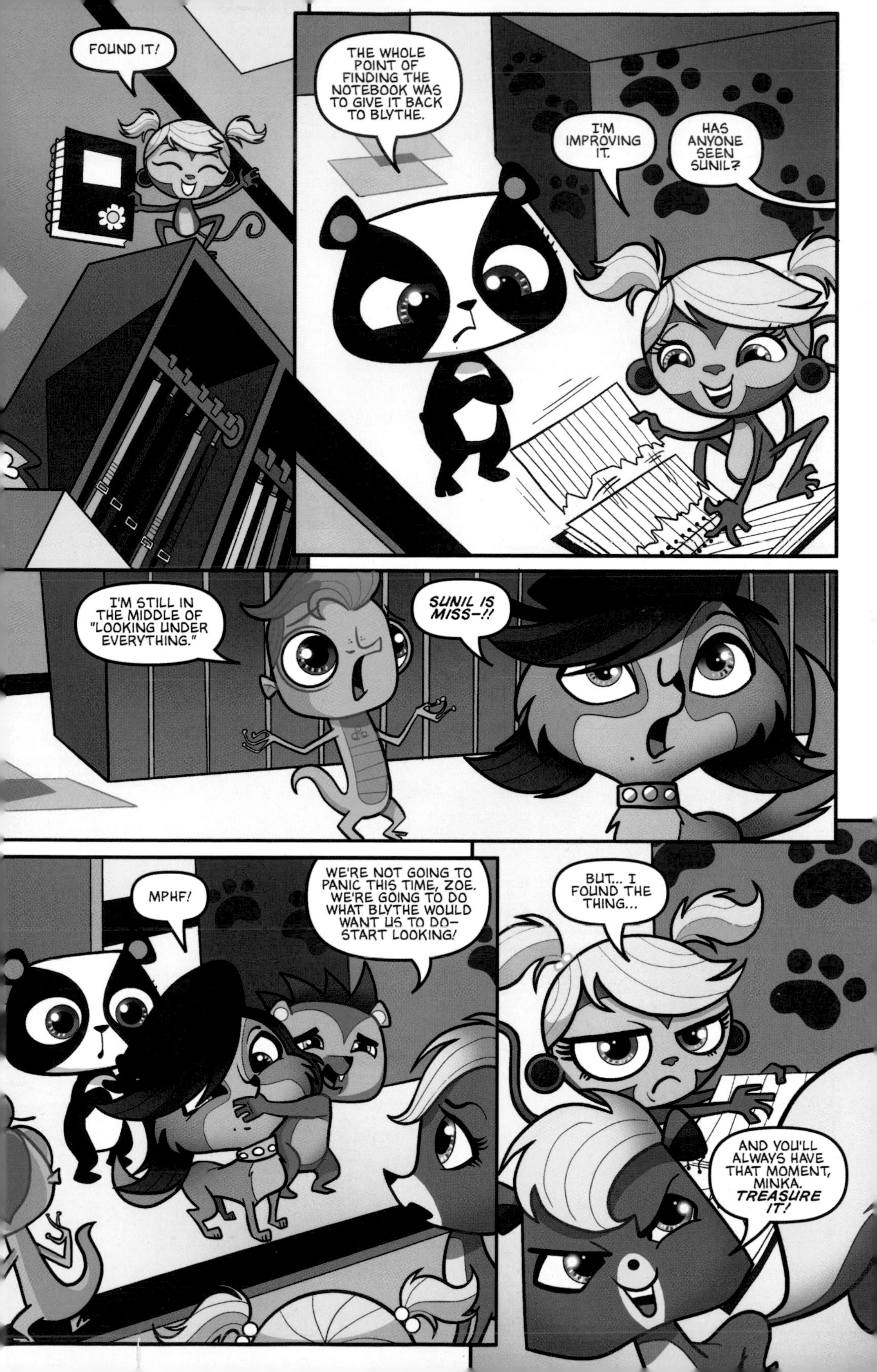
FOUND IT!
THE WHOLE POINT OF FINDING THE NOTEBOOK WAS TO GIVE IT BACK TO BLYTHE.
I'M IMPROVING IT.
HAS ANYONE SEEN SUNIL?
I'M STILL IN THE MIDDLE OF "LOOKING UNDER EVERYTHING."
SUNIL IS MISS-!!
MPHF!
WE'RE NOT GOING TO PANIC THIS TIME, ZOE. WE'RE GOING TO DO WHAT BLYTHE WOULD WANT US TO DO- START LOOKING!
BUT... I FOUND THE THING...
AND YOU'LL ALWAYS HAVE THAT MOMENT, MINKA. TREASURE IT!

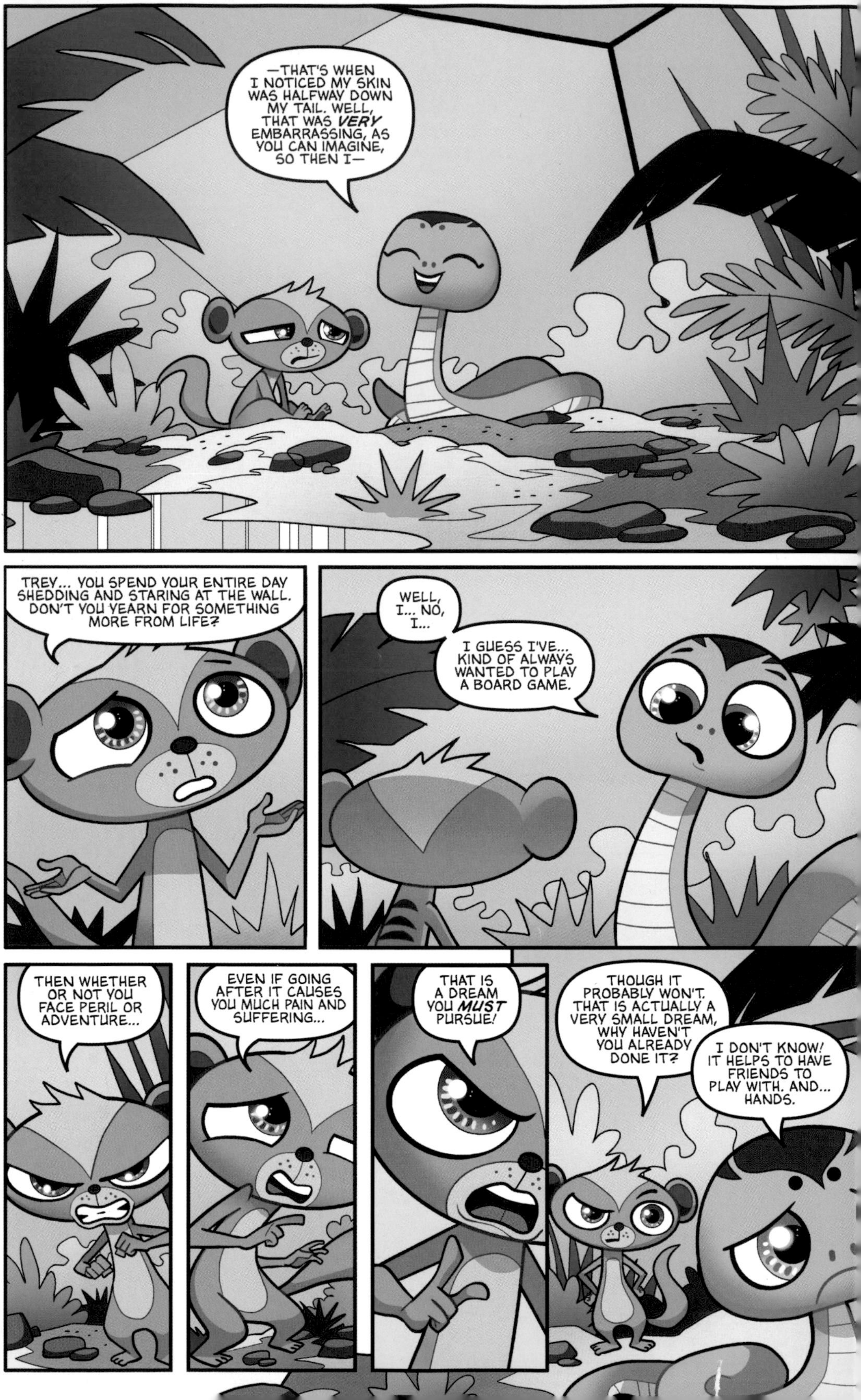
—THAT'S WHEN I NOTICED MY SKIN WAS HALFWAY DOWN MY TAIL. WELL, THAT WAS VERY EMBARRASSING, AS YOU CAN IMAGINE, SO THEN I—
TREY... YOU SPEND YOUR ENTIRE DAY SHEDDING AND STARING AT THE WALL. DON'T YOU YEARN FOR SOMETHING MORE FROM LIFE?
WELL, I... NO, I...
I GUESS I'VE... KIND OF ALWAYS WANTED TO PLAY A BOARD GAME.
THEN WHETHER OR NOT YOU FACE PERIL OR ADVENTURE...
EVEN IF GOING AFTER IT CAUSES YOU MUCH PAIN AND SUFFERING...
THAT IS A DREAM YOU MUST PURSUE!
THOUGH IT PROBABLY WON'T. THAT IS ACTUALLY A VERY SMALL DREAM. WHY HAVEN'T YOU ALREADY DONE IT?
I DON'T KNOW! IT HELPS TO HAVE FRIENDS TO PLAY WITH. AND... HANDS.

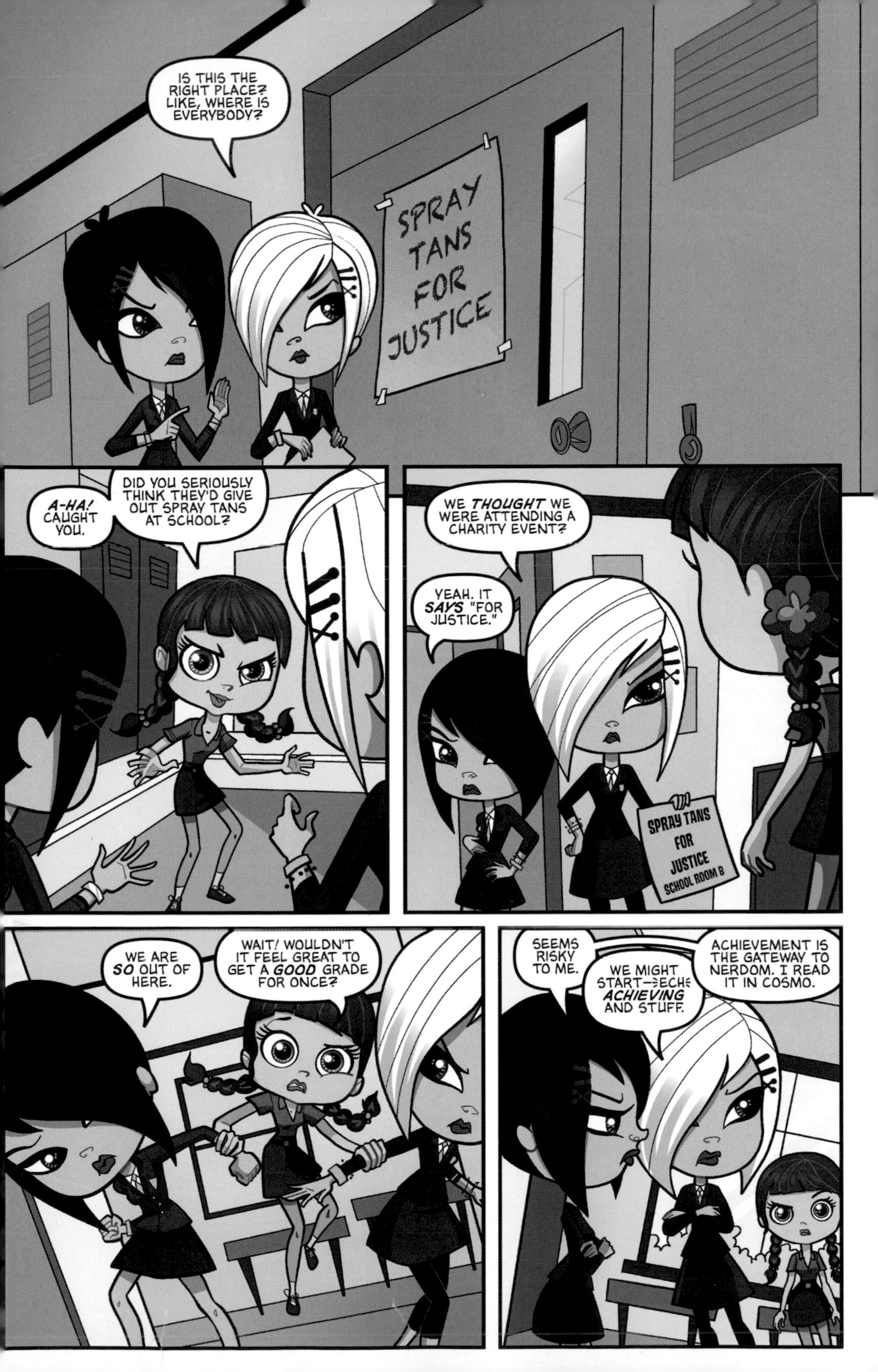

IS THIS THE RIGHT PLACE? LIKE, WHERE IS EVERYBODY?
SPRAY TANS FOR JUSTICE
A-HA! CAUGHT YOU.
DID YOU SERIOUSLY THINK THEY'D GIVE OUT SPRAY TANS AT SCHOOL?
WE *THOUGHT* WE WERE ATTENDING A CHARITY EVENT?
YEAH. IT *SAYS* "FOR JUSTICE."
SPRAY TANS FOR JUSTICE SCHOOL ROOM B
WE ARE *SO* OUT OF HERE.
WAIT! WOULDN'T IT FEEL GREAT TO GET A *GOOD* GRADE FOR ONCE?
SEEMS RISKY TO ME.
WE MIGHT START—ECH— *ACHIEVING* AND STUFF.
ACHIEVEMENT IS THE GATEWAY TO NERDOM. I READ IT IN COSMO.

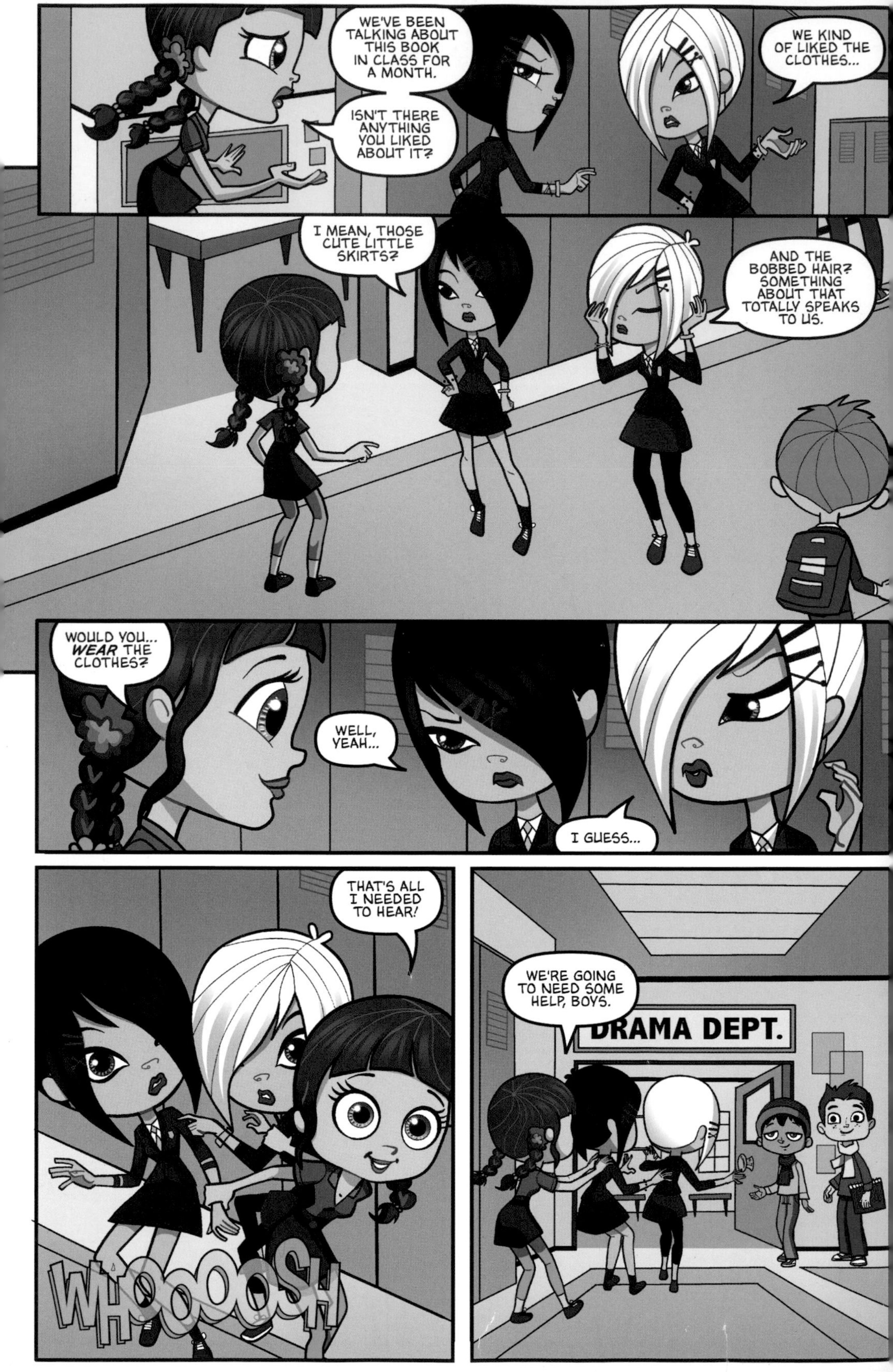
WE'VE BEEN TALKING ABOUT THIS BOOK IN CLASS FOR A MONTH.
ISN'T THERE ANYTHING YOU LIKED ABOUT IT?
WE KIND OF LIKED THE CLOTHES...
I MEAN, THOSE CUTE LITTLE SKIRTS?
AND THE BOBBED HAIR? SOMETHING ABOUT THAT TOTALLY SPEAKS TO US.
WOULD YOU... WEAR THE CLOTHES?
WELL, YEAH...
I GUESS...
THAT'S ALL I NEEDED TO HEAR!
WHOOOOOSH
WE'RE GOING TO NEED SOME HELP, BOYS.
DRAMA DEPT.

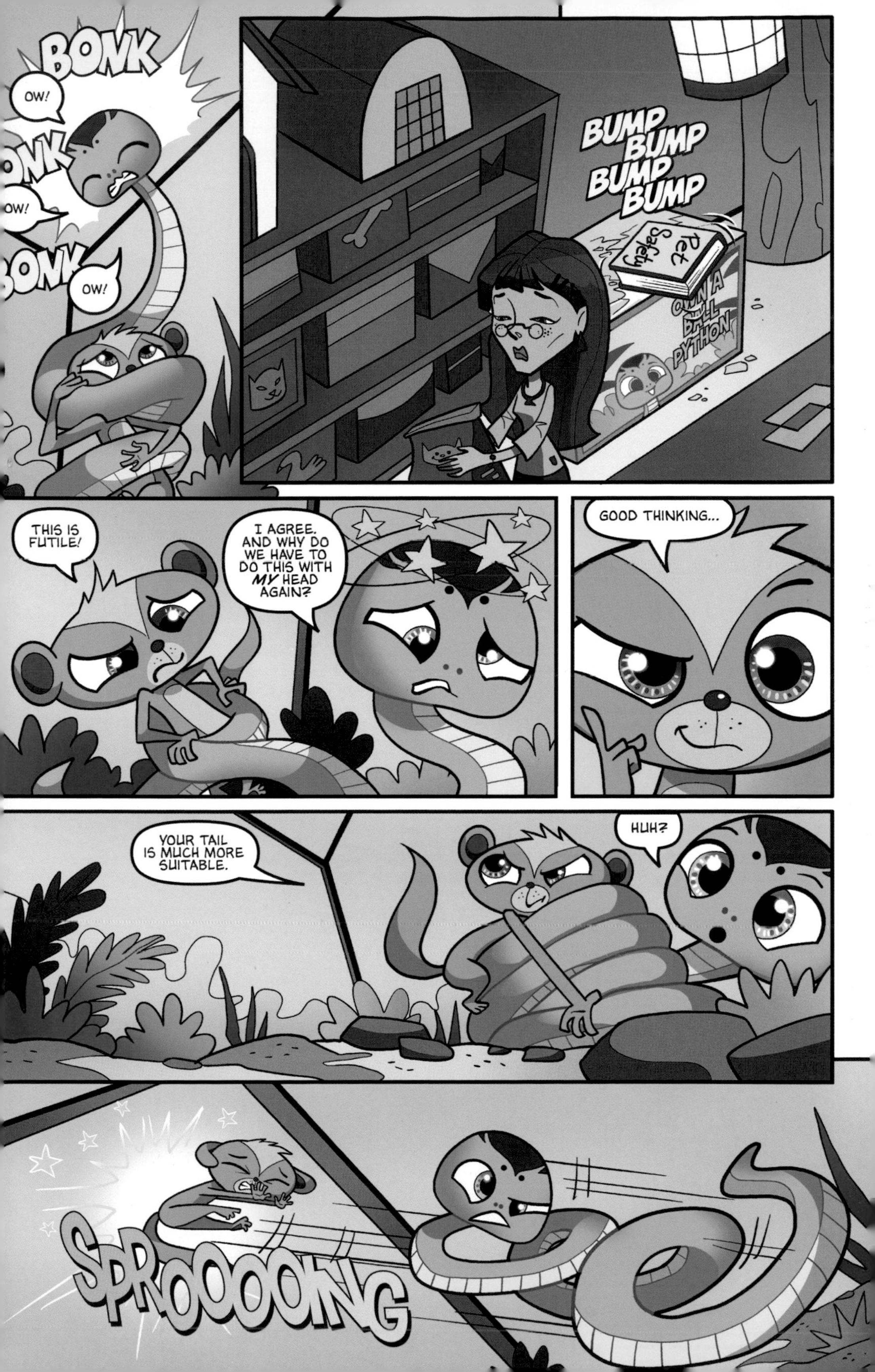
BONK
OW!
BONK
OW!
BONK
OW!
BUMP BUMP BUMP BUMP
Pet Safety
PYTHON
THIS IS FUTILE!
I AGREE. AND WHY DO WE HAVE TO DO THIS WITH MY HEAD AGAIN?
GOOD THINKING...
YOUR TAIL IS MUCH MORE SUITABLE.
HUH?
SPROOOOING

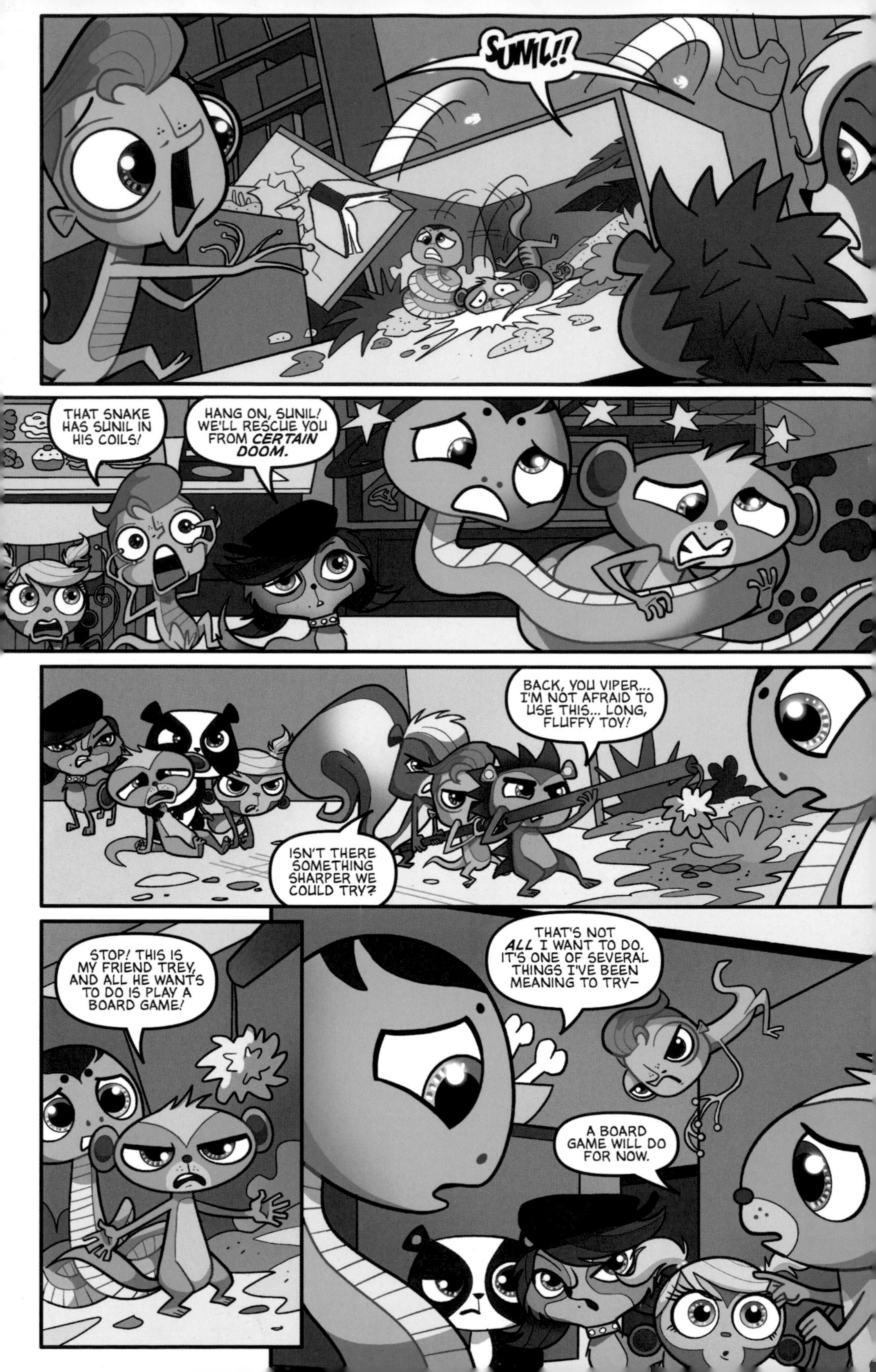
SUNIL!!
THAT SNAKE HAS SUNIL IN HIS COILS!
HANG ON, SUNIL! WE'LL RESCUE YOU FROM CERTAIN DOOM.
BACK, YOU VIPER... I'M NOT AFRAID TO USE THIS... LONG, FLUFFY TOY!
ISN'T THERE SOMETHING SHARPER WE COULD TRY?
STOP! THIS IS MY FRIEND TREY, AND ALL HE WANTS TO DO IS PLAY A BOARD GAME!
THAT'S NOT ALL I WANT TO DO. IT'S ONE OF SEVERAL THINGS I'VE BEEN MEANING TO TRY–
A BOARD GAME WILL DO FOR NOW.

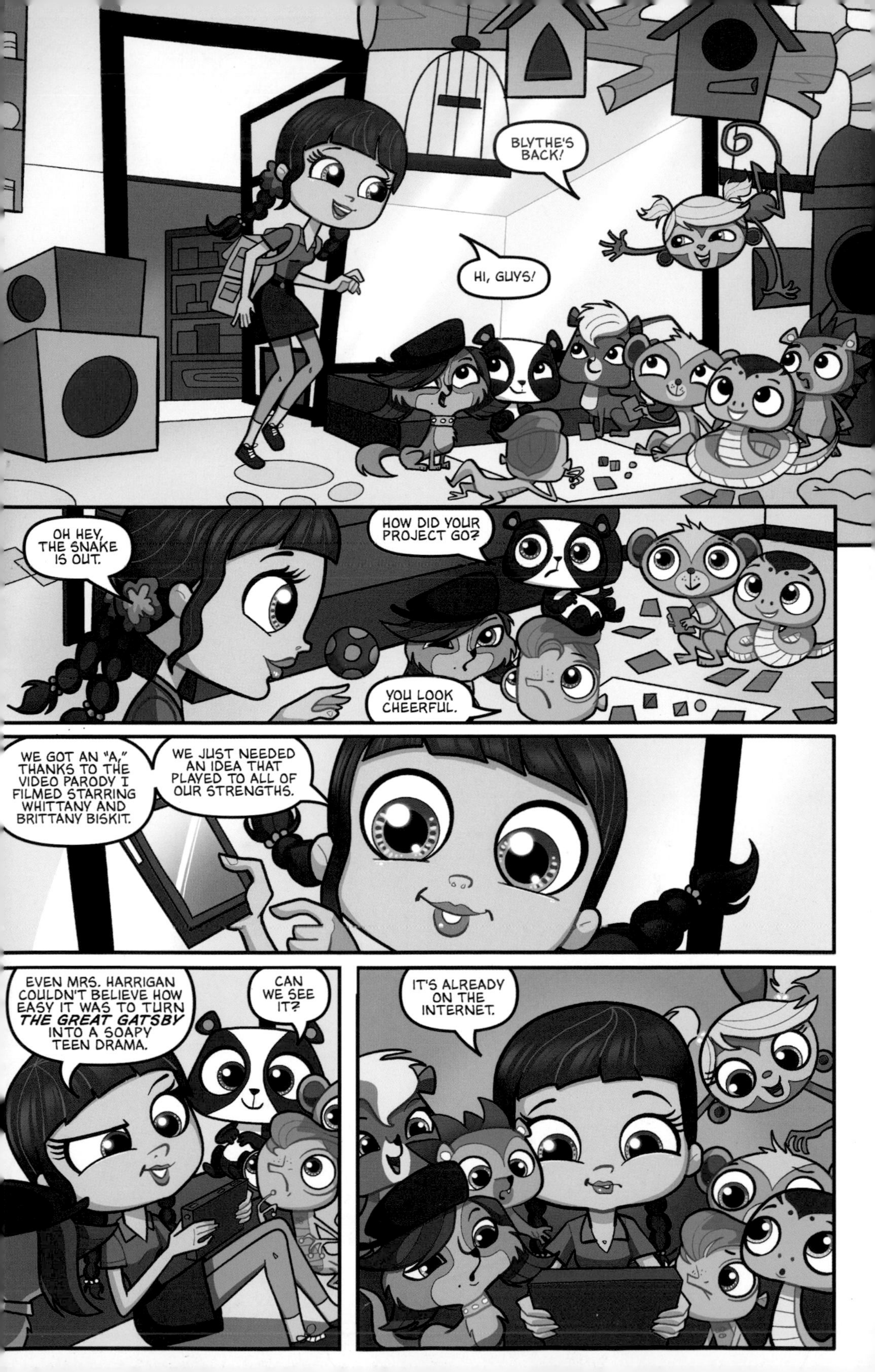
BLYTHE'S BACK!
HI, GUYS!
OH HEY, THE SNAKE IS OUT.
HOW DID YOUR PROJECT GO?
YOU LOOK CHEERFUL.
WE GOT AN "A," THANKS TO THE VIDEO PARODY I FILMED STARRING WHITTANY AND BRITTANY BISKIT.
WE JUST NEEDED AN IDEA THAT PLAYED TO ALL OF OUR STRENGTHS.
EVEN MRS. HARRIGAN COULDN'T BELIEVE HOW EASY IT WAS TO TURN ***THE GREAT GATSBY*** INTO A SOAPY TEEN DRAMA.
CAN WE SEE IT?
IT'S ALREADY ON THE INTERNET.

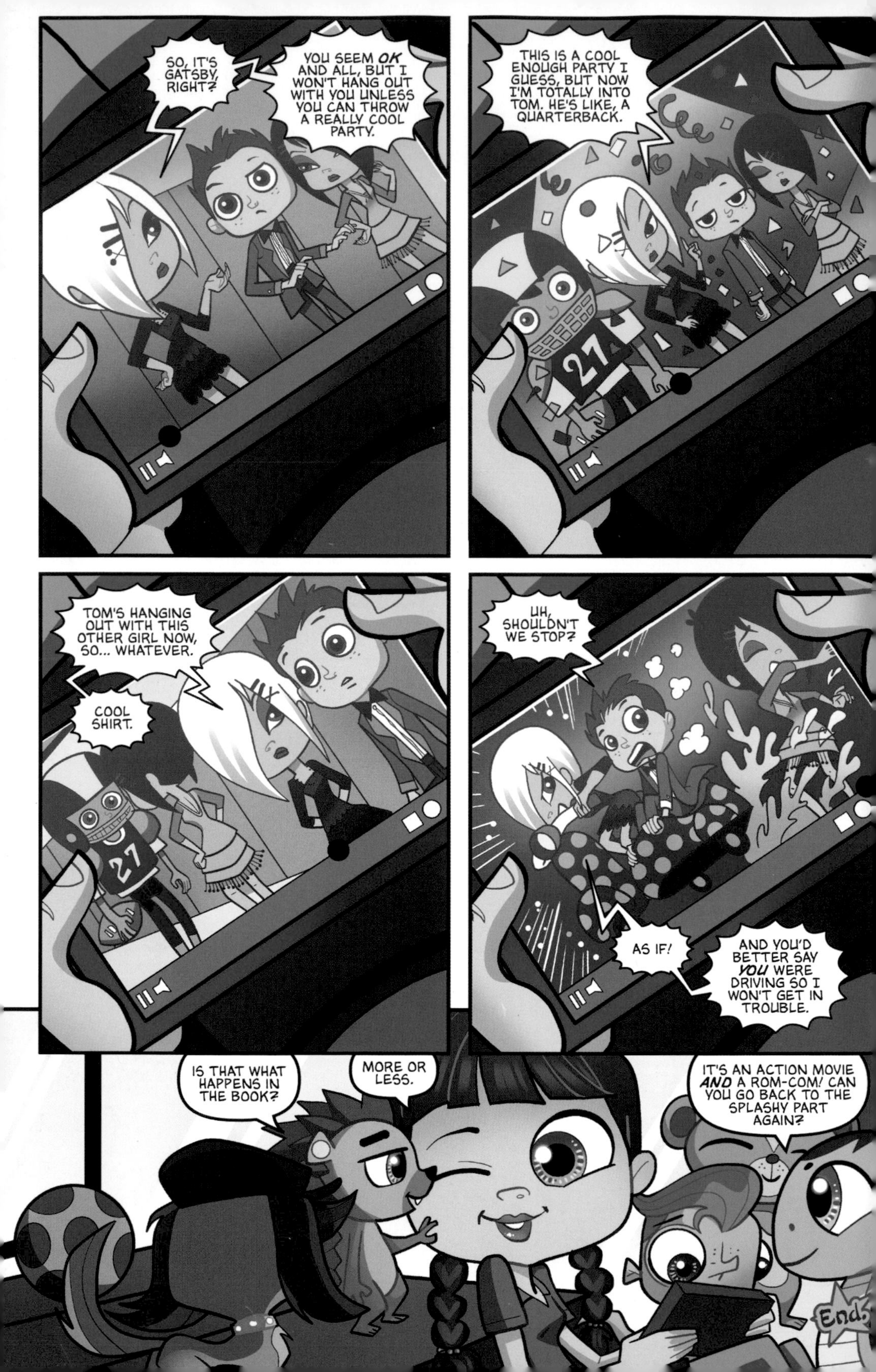
SO, IT'S GATSBY, RIGHT?
YOU SEEM OK AND ALL, BUT I WON'T HANG OUT WITH YOU UNLESS YOU CAN THROW A REALLY COOL PARTY.
THIS IS A COOL ENOUGH PARTY I GUESS, BUT NOW I'M TOTALLY INTO TOM. HE'S LIKE, A QUARTERBACK.
27
TOM'S HANGING OUT WITH THIS OTHER GIRL NOW, SO... WHATEVER.
COOL SHIRT.
27
UH, SHOULDN'T WE STOP?
AS IF!
AND YOU'D BETTER SAY YOU WERE DRIVING SO I WON'T GET IN TROUBLE.
IS THAT WHAT HAPPENS IN THE BOOK?
MORE OR LESS.
IT'S AN ACTION MOVIE AND A ROM-COM! CAN YOU GO BACK TO THE SPLASHY PART AGAIN?
End.

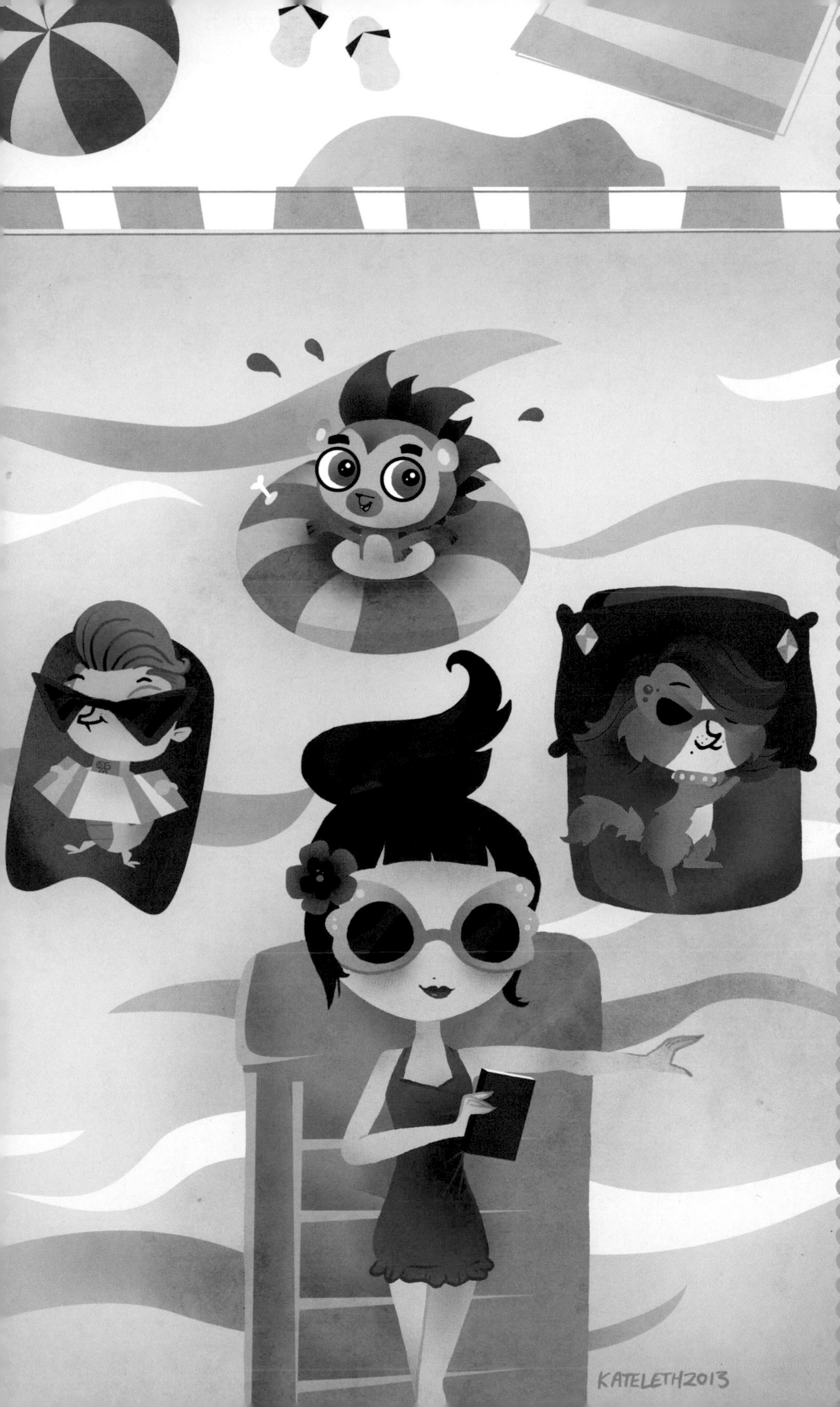
KATELETH2013

art by: Kate Leth

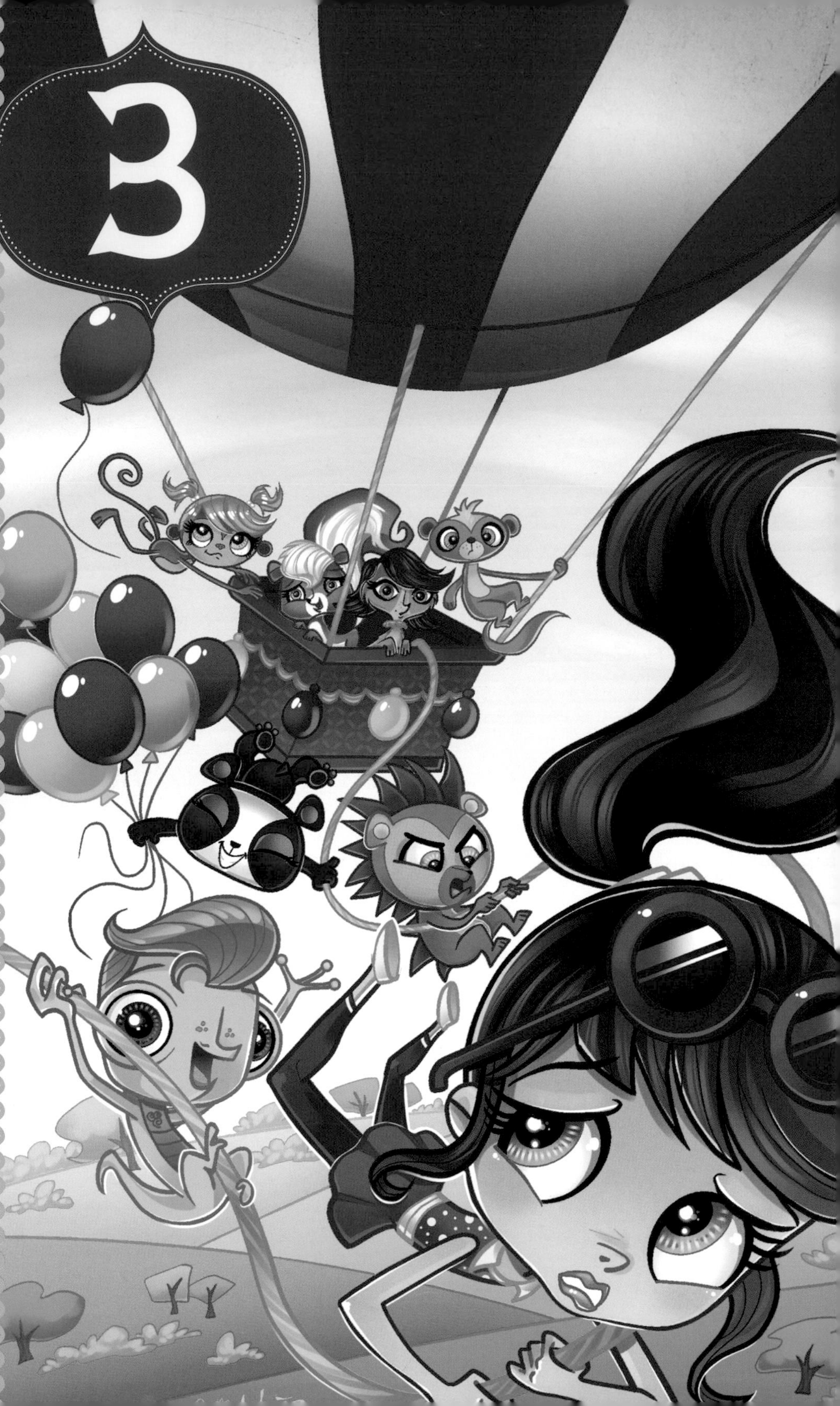
3

art by: Nicanor Peña • colors by: Victoria Robado

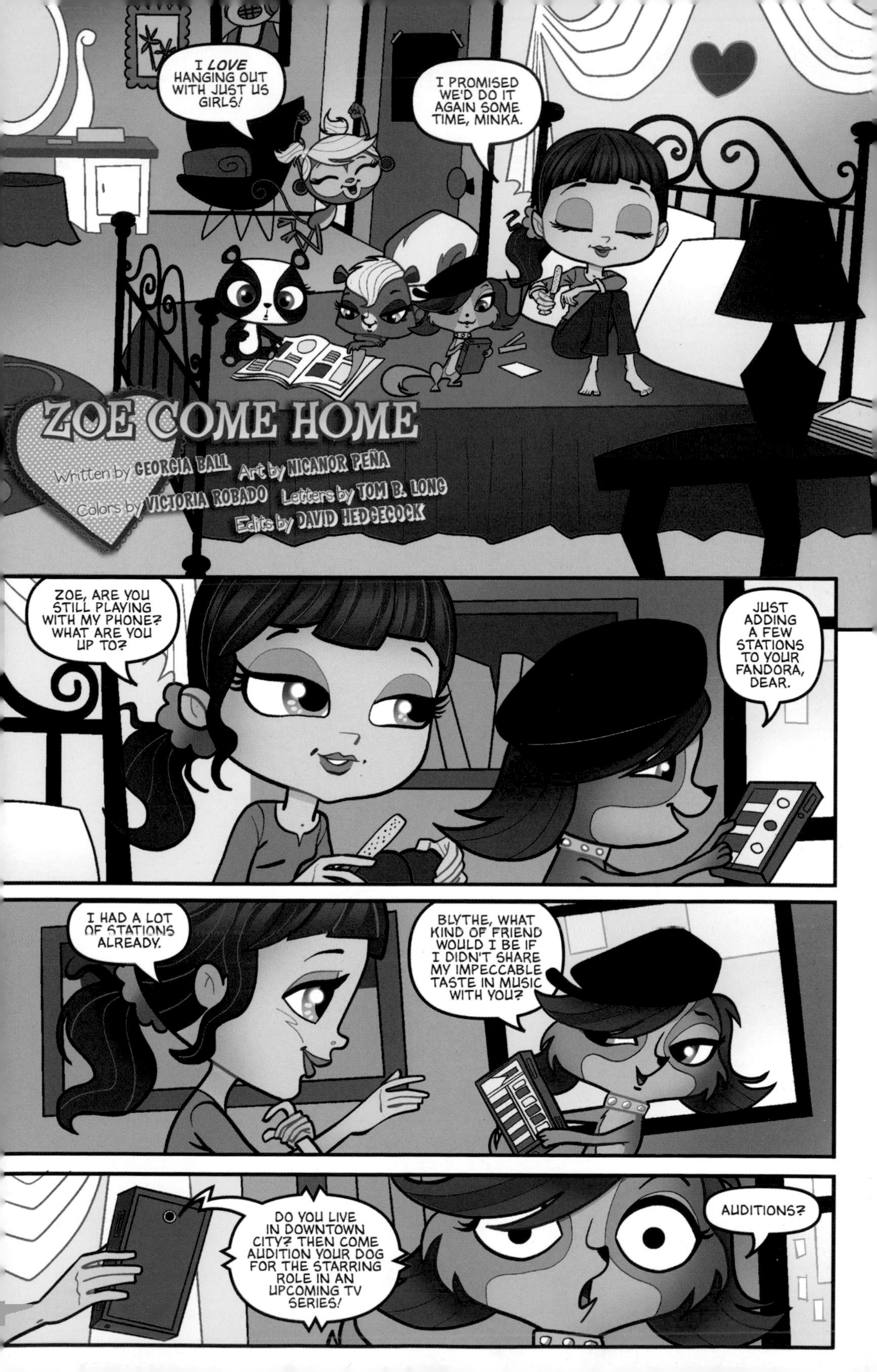
I LOVE HANGING OUT WITH JUST US GIRLS!
I PROMISED WE'D DO IT AGAIN SOME TIME, MINKA.
ZOE COME HOME
Written by GEORGIA BALL Art by NICANOR PEÑA
Colors by VICTORIA ROBADO Letters by TOM B. LONG
Edits by DAVID HEDGECOCK
ZOE, ARE YOU STILL PLAYING WITH MY PHONE? WHAT ARE YOU UP TO?
JUST ADDING A FEW STATIONS TO YOUR FANDORA, DEAR.
I HAD A LOT OF STATIONS ALREADY.
BLYTHE, WHAT KIND OF FRIEND WOULD I BE IF I DIDN'T SHARE MY IMPECCABLE TASTE IN MUSIC WITH YOU?
DO YOU LIVE IN DOWNTOWN CITY? THEN COME AUDITION YOUR DOG FOR THE STARRING ROLE IN AN UPCOMING TV SERIES!
AUDITIONS?

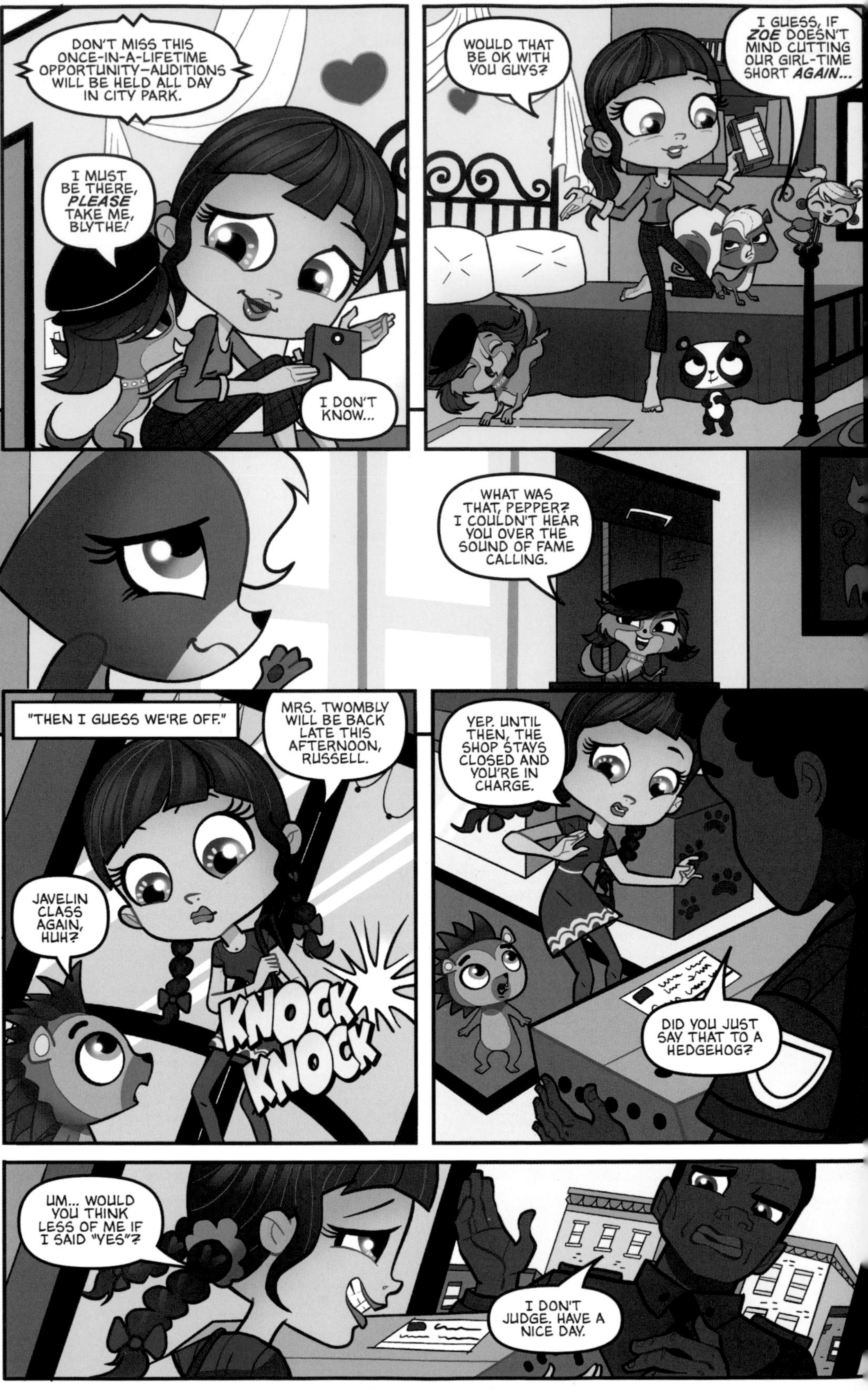
DON'T MISS THIS ONCE-IN-A-LIFETIME OPPORTUNITY—AUDITIONS WILL BE HELD ALL DAY IN CITY PARK.
I MUST BE THERE, PLEASE TAKE ME, BLYTHE!
I DON'T KNOW...
WOULD THAT BE OK WITH YOU GUYS?
I GUESS, IF ZOE DOESN'T MIND CUTTING OUR GIRL-TIME SHORT AGAIN...
WHAT WAS THAT, PEPPER? I COULDN'T HEAR YOU OVER THE SOUND OF FAME CALLING.
"THEN I GUESS WE'RE OFF."
MRS. TWOMBLY WILL BE BACK LATE THIS AFTERNOON, RUSSELL.
JAVELIN CLASS AGAIN, HUH?
KNOCK KNOCK
YEP. UNTIL THEN, THE SHOP STAYS CLOSED AND YOU'RE IN CHARGE.
DID YOU JUST SAY THAT TO A HEDGEHOG?
UM... WOULD YOU THINK LESS OF ME IF I SAID "YES"?
I DON'T JUDGE. HAVE A NICE DAY.

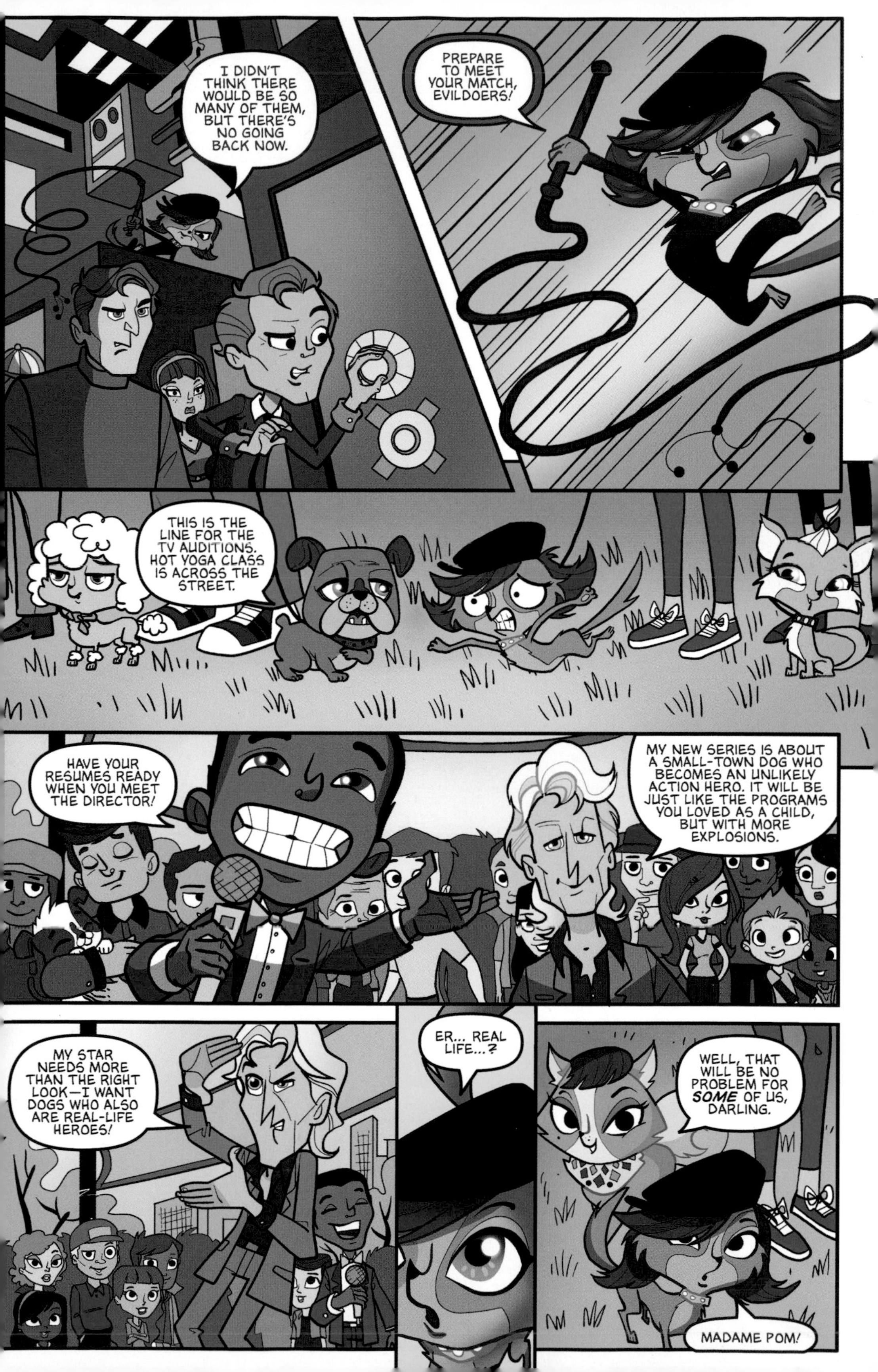
I DIDN'T THINK THERE WOULD BE SO MANY OF THEM, BUT THERE'S NO GOING BACK NOW.
PREPARE TO MEET YOUR MATCH, EVILDOERS!
THIS IS THE LINE FOR THE TV AUDITIONS. HOT YOGA CLASS IS ACROSS THE STREET.
HAVE YOUR RESUMES READY WHEN YOU MEET THE DIRECTOR!
MY NEW SERIES IS ABOUT A SMALL-TOWN DOG WHO BECOMES AN UNLIKELY ACTION HERO. IT WILL BE JUST LIKE THE PROGRAMS YOU LOVED AS A CHILD, BUT WITH MORE EXPLOSIONS.
MY STAR NEEDS MORE THAN THE RIGHT LOOK—I WANT DOGS WHO ALSO ARE REAL-LIFE HEROES!
ER... REAL LIFE...?
WELL, THAT WILL BE NO PROBLEM FOR *SOME* OF US, DARLING.
MADAME POM!

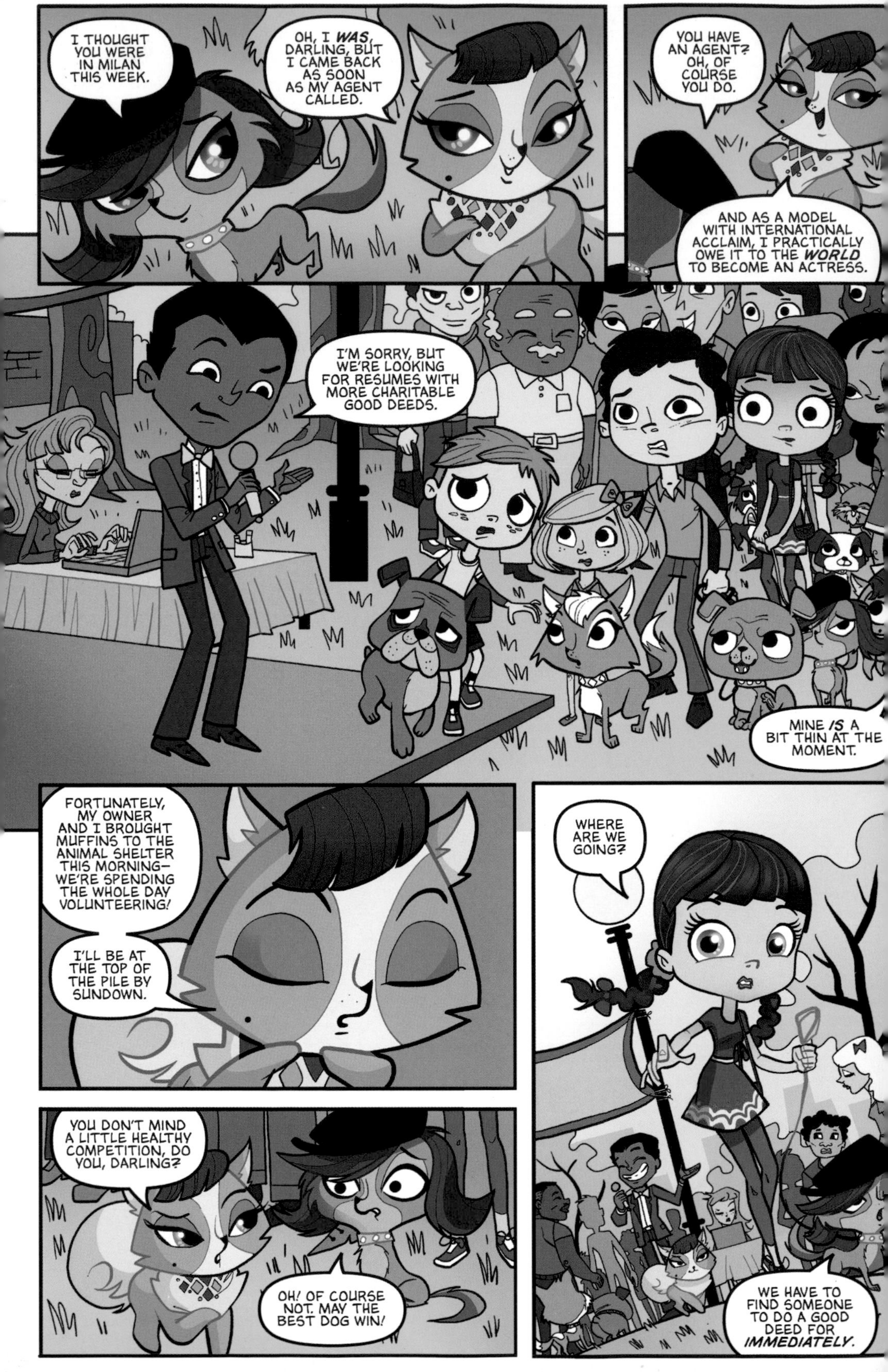
I THOUGHT YOU WERE IN MILAN THIS WEEK.
OH, I WAS, DARLING, BUT I CAME BACK AS SOON AS MY AGENT CALLED.
YOU HAVE AN AGENT? OH, OF COURSE YOU DO.
AND AS A MODEL WITH INTERNATIONAL ACCLAIM, I PRACTICALLY OWE IT TO THE WORLD TO BECOME AN ACTRESS.
I'M SORRY, BUT WE'RE LOOKING FOR RESUMES WITH MORE CHARITABLE GOOD DEEDS.
MINE IS A BIT THIN AT THE MOMENT.
FORTUNATELY, MY OWNER AND I BROUGHT MUFFINS TO THE ANIMAL SHELTER THIS MORNING– WE'RE SPENDING THE WHOLE DAY VOLUNTEERING!
I'LL BE AT THE TOP OF THE PILE BY SUNDOWN.
YOU DON'T MIND A LITTLE HEALTHY COMPETITION, DO YOU, DARLING?
OH! OF COURSE NOT. MAY THE BEST DOG WIN!
WHERE ARE WE GOING?
WE HAVE TO FIND SOMEONE TO DO A GOOD DEED FOR IMMEDIATELY.

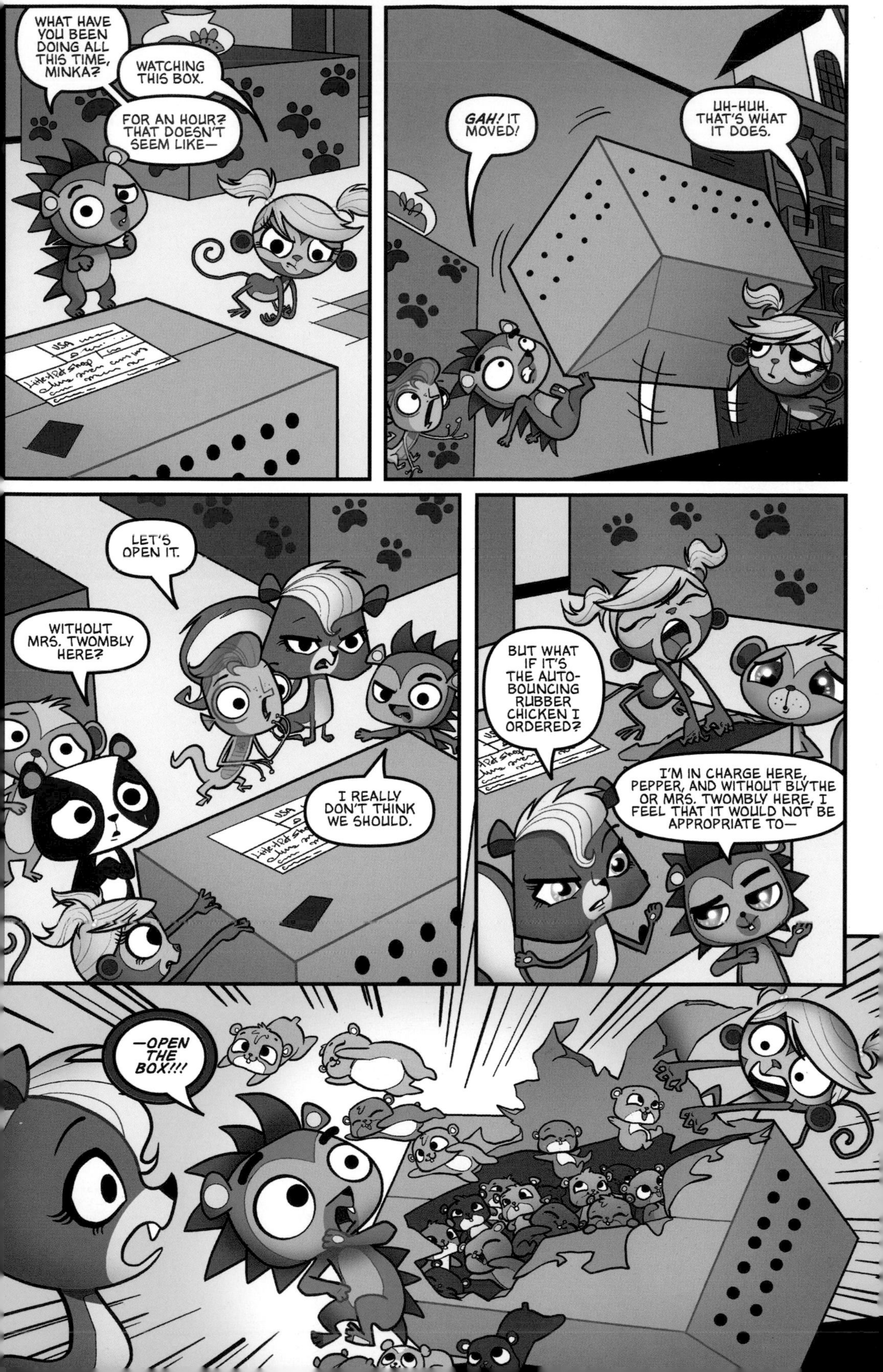
WHAT HAVE YOU BEEN DOING ALL THIS TIME, MINKA?
WATCHING THIS BOX.
FOR AN HOUR? THAT DOESN'T SEEM LIKE—
GAH! IT MOVED!
UH-HUH. THAT'S WHAT IT DOES.
LET'S OPEN IT.
WITHOUT MRS. TWOMBLY HERE?
I REALLY DON'T THINK WE SHOULD.
BUT WHAT IF IT'S THE AUTO-BOUNCING RUBBER CHICKEN I ORDERED?
I'M IN CHARGE HERE, PEPPER, AND WITHOUT BLYTHE OR MRS. TWOMBLY HERE, I FEEL THAT IT WOULD NOT BE APPROPRIATE TO—
—OPEN THE BOX!!!

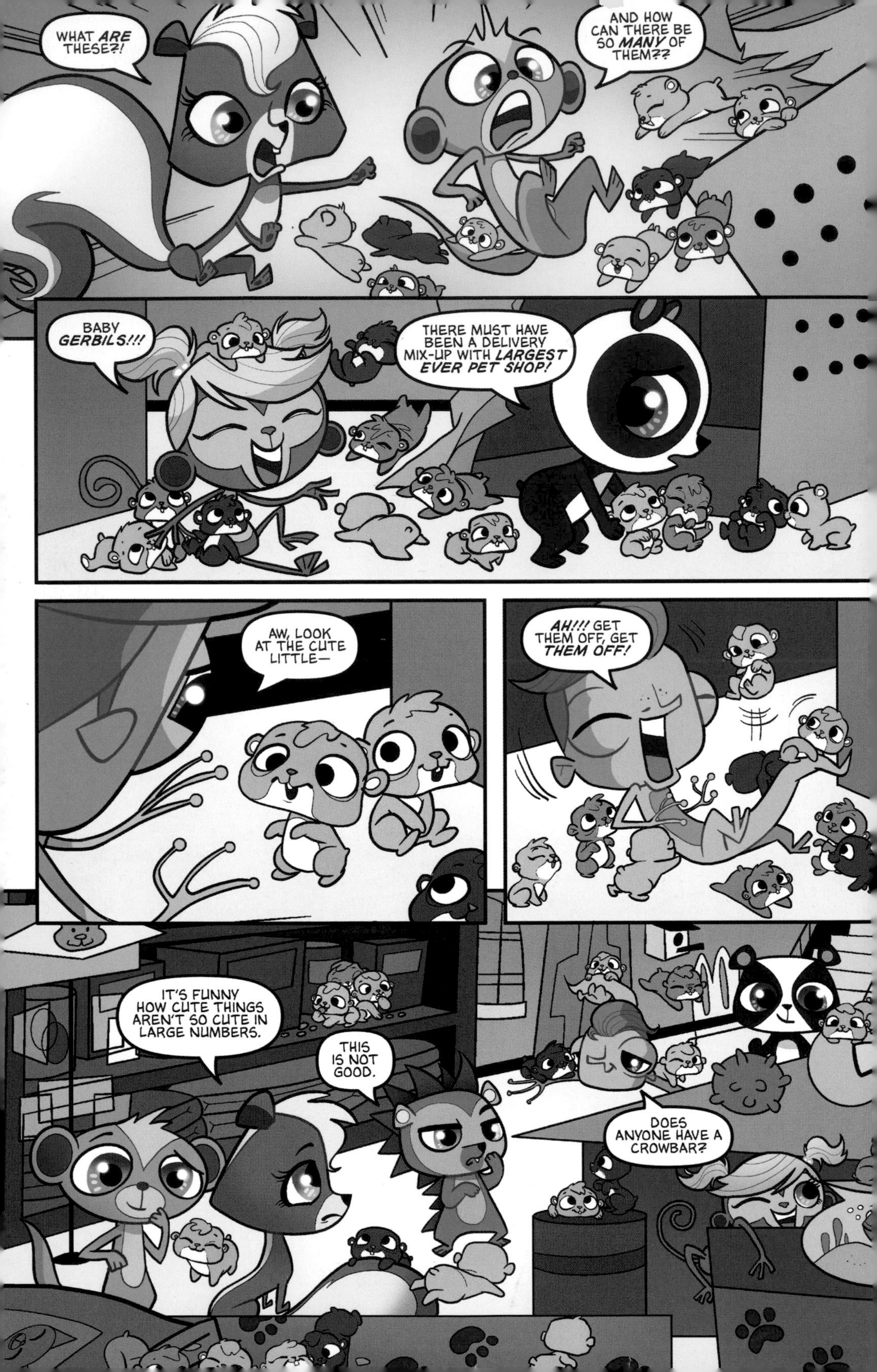
WHAT ARE THESE?!
AND HOW CAN THERE BE SO MANY OF THEM??
BABY GERBILS!!!
THERE MUST HAVE BEEN A DELIVERY MIX-UP WITH LARGEST EVER PET SHOP!
AW, LOOK AT THE CUTE LITTLE—
AH!!! GET THEM OFF, GET THEM OFF!
IT'S FUNNY HOW CUTE THINGS AREN'T SO CUTE IN LARGE NUMBERS.
THIS IS NOT GOOD.
DOES ANYONE HAVE A CROWBAR?

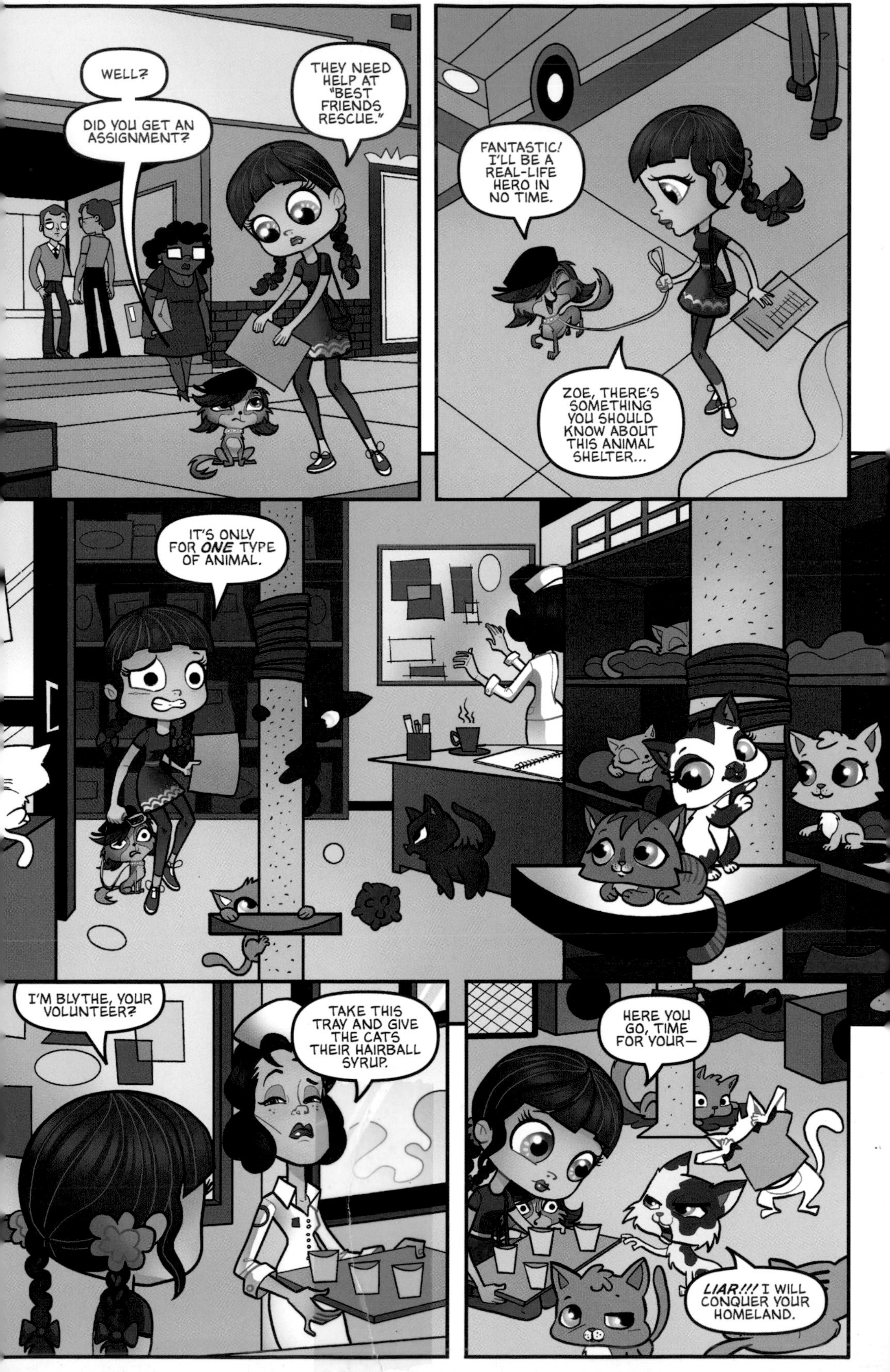
WELL?
DID YOU GET AN ASSIGNMENT?
THEY NEED HELP AT "BEST FRIENDS RESCUE."
FANTASTIC! I'LL BE A REAL-LIFE HERO IN NO TIME.
ZOE, THERE'S SOMETHING YOU SHOULD KNOW ABOUT THIS ANIMAL SHELTER...
IT'S ONLY FOR *ONE* TYPE OF ANIMAL.
I'M BLYTHE, YOUR VOLUNTEER?
TAKE THIS TRAY AND GIVE THE CATS THEIR HAIRBALL SYRUP.
HERE YOU GO, TIME FOR YOUR—
LIAR!!! I WILL CONQUER YOUR HOMELAND.

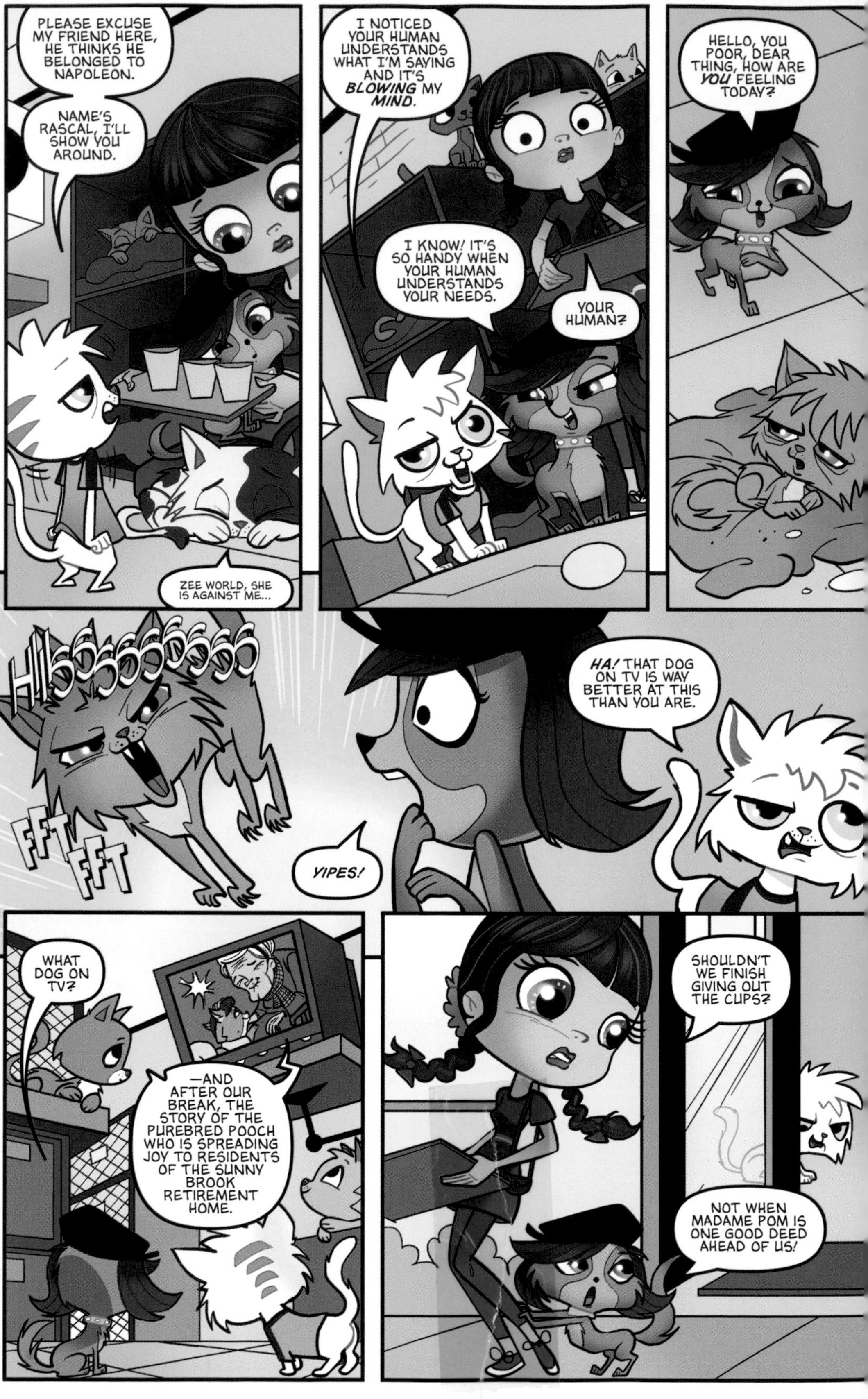
PLEASE EXCUSE MY FRIEND HERE, HE THINKS HE BELONGED TO NAPOLEON.
NAME'S RASCAL, I'LL SHOW YOU AROUND.
ZEE WORLD, SHE IS AGAINST ME...
I NOTICED YOUR HUMAN UNDERSTANDS WHAT I'M SAYING AND IT'S *BLOWING* MY *MIND*.
I KNOW! IT'S SO HANDY WHEN YOUR HUMAN UNDERSTANDS YOUR NEEDS.
YOUR HUMAN?
HELLO, YOU POOR, DEAR THING, HOW ARE *YOU* FEELING TODAY?
HISSSSSSSSS
FFT FFT
YIPES!
HA! THAT DOG ON TV IS WAY BETTER AT THIS THAN YOU ARE.
WHAT DOG ON TV?
—AND AFTER OUR BREAK, THE STORY OF THE PUREBRED POOCH WHO IS SPREADING JOY TO RESIDENTS OF THE SUNNY BROOK RETIREMENT HOME.
SHOULDN'T WE FINISH GIVING OUT THE CUPS?
NOT WHEN MADAME POM IS ONE GOOD DEED AHEAD OF US!

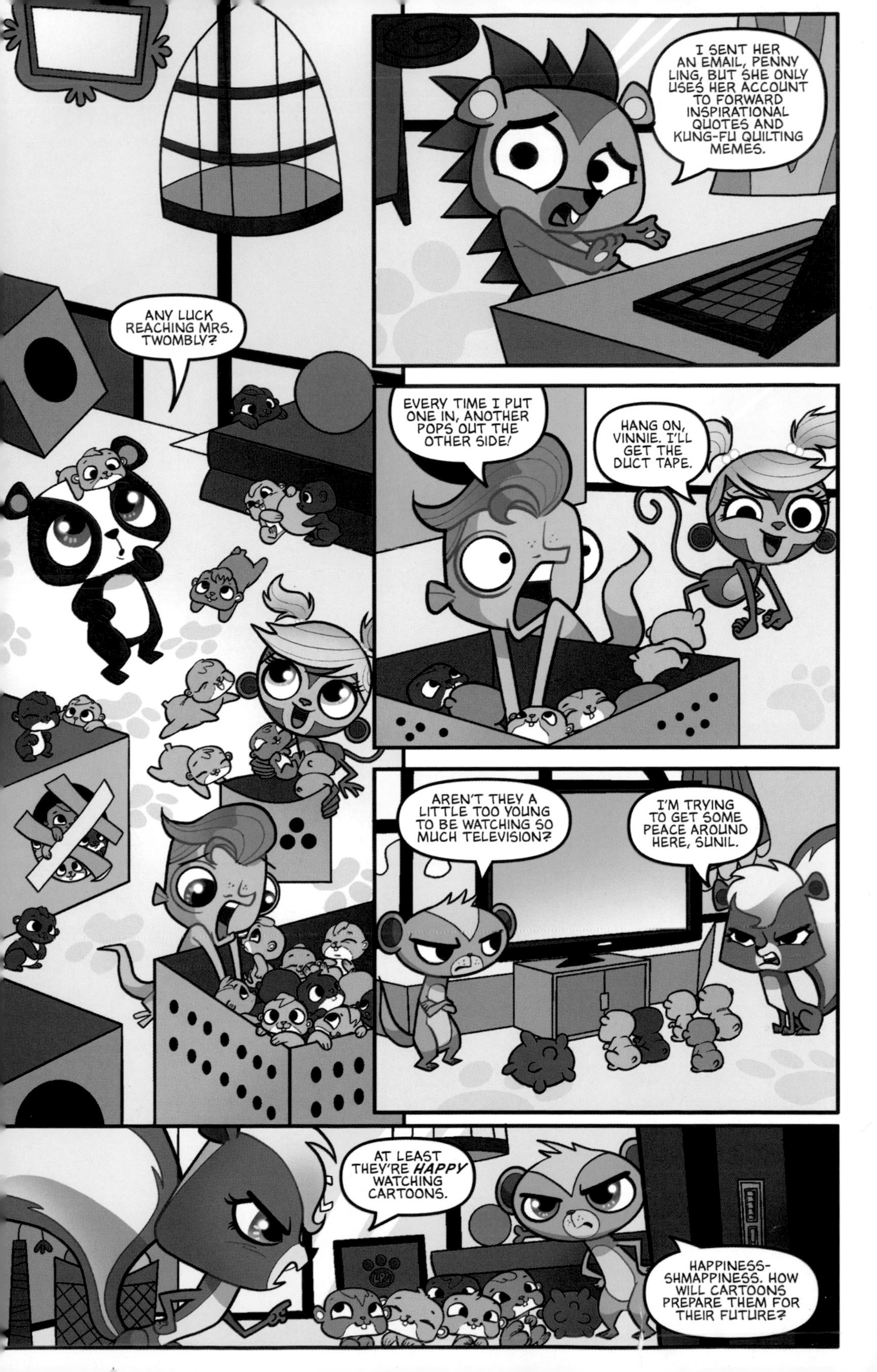
ANY LUCK REACHING MRS. TWOMBLY?
I SENT HER AN EMAIL, PENNY LING, BUT SHE ONLY USES HER ACCOUNT TO FORWARD INSPIRATIONAL QUOTES AND KUNG-FU QUILTING MEMES.
EVERY TIME I PUT ONE IN, ANOTHER POPS OUT THE OTHER SIDE!
HANG ON, VINNIE. I'LL GET THE DUCT TAPE.
AREN'T THEY A LITTLE TOO YOUNG TO BE WATCHING SO MUCH TELEVISION?
I'M TRYING TO GET SOME PEACE AROUND HERE, SUNIL.
AT LEAST THEY'RE *HAPPY* WATCHING CARTOONS.
HAPPINESS-SHMAPPINESS. HOW WILL CARTOONS PREPARE THEM FOR THEIR FUTURE?

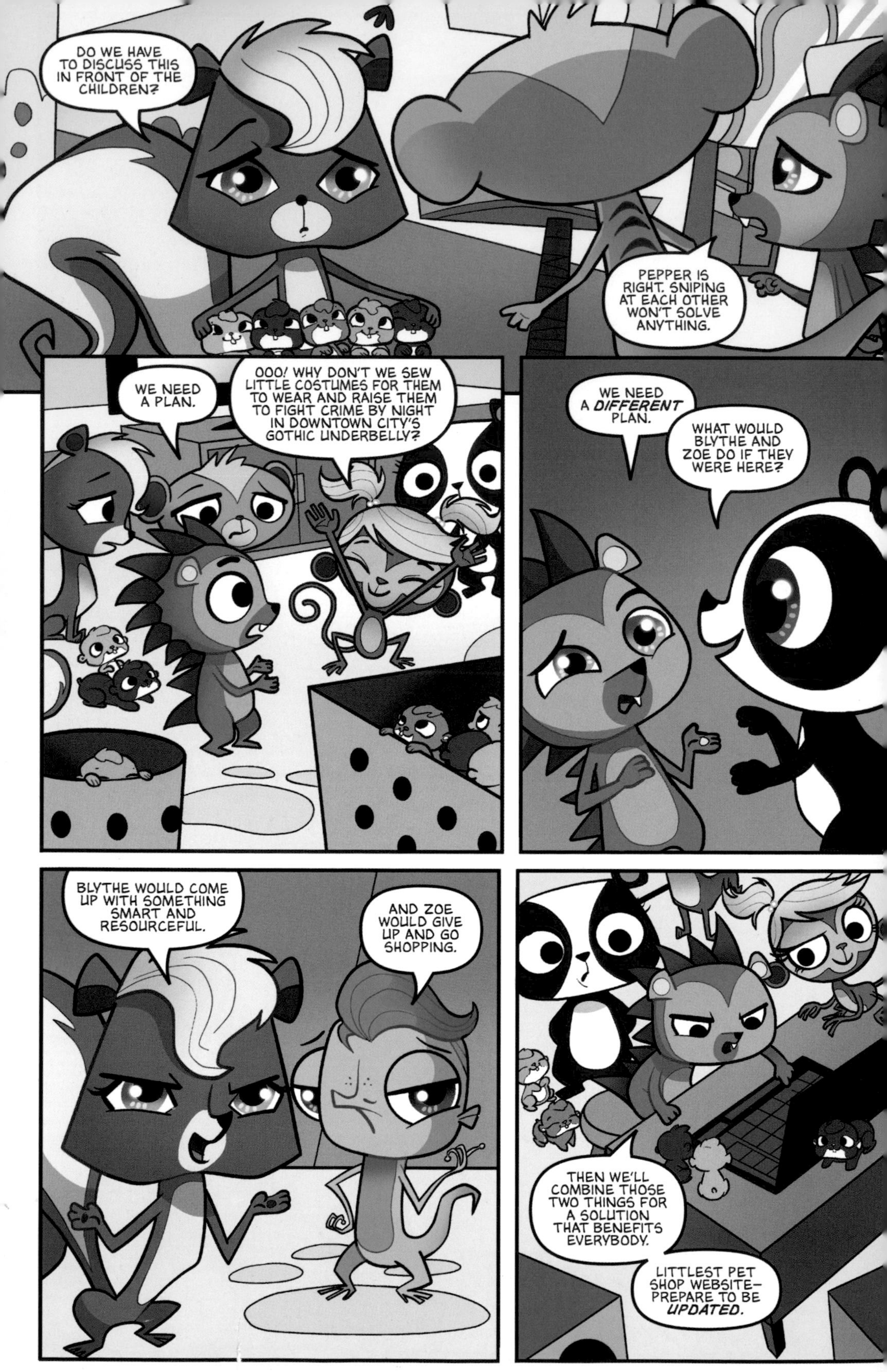
DO WE HAVE TO DISCUSS THIS IN FRONT OF THE CHILDREN?
PEPPER IS RIGHT. SNIPING AT EACH OTHER WON'T SOLVE ANYTHING.
WE NEED A PLAN.
OOO! WHY DON'T WE SEW LITTLE COSTUMES FOR THEM TO WEAR AND RAISE THEM TO FIGHT CRIME BY NIGHT IN DOWNTOWN CITY'S GOTHIC UNDERBELLY?
WE NEED A *DIFFERENT* PLAN.
WHAT WOULD BLYTHE AND ZOE DO IF THEY WERE HERE?
BLYTHE WOULD COME UP WITH SOMETHING SMART AND RESOURCEFUL.
AND ZOE WOULD GIVE UP AND GO SHOPPING.
THEN WE'LL COMBINE THOSE TWO THINGS FOR A SOLUTION THAT BENEFITS EVERYBODY.
LITTLEST PET SHOP WEBSITE– PREPARE TO BE *UPDATED*.

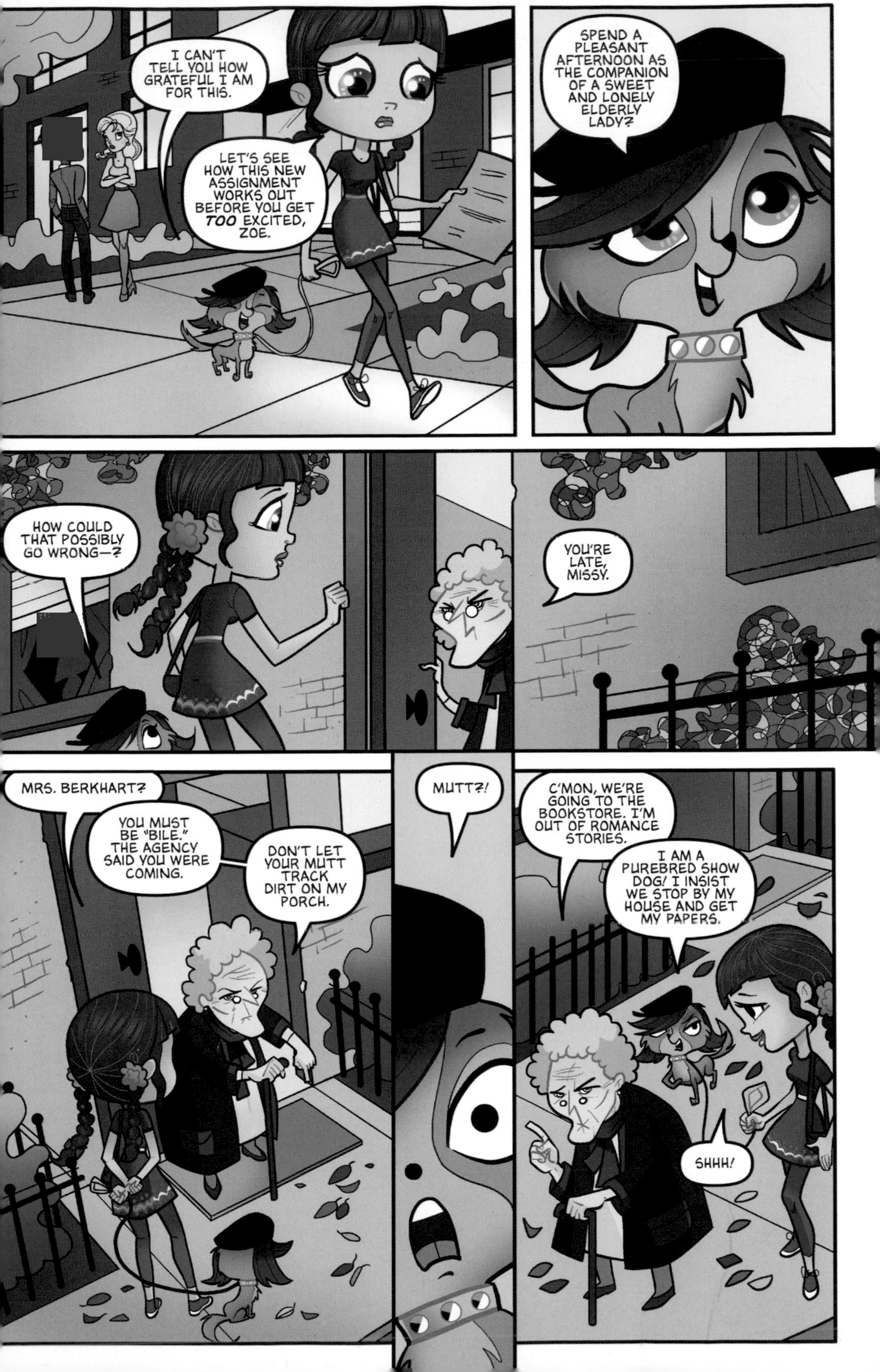

I CAN'T TELL YOU HOW GRATEFUL I AM FOR THIS.
LET'S SEE HOW THIS NEW ASSIGNMENT WORKS OUT BEFORE YOU GET *TOO* EXCITED, ZOE.
SPEND A PLEASANT AFTERNOON AS THE COMPANION OF A SWEET AND LONELY ELDERLY LADY?
HOW COULD THAT POSSIBLY GO WRONG—?
YOU'RE LATE, MISSY.
MRS. BERKHART?
YOU MUST BE "BILE." THE AGENCY SAID YOU WERE COMING.
DON'T LET YOUR MUTT TRACK DIRT ON MY PORCH.
MUTT?!
C'MON, WE'RE GOING TO THE BOOKSTORE. I'M OUT OF ROMANCE STORIES.
I AM A PUREBRED SHOW DOG! I INSIST WE STOP BY MY HOUSE AND GET MY PAPERS.
SHHH!

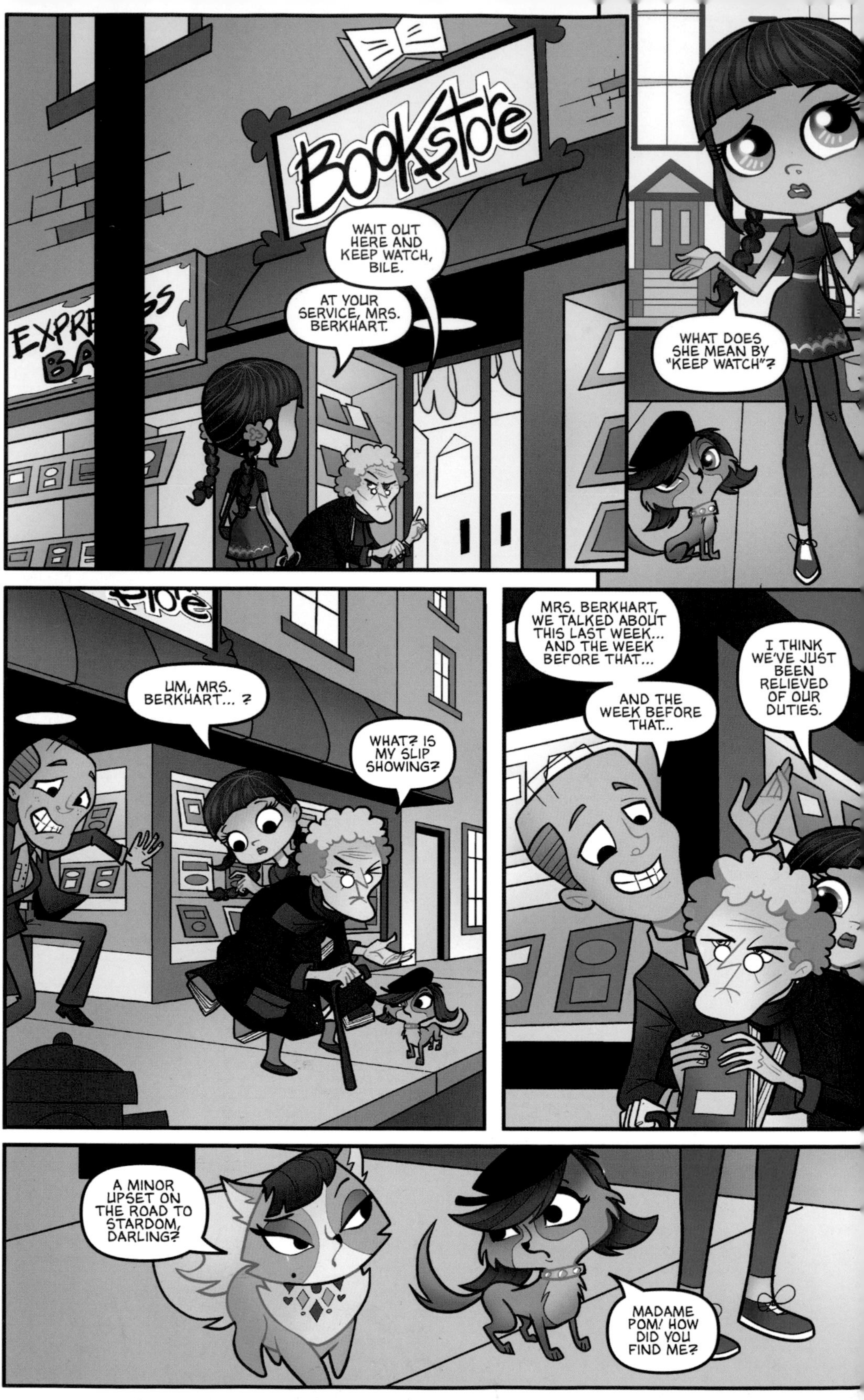
Bookstore
EXPRESS BA
WAIT OUT HERE AND KEEP WATCH, BILE.
AT YOUR SERVICE, MRS. BERKHART.
WHAT DOES SHE MEAN BY "KEEP WATCH"?
UM, MRS. BERKHART... ?
WHAT? IS MY SLIP SHOWING?
MRS. BERKHART, WE TALKED ABOUT THIS LAST WEEK... AND THE WEEK BEFORE THAT...
AND THE WEEK BEFORE THAT...
I THINK WE'VE JUST BEEN RELIEVED OF OUR DUTIES.
A MINOR UPSET ON THE ROAD TO STARDOM, DARLING?
MADAME POM! HOW DID YOU FIND ME?

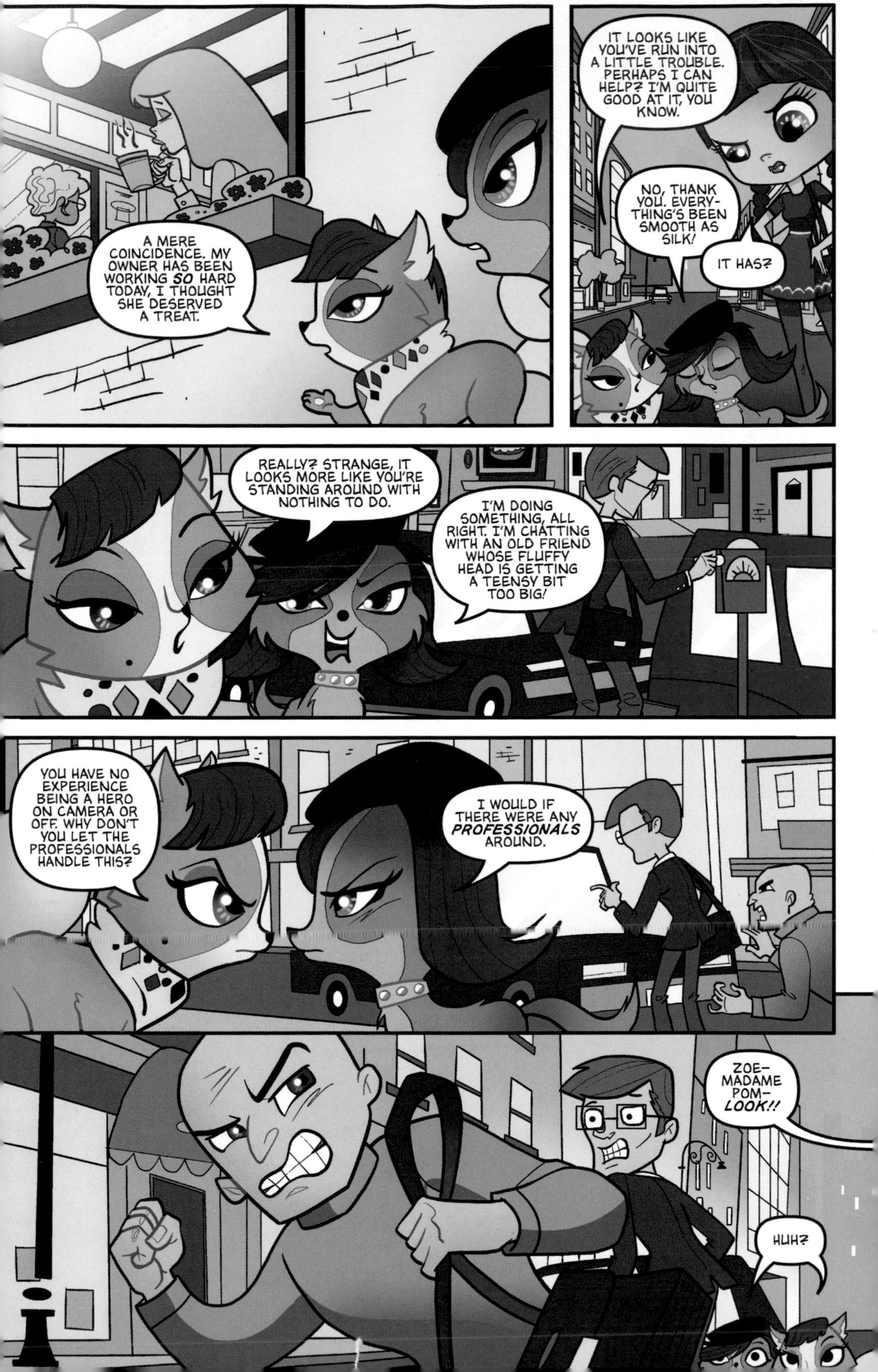
A MERE COINCIDENCE. MY OWNER HAS BEEN WORKING SO HARD TODAY, I THOUGHT SHE DESERVED A TREAT.
IT LOOKS LIKE YOU'VE RUN INTO A LITTLE TROUBLE. PERHAPS I CAN HELP? I'M QUITE GOOD AT IT, YOU KNOW.
NO, THANK YOU. EVERY-THING'S BEEN SMOOTH AS SILK!
IT HAS?
REALLY? STRANGE, IT LOOKS MORE LIKE YOU'RE STANDING AROUND WITH NOTHING TO DO.
I'M DOING SOMETHING, ALL RIGHT. I'M CHATTING WITH AN OLD FRIEND WHOSE FLUFFY HEAD IS GETTING A TEENSY BIT TOO BIG!
YOU HAVE NO EXPERIENCE BEING A HERO ON CAMERA OR OFF. WHY DON'T YOU LET THE PROFESSIONALS HANDLE THIS?
I WOULD IF THERE WERE ANY PROFESSIONALS AROUND.
ZOE-MADAME POM-LOOK!!
HUH?

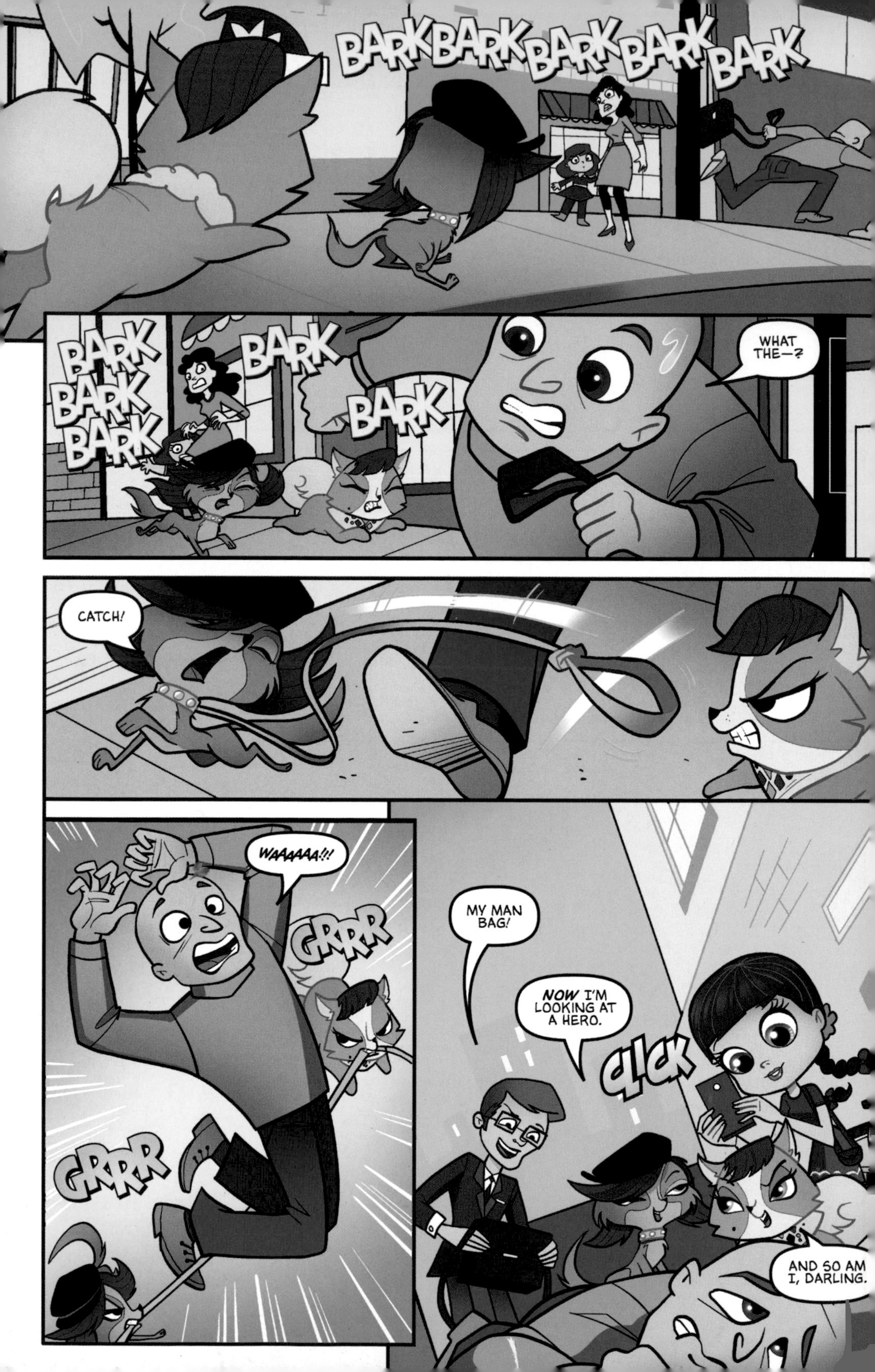

BARK BARK BARK BARK BARK
BARK BARK BARK
BARK
BARK
WHAT THE—?
CATCH!
WAAAAAA!!!
GRRR
GRRR
MY MAN BAG!
NOW I'M LOOKING AT A HERO.
CLICK
AND SO AM I, DARLING.

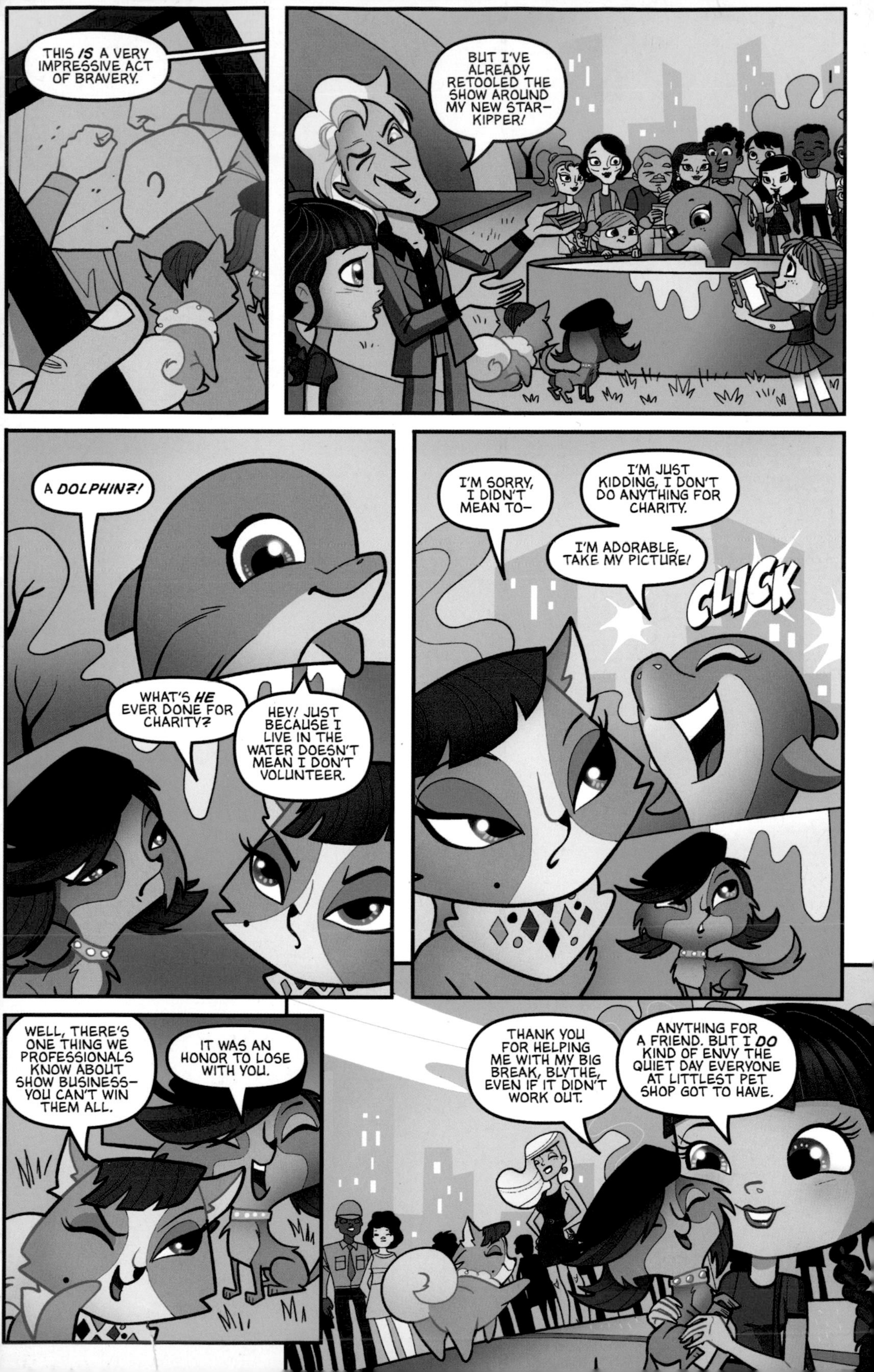
THIS *IS* A VERY IMPRESSIVE ACT OF BRAVERY.
BUT I'VE ALREADY RETOOLED THE SHOW AROUND MY NEW STAR-KIPPER!
A ***DOLPHIN?!***
WHAT'S ***HE*** EVER DONE FOR CHARITY?
HEY! JUST BECAUSE I LIVE IN THE WATER DOESN'T MEAN I DON'T VOLUNTEER.
I'M SORRY, I DIDN'T MEAN TO–
I'M JUST KIDDING, I DON'T DO ANYTHING FOR CHARITY.
I'M ADORABLE, TAKE MY PICTURE!
CLICK
WELL, THERE'S ONE THING WE PROFESSIONALS KNOW ABOUT SHOW BUSINESS– YOU CAN'T WIN THEM ALL.
IT WAS AN HONOR TO LOSE WITH YOU.
THANK YOU FOR HELPING ME WITH MY BIG BREAK, BLYTHE, EVEN IF IT DIDN'T WORK OUT.
ANYTHING FOR A FRIEND. BUT I ***DO*** KIND OF ENVY THE QUIET DAY EVERYONE AT LITTLEST PET SHOP GOT TO HAVE.

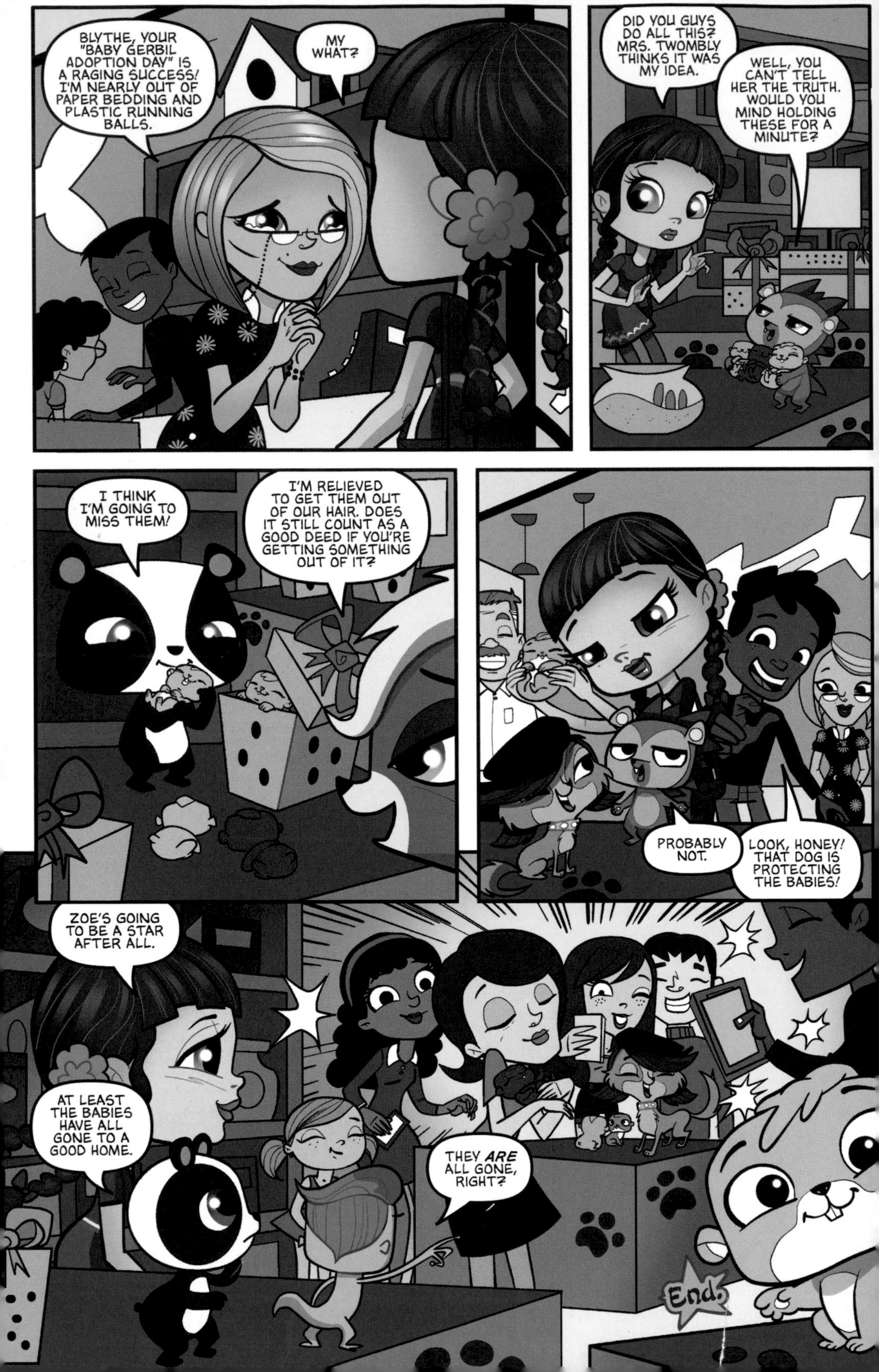
BLYTHE, YOUR "BABY GERBIL ADOPTION DAY" IS A RAGING SUCCESS! I'M NEARLY OUT OF PAPER BEDDING AND PLASTIC RUNNING BALLS.
MY WHAT?
DID YOU GUYS DO ALL THIS? MRS. TWOMBLY THINKS IT WAS MY IDEA.
WELL, YOU CAN'T TELL HER THE TRUTH. WOULD YOU MIND HOLDING THESE FOR A MINUTE?
I THINK I'M GOING TO MISS THEM!
I'M RELIEVED TO GET THEM OUT OF OUR HAIR. DOES IT STILL COUNT AS A GOOD DEED IF YOU'RE GETTING SOMETHING OUT OF IT?
PROBABLY NOT.
LOOK, HONEY! THAT DOG IS PROTECTING THE BABIES!
ZOE'S GOING TO BE A STAR AFTER ALL.
AT LEAST THE BABIES HAVE ALL GONE TO A GOOD HOME.
THEY *ARE* ALL GONE, RIGHT?
End.

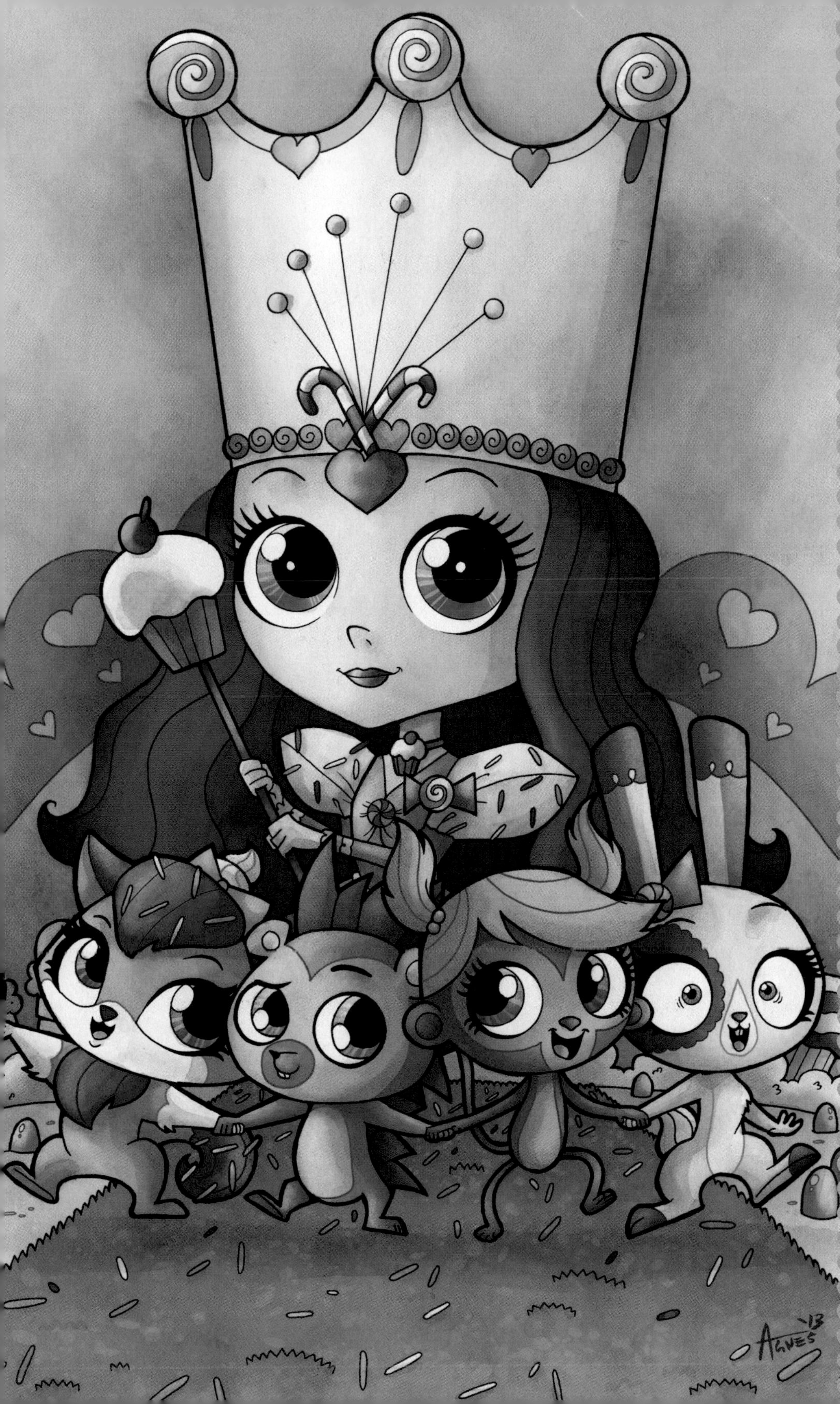
AGNES '13

art by: Agnes Garbowska

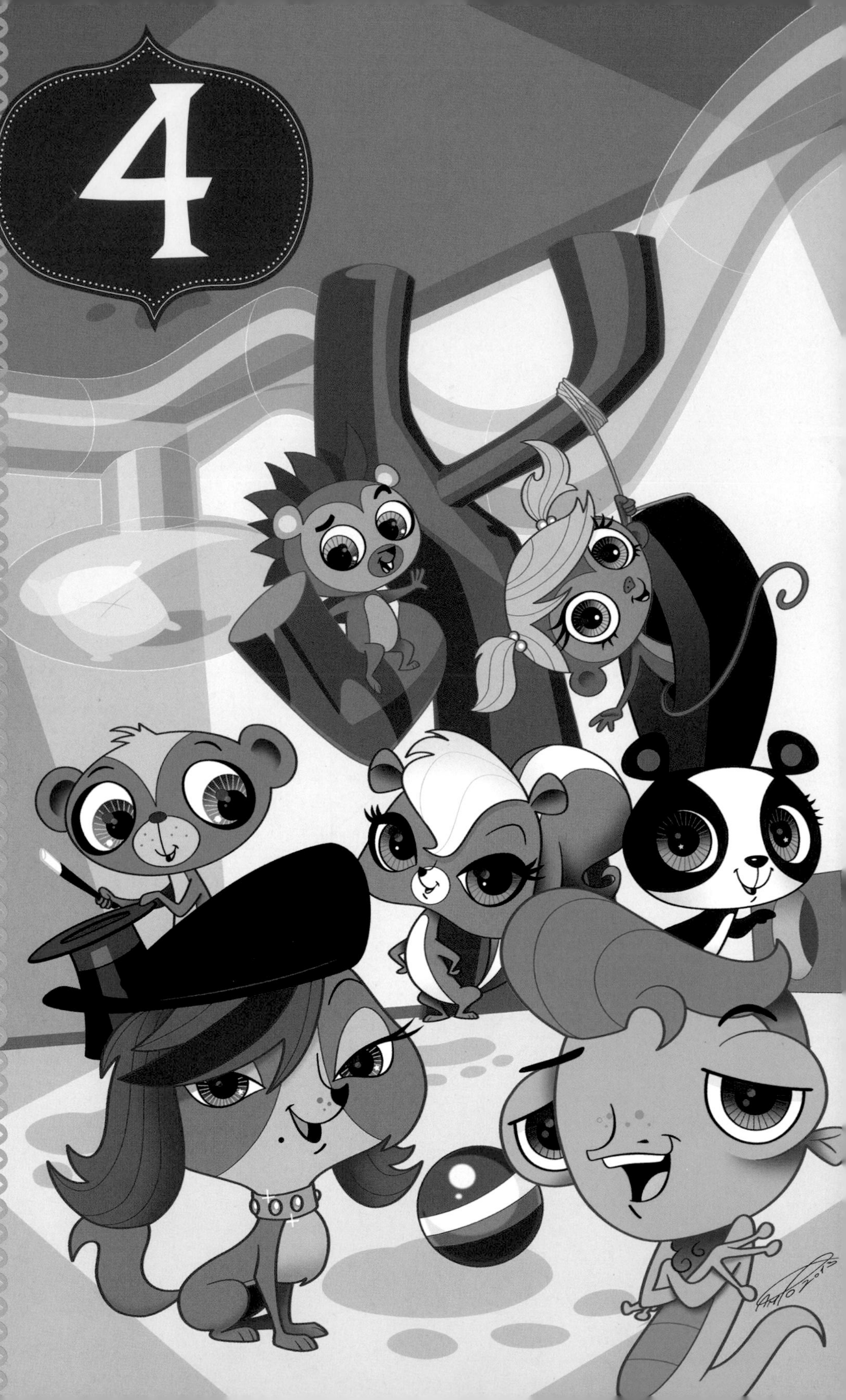
4

art by: Antonio Campo • colors by: Diego Rodriguez

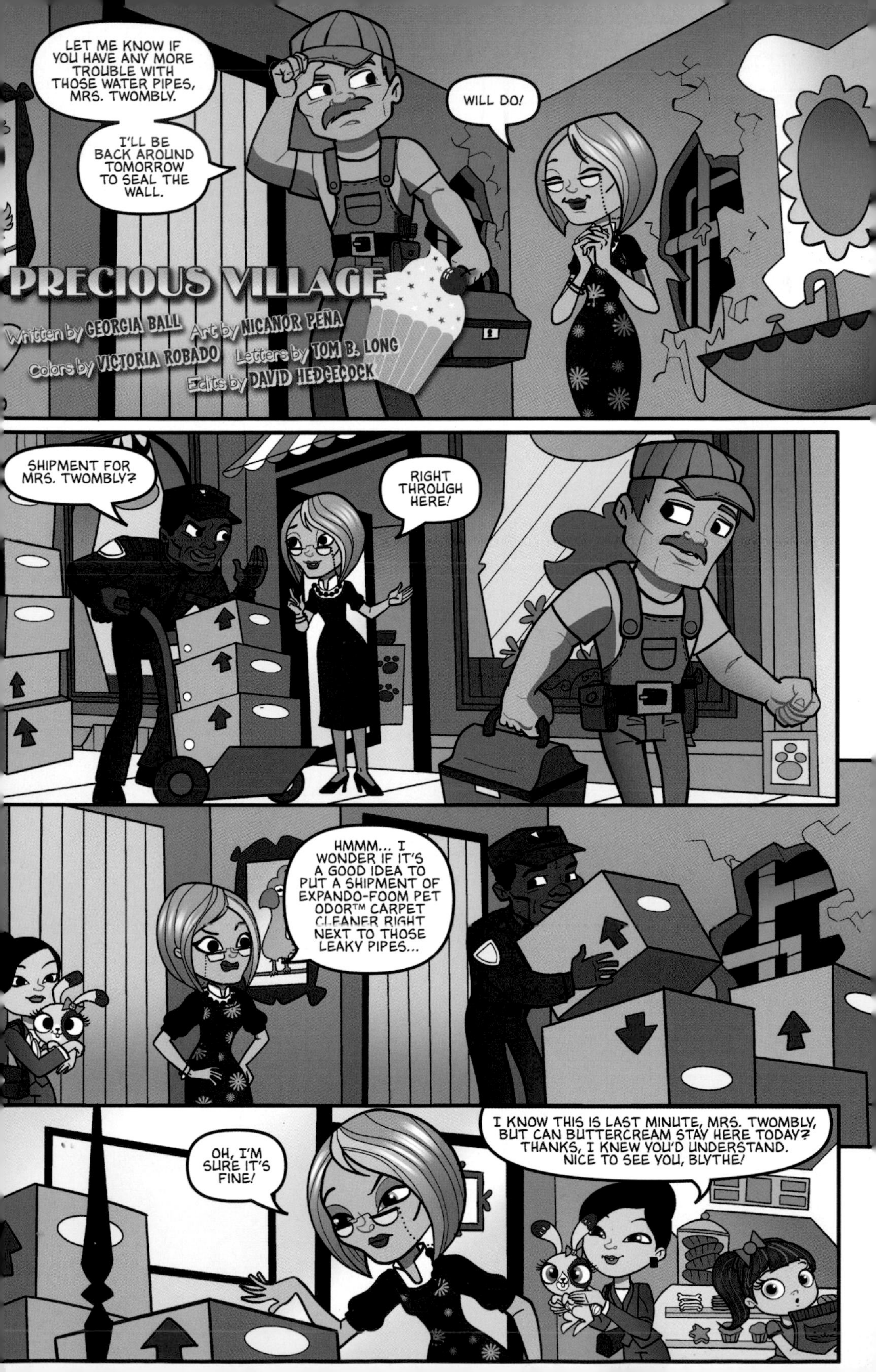
LET ME KNOW IF YOU HAVE ANY MORE TROUBLE WITH THOSE WATER PIPES, MRS. TWOMBLY.
I'LL BE BACK AROUND TOMORROW TO SEAL THE WALL.
WILL DO!
PRECIOUS VILLAGE
Written by GEORGIA BALL Art by NICANOR PEÑA
Colors by VICTORIA ROBADO Letters by TOM B. LONG
Edits by DAVID HEDGECOCK
SHIPMENT FOR MRS. TWOMBLY?
RIGHT THROUGH HERE!
HMMM... I WONDER IF IT'S A GOOD IDEA TO PUT A SHIPMENT OF EXPANDO-FOOM PET ODOR™ CARPET CLEANER RIGHT NEXT TO THOSE LEAKY PIPES...
OH, I'M SURE IT'S FINE!
I KNOW THIS IS LAST MINUTE, MRS. TWOMBLY, BUT CAN BUTTERCREAM STAY HERE TODAY? THANKS, I KNEW YOU'D UNDERSTAND. NICE TO SEE YOU, BLYTHE!

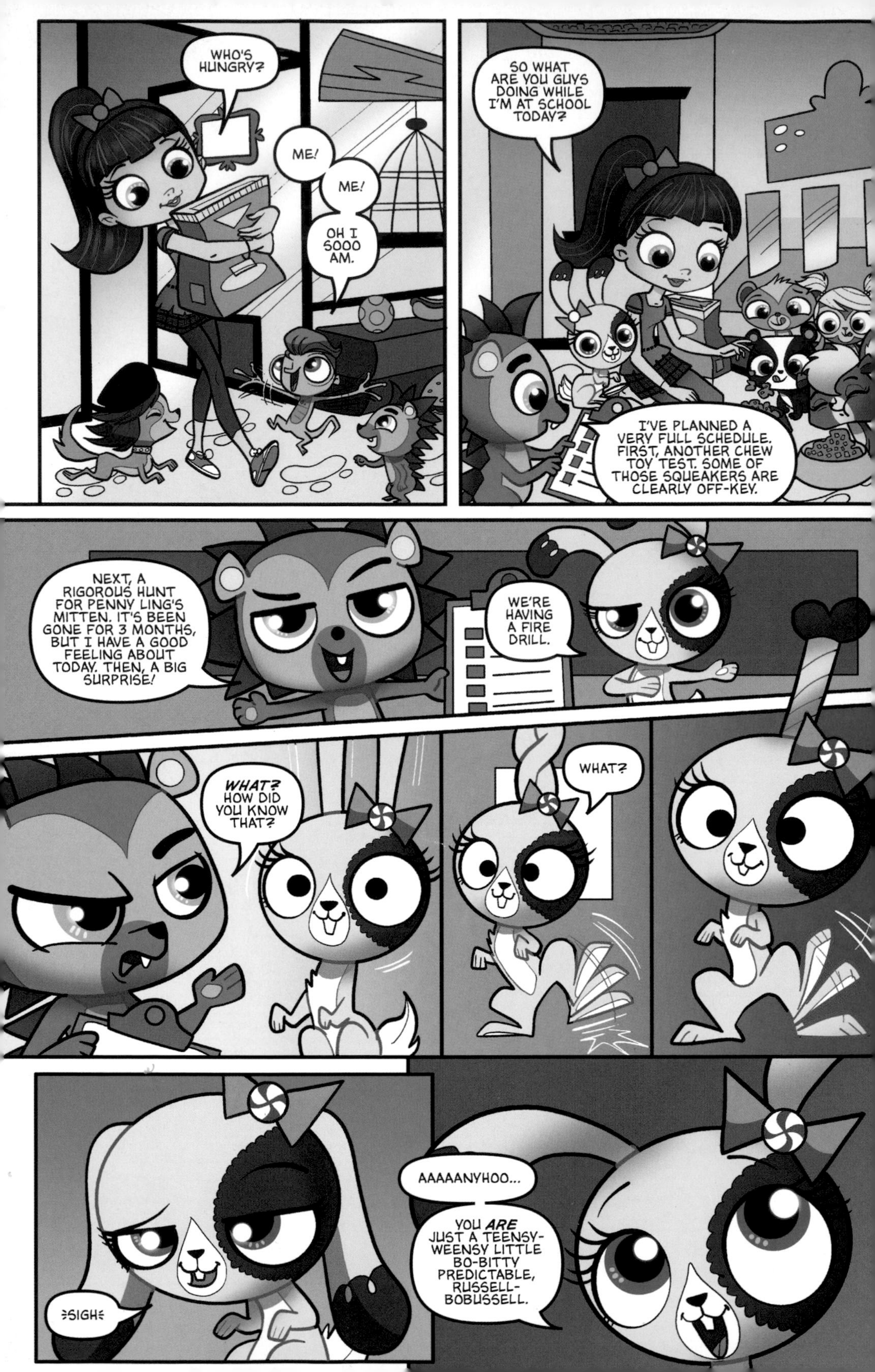
WHO'S HUNGRY?
ME!
ME!
OH I SOOO AM.
SO WHAT ARE YOU GUYS DOING WHILE I'M AT SCHOOL TODAY?
I'VE PLANNED A VERY FULL SCHEDULE. FIRST, ANOTHER CHEW TOY TEST. SOME OF THOSE SQUEAKERS ARE CLEARLY OFF-KEY.
NEXT, A RIGOROUS HUNT FOR PENNY LING'S MITTEN. IT'S BEEN GONE FOR 3 MONTHS, BUT I HAVE A GOOD FEELING ABOUT TODAY. THEN, A BIG SURPRISE!
WE'RE HAVING A FIRE DRILL.
WHAT? HOW DID YOU KNOW THAT?
WHAT?
SIGH
AAAAANYHOO...
YOU ARE JUST A TEENSY-WEENSY LITTLE BO-BITTY PREDICTABLE, RUSSELL-BOBUSSELL.

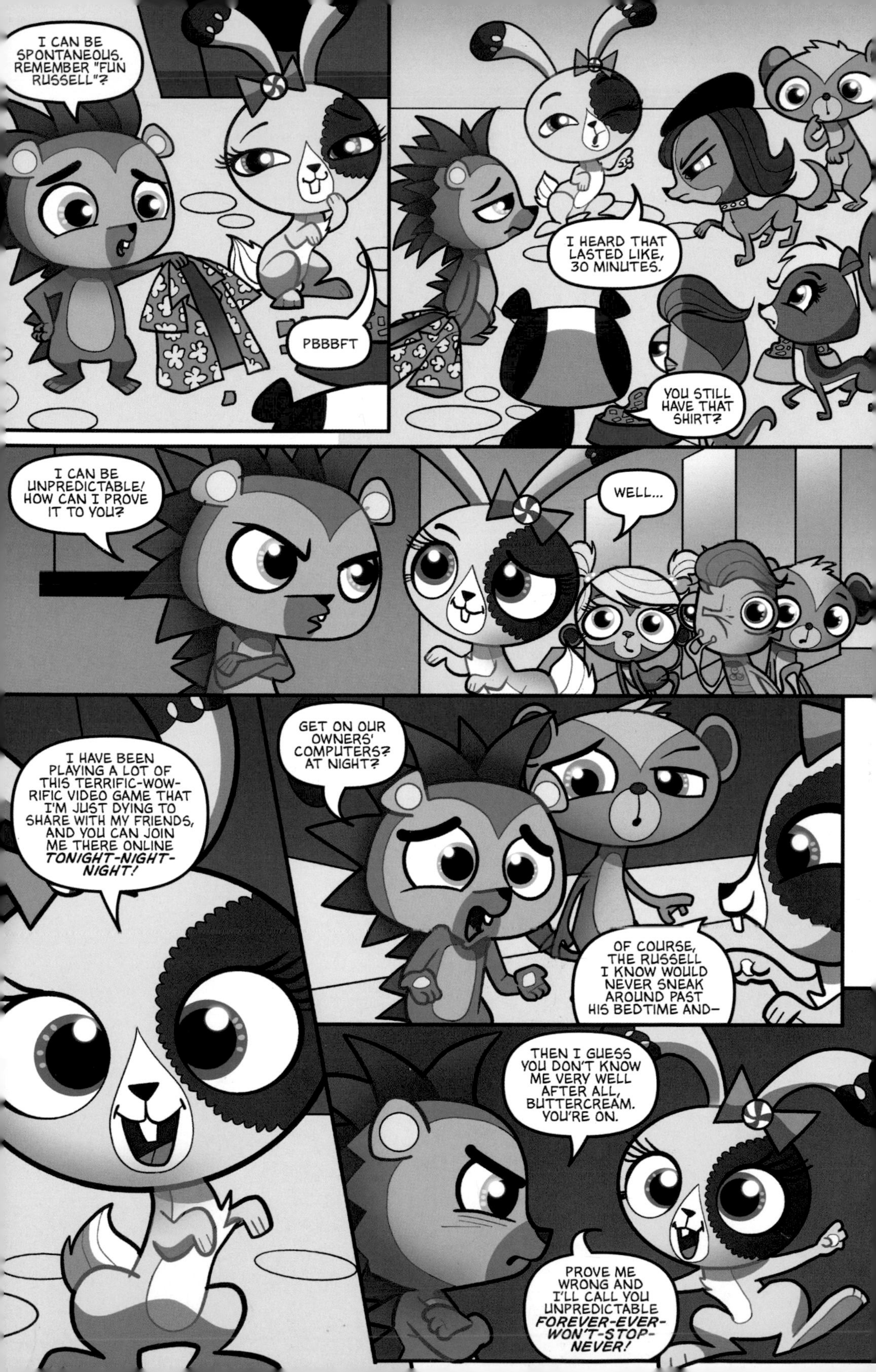

I CAN BE SPONTANEOUS. REMEMBER "FUN RUSSELL"?
PBBBFT
I HEARD THAT LASTED LIKE, 30 MINUTES.
YOU STILL HAVE THAT SHIRT?
I CAN BE UNPREDICTABLE! HOW CAN I PROVE IT TO YOU?
WELL...
I HAVE BEEN PLAYING A LOT OF THIS TERRIFIC-WOW-RIFIC VIDEO GAME THAT I'M JUST DYING TO SHARE WITH MY FRIENDS, AND YOU CAN JOIN ME THERE ONLINE *TONIGHT-NIGHT-NIGHT!*
GET ON OUR OWNERS' COMPUTERS? AT NIGHT?
OF COURSE, THE RUSSELL I KNOW WOULD NEVER SNEAK AROUND PAST HIS BEDTIME AND—
THEN I GUESS YOU DON'T KNOW ME VERY WELL AFTER ALL, BUTTERCREAM. YOU'RE ON.
PROVE ME WRONG AND I'LL CALL YOU UNPREDICTABLE *FOREVER-EVER-WON'T-STOP-NEVER!*

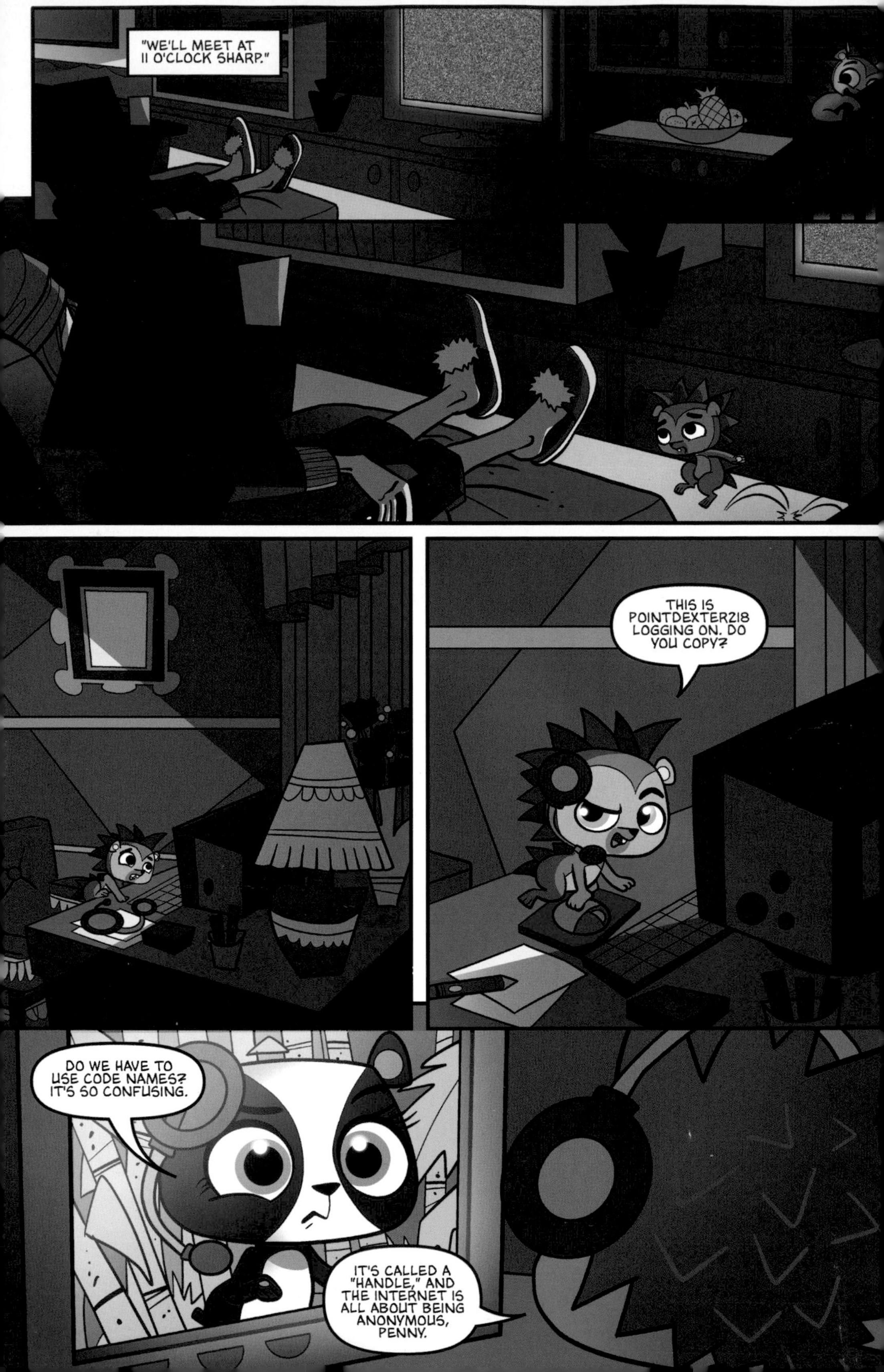
"WE'LL MEET AT
11 O'CLOCK SHARP."
THIS IS POINTDEXTER218 LOGGING ON. DO YOU COPY?
DO WE HAVE TO USE CODE NAMES? IT'S SO CONFUSING.
IT'S CALLED A "HANDLE," AND THE INTERNET IS ALL ABOUT BEING ANONYMOUS, PENNY.

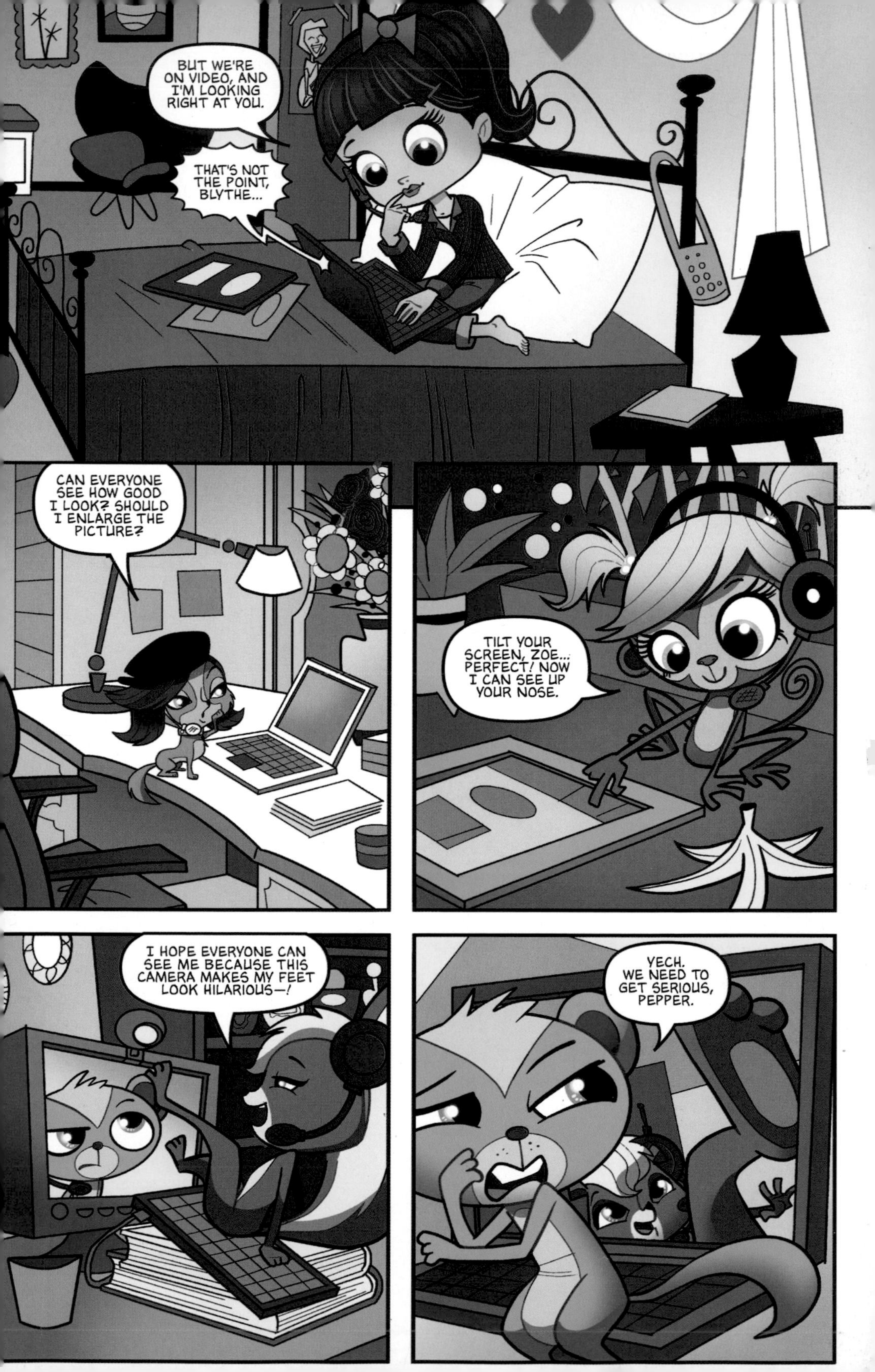
BUT WE'RE ON VIDEO, AND I'M LOOKING RIGHT AT YOU.
THAT'S NOT THE POINT, BLYTHE...
CAN EVERYONE SEE HOW GOOD I LOOK? SHOULD I ENLARGE THE PICTURE?
TILT YOUR SCREEN, ZOE... PERFECT! NOW I CAN SEE UP YOUR NOSE.
I HOPE EVERYONE CAN SEE ME BECAUSE THIS CAMERA MAKES MY FEET LOOK HILARIOUS—!
YECH. WE NEED TO GET SERIOUS, PEPPER.

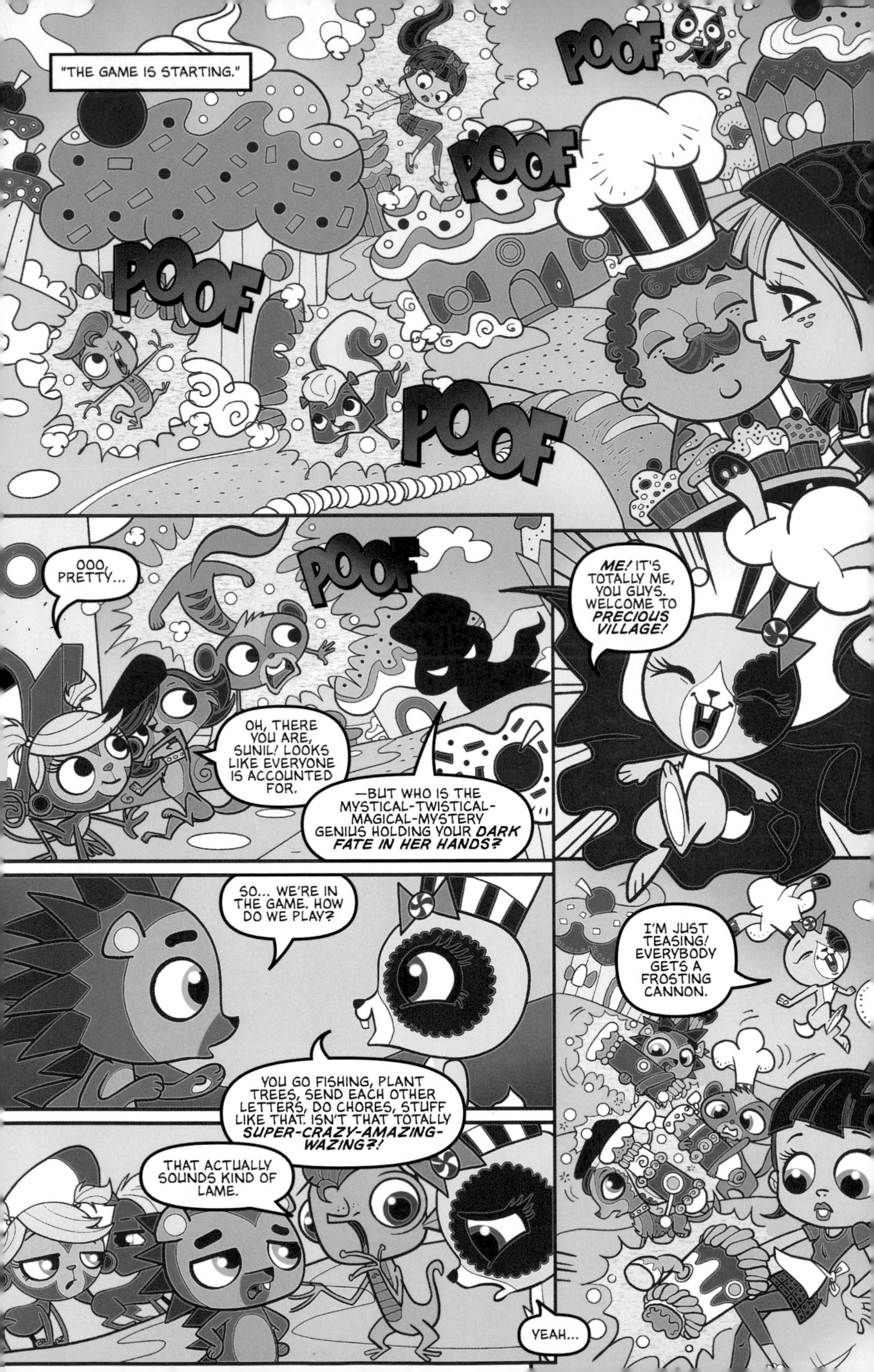
"THE GAME IS STARTING."
POOF
POOF
POOF
POOF
OOO, PRETTY...
POOF
OH, THERE YOU ARE, SUNIL! LOOKS LIKE EVERYONE IS ACCOUNTED FOR.
—BUT WHO IS THE MYSTICAL-TWISTICAL-MAGICAL-MYSTERY GENIUS HOLDING YOUR DARK FATE IN HER HANDS?
ME! IT'S TOTALLY ME, YOU GUYS. WELCOME TO PRECIOUS VILLAGE!
SO... WE'RE IN THE GAME. HOW DO WE PLAY?
YOU GO FISHING, PLANT TREES, SEND EACH OTHER LETTERS, DO CHORES, STUFF LIKE THAT. ISN'T THAT TOTALLY SUPER-CRAZY-AMAZING-WAZING?!
THAT ACTUALLY SOUNDS KIND OF LAME.
YEAH...
I'M JUST TEASING! EVERYBODY GETS A FROSTING CANNON.

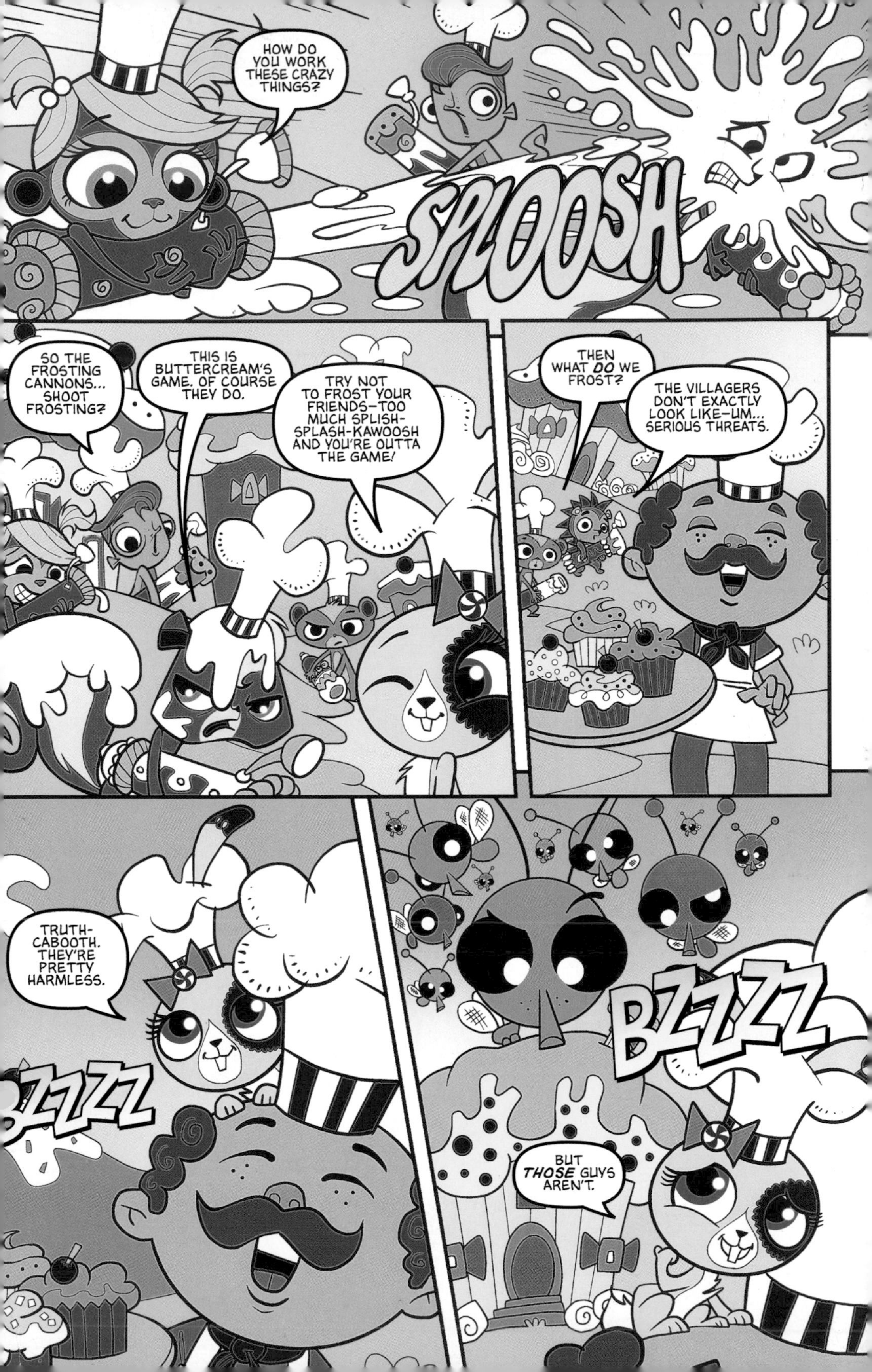
HOW DO YOU WORK THESE CRAZY THINGS?
SPLOOSH
SO THE FROSTING CANNONS... SHOOT FROSTING?
THIS IS BUTTERCREAM'S GAME. OF COURSE THEY DO.
TRY NOT TO FROST YOUR FRIENDS—TOO MUCH SPLISH-SPLASH-KAWOOSH AND YOU'RE OUTTA THE GAME!
THEN WHAT DO WE FROST?
THE VILLAGERS DON'T EXACTLY LOOK LIKE—UM... SERIOUS THREATS.
TRUTH-CABOOTH. THEY'RE PRETTY HARMLESS.
BZZZZ
BZZZZ
BUT THOSE GUYS AREN'T.

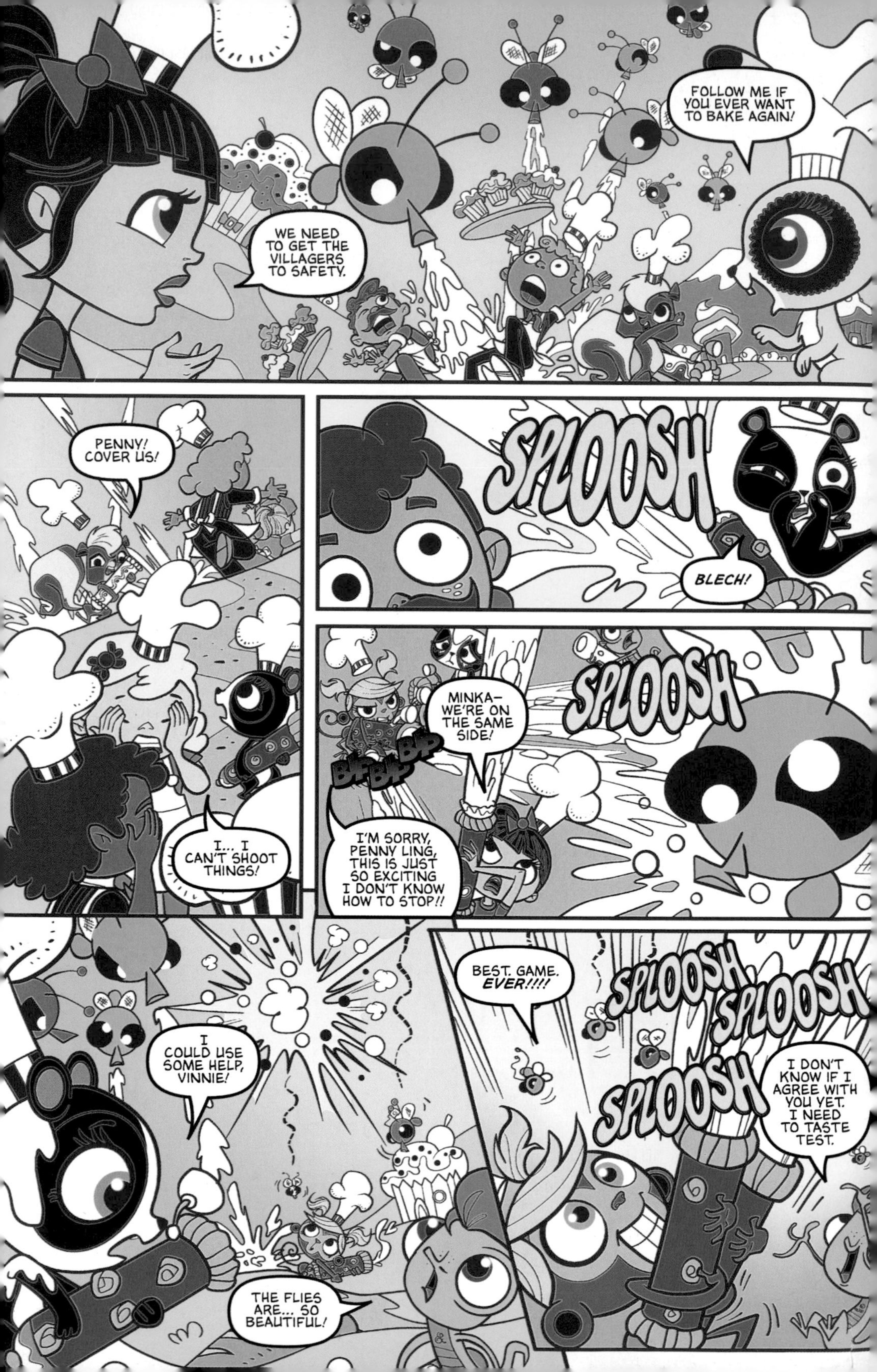
WE NEED TO GET THE VILLAGERS TO SAFETY.
FOLLOW ME IF YOU EVER WANT TO BAKE AGAIN!
PENNY! COVER US!
I... I CAN'T SHOOT THINGS!
SPLOOSH
BLECH!
SPLOOSH
MINKA– WE'RE ON THE SAME SIDE!
BIP BIP BIP
I'M SORRY, PENNY LING, THIS IS JUST SO EXCITING I DON'T KNOW HOW TO STOP!!
I COULD USE SOME HELP, VINNIE!
THE FLIES ARE... SO BEAUTIFUL!
BEST. GAME. EVER!!!!
SPLOOSH SPLOOSH SPLOOSH
I DON'T KNOW IF I AGREE WITH YOU YET. I NEED TO TASTE TEST.

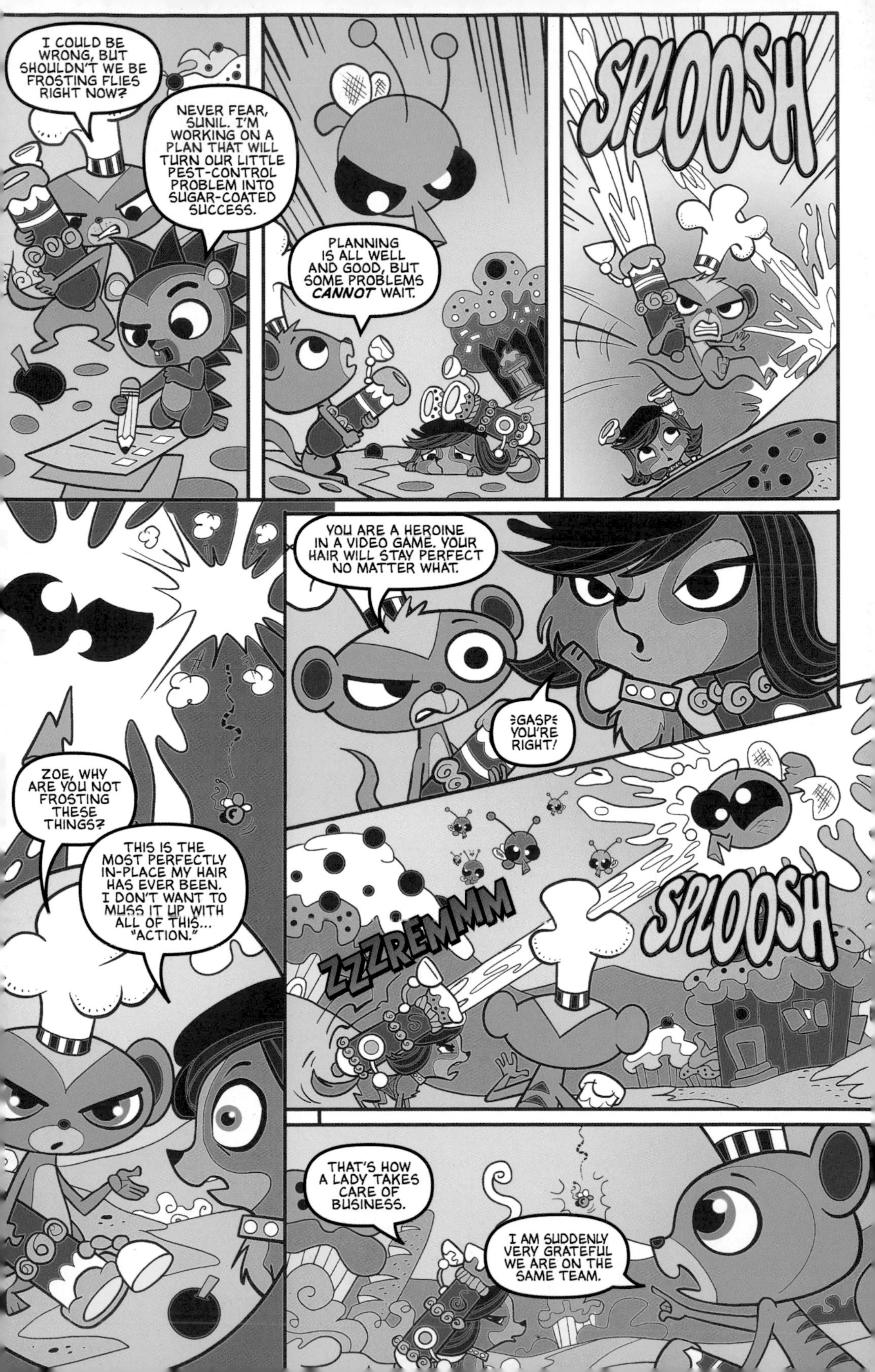
I COULD BE WRONG, BUT SHOULDN'T WE BE FROSTING FLIES RIGHT NOW?
NEVER FEAR, SUNIL. I'M WORKING ON A PLAN THAT WILL TURN OUR LITTLE PEST-CONTROL PROBLEM INTO SUGAR-COATED SUCCESS.
PLANNING IS ALL WELL AND GOOD, BUT SOME PROBLEMS *CANNOT* WAIT.
SPLOOSH
ZOE, WHY ARE YOU NOT FROSTING THESE THINGS?
THIS IS THE MOST PERFECTLY IN-PLACE MY HAIR HAS EVER BEEN. I DON'T WANT TO MUSS IT UP WITH ALL OF THIS... "ACTION."
YOU ARE A HEROINE IN A VIDEO GAME. YOUR HAIR WILL STAY PERFECT NO MATTER WHAT.
GASP YOU'RE RIGHT!
ZZZREMMMM
SPLOOSH
THAT'S HOW A LADY TAKES CARE OF BUSINESS.
I AM SUDDENLY VERY GRATEFUL WE ARE ON THE SAME TEAM.

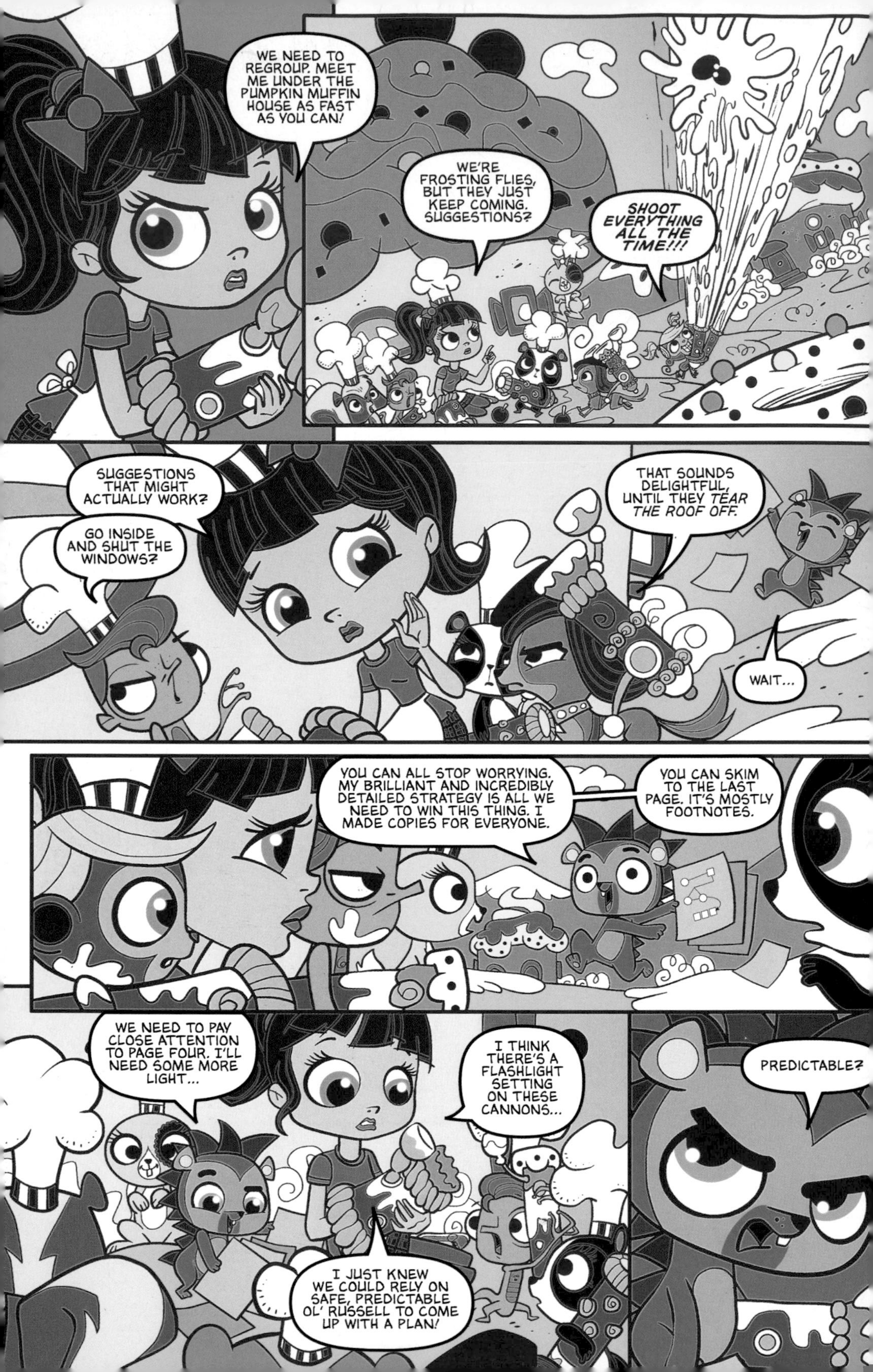
WE NEED TO REGROUP. MEET ME UNDER THE PUMPKIN MUFFIN HOUSE AS FAST AS YOU CAN!
WE'RE FROSTING FLIES, BUT THEY JUST KEEP COMING. SUGGESTIONS?
SHOOT EVERYTHING ALL THE TIME!!!
SUGGESTIONS THAT MIGHT ACTUALLY WORK?
GO INSIDE AND SHUT THE WINDOWS?
THAT SOUNDS DELIGHTFUL, UNTIL THEY *TEAR THE ROOF OFF.*
WAIT...
YOU CAN ALL STOP WORRYING. MY BRILLIANT AND INCREDIBLY DETAILED STRATEGY IS ALL WE NEED TO WIN THIS THING. I MADE COPIES FOR EVERYONE.
YOU CAN SKIM TO THE LAST PAGE. IT'S MOSTLY FOOTNOTES.
WE NEED TO PAY CLOSE ATTENTION TO PAGE FOUR. I'LL NEED SOME MORE LIGHT...
I THINK THERE'S A FLASHLIGHT SETTING ON THESE CANNONS...
I JUST KNEW WE COULD RELY ON SAFE, PREDICTABLE OL' RUSSELL TO COME UP WITH A PLAN!
PREDICTABLE?

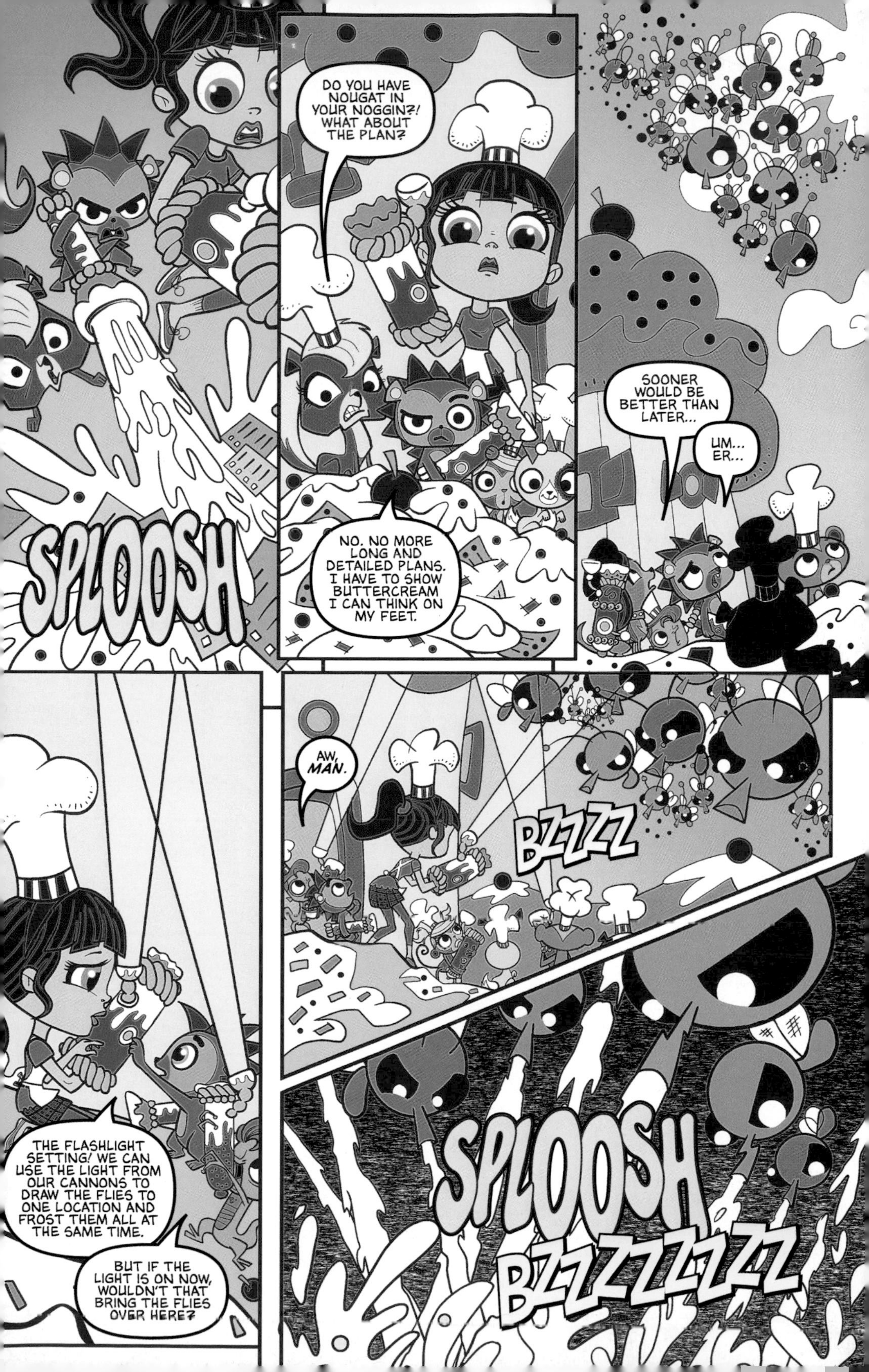
SPLOOSH
DO YOU HAVE NOUGAT IN YOUR NOGGIN?! WHAT ABOUT THE PLAN?
NO. NO MORE LONG AND DETAILED PLANS. I HAVE TO SHOW BUTTERCREAM I CAN THINK ON MY FEET.
SOONER WOULD BE BETTER THAN LATER...
UM... ER...
THE FLASHLIGHT SETTING! WE CAN USE THE LIGHT FROM OUR CANNONS TO DRAW THE FLIES TO ONE LOCATION AND FROST THEM ALL AT THE SAME TIME.
BUT IF THE LIGHT IS ON NOW, WOULDN'T THAT BRING THE FLIES OVER HERE?
AW, *MAN.*
BZZZZ
SPLOOSH
BZZZZZZZZ

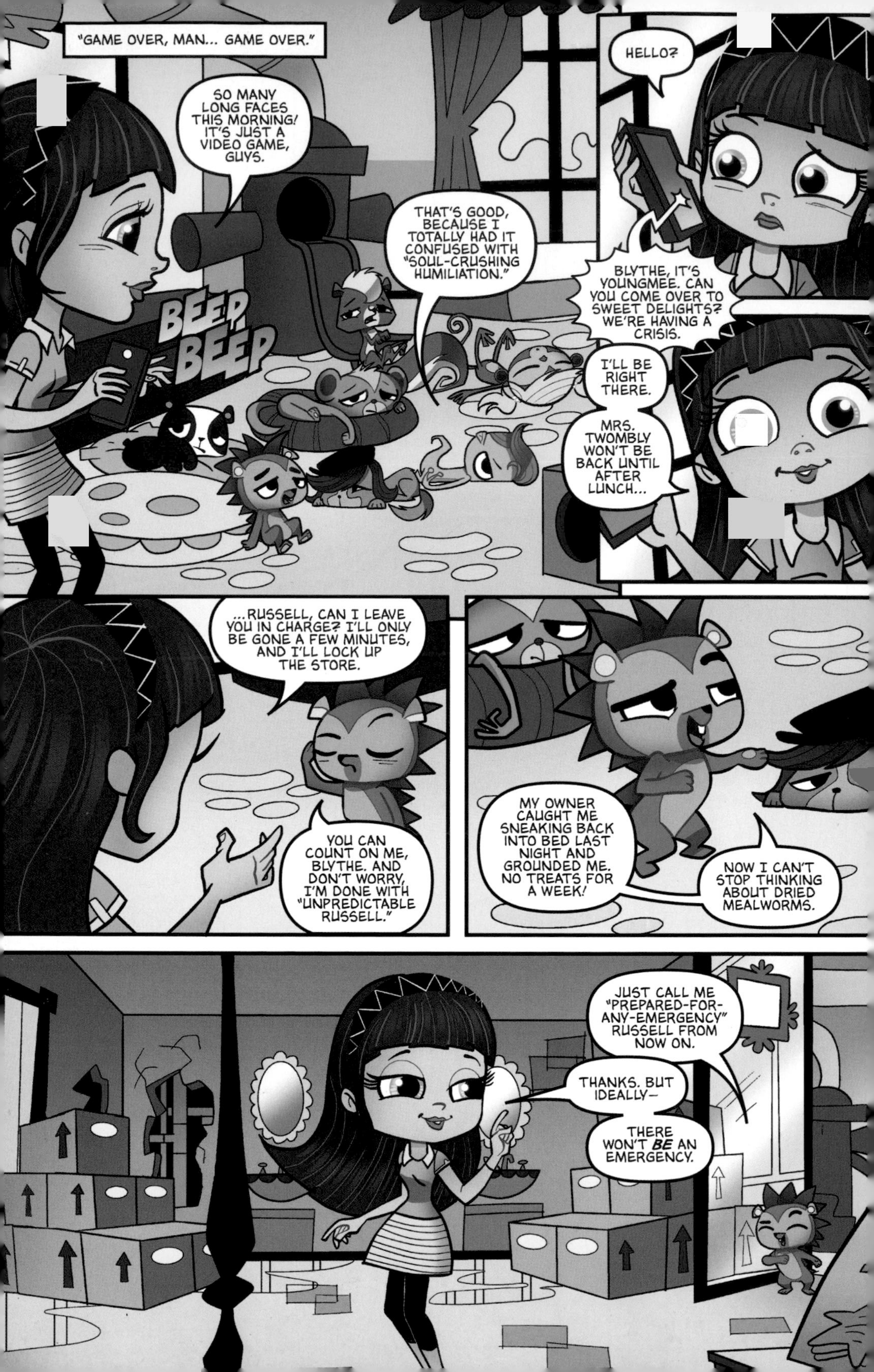
"GAME OVER, MAN... GAME OVER."
SO MANY LONG FACES THIS MORNING! IT'S JUST A VIDEO GAME, GUYS.
THAT'S GOOD, BECAUSE I TOTALLY HAD IT CONFUSED WITH "SOUL-CRUSHING HUMILIATION."
BEEP BEEP
HELLO?
BLYTHE, IT'S YOUNGMEE. CAN YOU COME OVER TO SWEET DELIGHTS? WE'RE HAVING A CRISIS.
I'LL BE RIGHT THERE.
MRS. TWOMBLY WON'T BE BACK UNTIL AFTER LUNCH...
...RUSSELL, CAN I LEAVE YOU IN CHARGE? I'LL ONLY BE GONE A FEW MINUTES, AND I'LL LOCK UP THE STORE.
YOU CAN COUNT ON ME, BLYTHE. AND DON'T WORRY, I'M DONE WITH "UNPREDICTABLE RUSSELL."
MY OWNER CAUGHT ME SNEAKING BACK INTO BED LAST NIGHT AND GROUNDED ME. NO TREATS FOR A WEEK!
NOW I CAN'T STOP THINKING ABOUT DRIED MEALWORMS.
JUST CALL ME "PREPARED-FOR-ANY-EMERGENCY" RUSSELL FROM NOW ON.
THANKS. BUT IDEALLY—
THERE WON'T BE AN EMERGENCY.

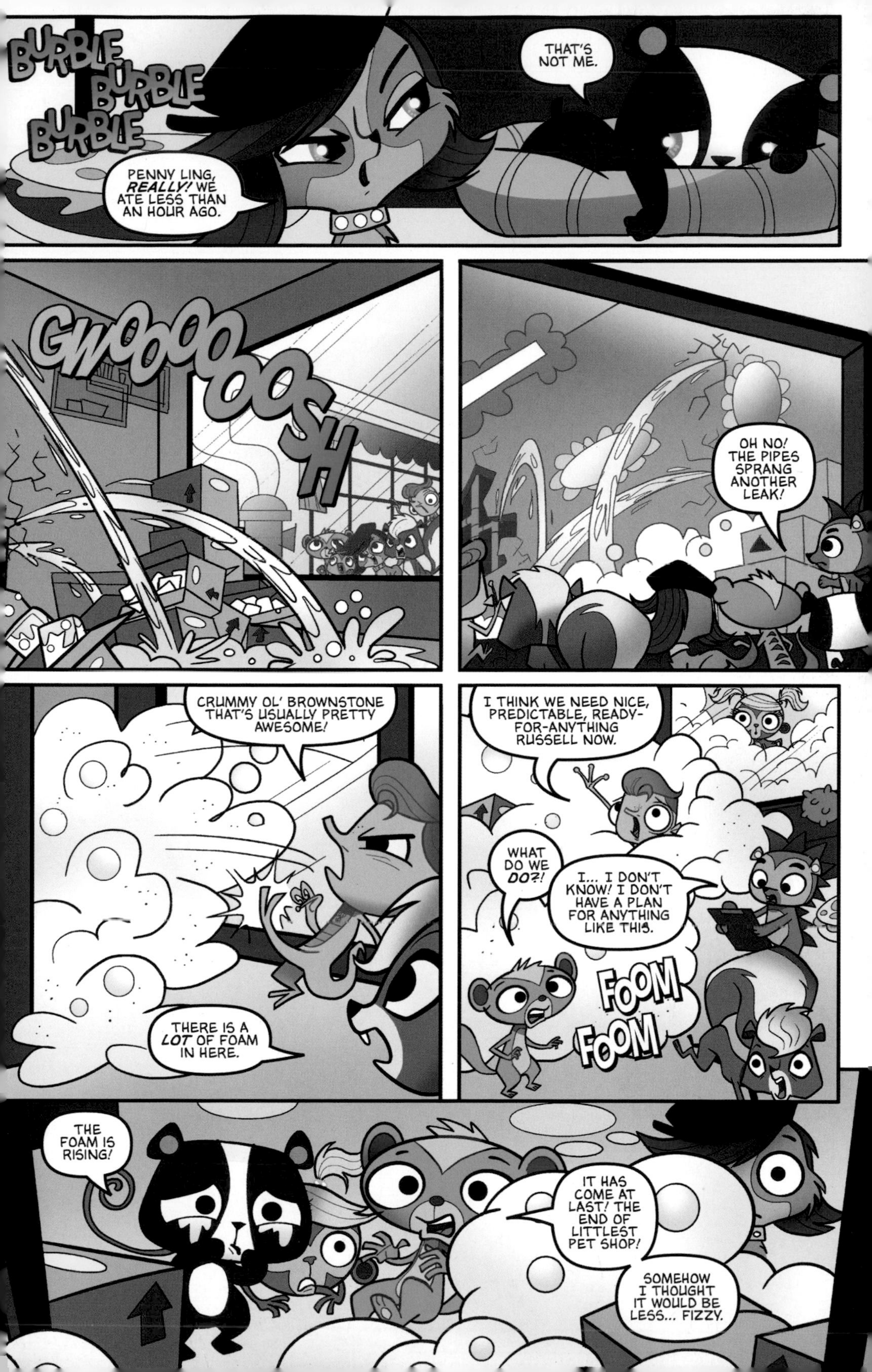
BURBLE BURBLE BURBLE
PENNY LING, REALLY! WE ATE LESS THAN AN HOUR AGO.
THAT'S NOT ME.
GWOOOOOOOSH
OH NO! THE PIPES SPRANG ANOTHER LEAK!
CRUMMY OL' BROWNSTONE THAT'S USUALLY PRETTY AWESOME!
THERE IS A LOT OF FOAM IN HERE.
I THINK WE NEED NICE, PREDICTABLE, READY-FOR-ANYTHING RUSSELL NOW.
WHAT DO WE DO?!
I... I DON'T KNOW! I DON'T HAVE A PLAN FOR ANYTHING LIKE THIS.
FOOM FOOM
THE FOAM IS RISING!
IT HAS COME AT LAST! THE END OF LITTLEST PET SHOP!
SOMEHOW I THOUGHT IT WOULD BE LESS... FIZZY.

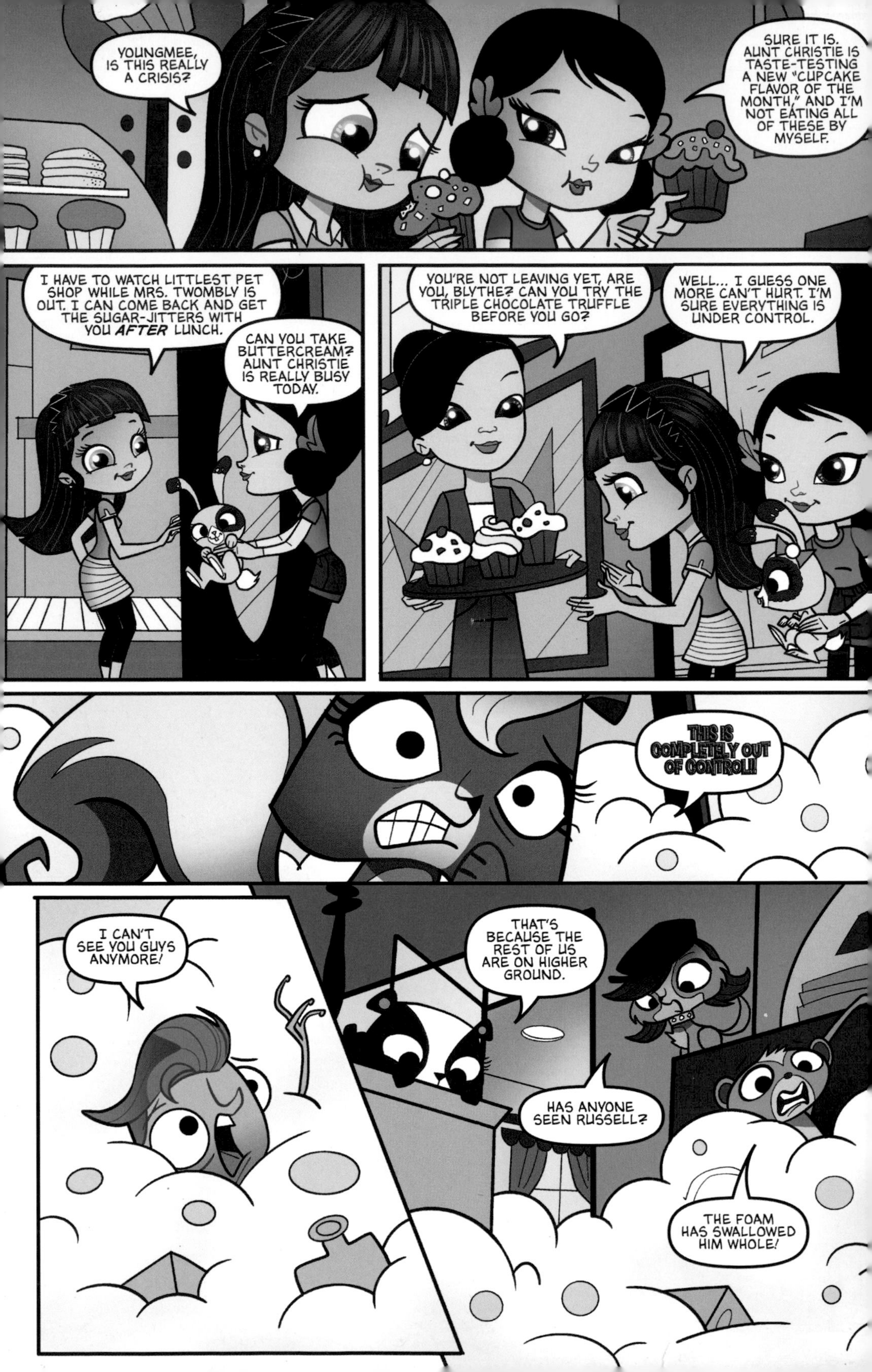
YOUNGMEE, IS THIS REALLY A CRISIS?
SURE IT IS. AUNT CHRISTIE IS TASTE-TESTING A NEW "CUPCAKE FLAVOR OF THE MONTH," AND I'M NOT EATING ALL OF THESE BY MYSELF.
I HAVE TO WATCH LITTLEST PET SHOP WHILE MRS. TWOMBLY IS OUT. I CAN COME BACK AND GET THE SUGAR-JITTERS WITH YOU AFTER LUNCH.
CAN YOU TAKE BUTTERCREAM? AUNT CHRISTIE IS REALLY BUSY TODAY.
YOU'RE NOT LEAVING YET, ARE YOU, BLYTHE? CAN YOU TRY THE TRIPLE CHOCOLATE TRUFFLE BEFORE YOU GO?
WELL... I GUESS ONE MORE CAN'T HURT. I'M SURE EVERYTHING IS UNDER CONTROL.
THIS IS COMPLETELY OUT OF CONTROL!!
I CAN'T SEE YOU GUYS ANYMORE!
THAT'S BECAUSE THE REST OF US ARE ON HIGHER GROUND.
HAS ANYONE SEEN RUSSELL?
THE FOAM HAS SWALLOWED HIM WHOLE!

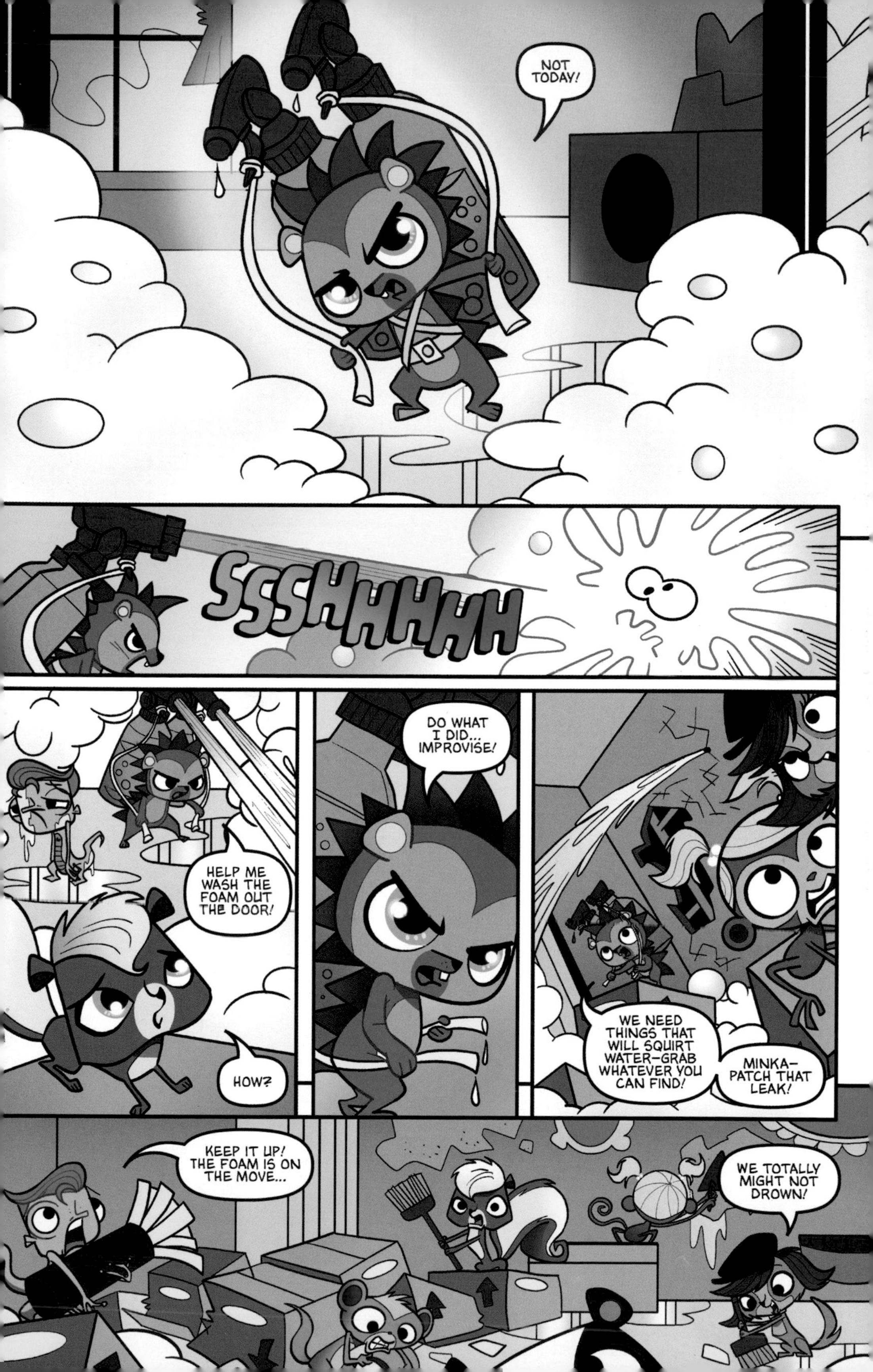
NOT TODAY!
SSSHHHHHH
DO WHAT I DID... IMPROVISE!
HELP ME WASH THE FOAM OUT THE DOOR!
HOW?
WE NEED THINGS THAT WILL SQUIRT WATER–GRAB WHATEVER YOU CAN FIND!
MINKA–PATCH THAT LEAK!
KEEP IT UP! THE FOAM IS ON THE MOVE...
WE TOTALLY MIGHT NOT DROWN!

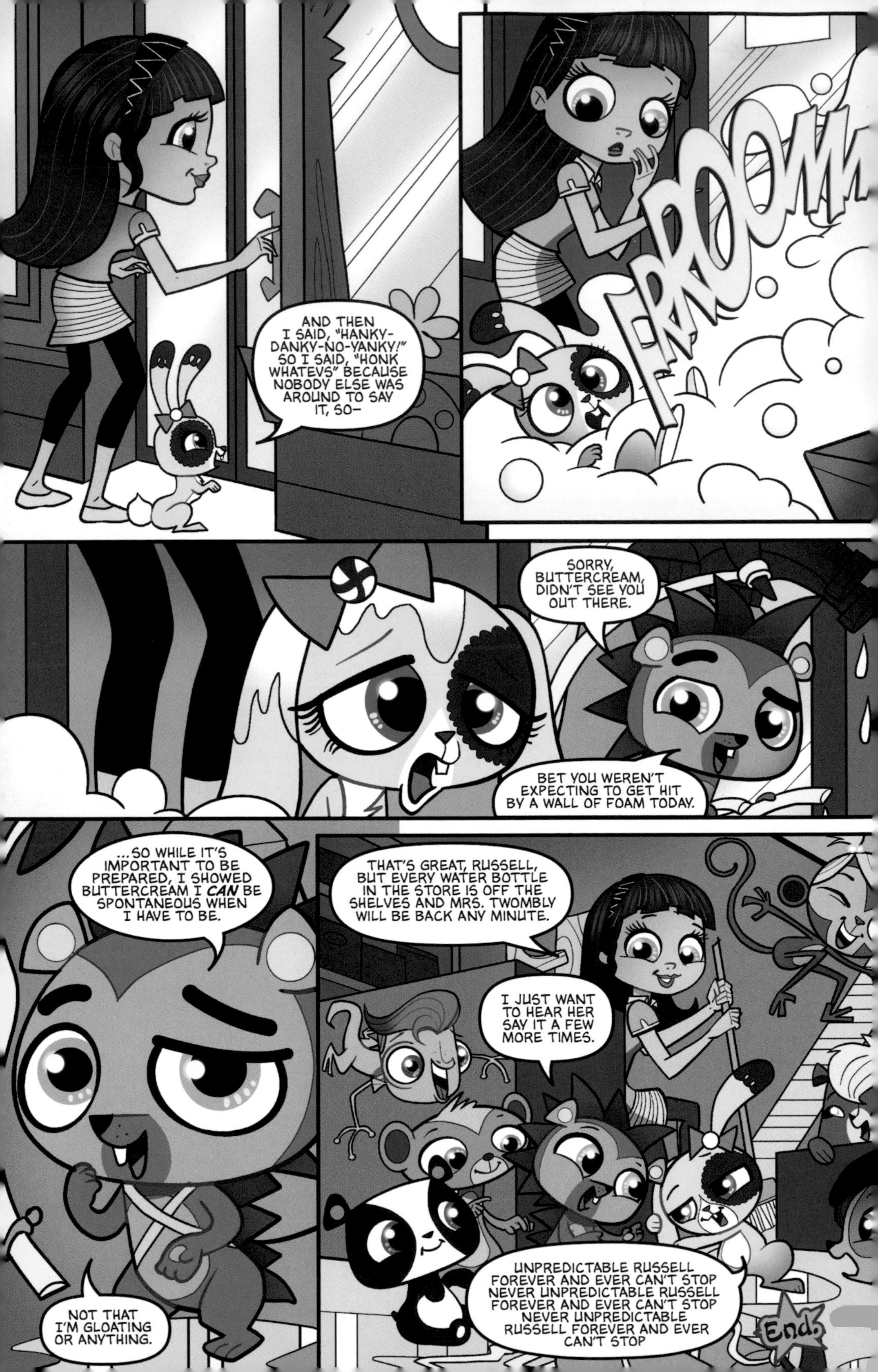
AND THEN I SAID, "HANKY-DANKY-NO-YANKY!" SO I SAID, "HONK WHATEVS" BECAUSE NOBODY ELSE WAS AROUND TO SAY IT, SO–
FRROOMM
SORRY, BUTTERCREAM, DIDN'T SEE YOU OUT THERE.
BET YOU WEREN'T EXPECTING TO GET HIT BY A WALL OF FOAM TODAY.
...SO WHILE IT'S IMPORTANT TO BE PREPARED, I SHOWED BUTTERCREAM I *CAN* BE SPONTANEOUS WHEN I HAVE TO BE.
NOT THAT I'M GLOATING OR ANYTHING.
THAT'S GREAT, RUSSELL, BUT EVERY WATER BOTTLE IN THE STORE IS OFF THE SHELVES AND MRS. TWOMBLY WILL BE BACK ANY MINUTE.
I JUST WANT TO HEAR HER SAY IT A FEW MORE TIMES.
UNPREDICTABLE RUSSELL FOREVER AND EVER CAN'T STOP NEVER UNPREDICTABLE RUSSELL FOREVER AND EVER CAN'T STOP NEVER UNPREDICTABLE RUSSELL FOREVER AND EVER CAN'T STOP
End.

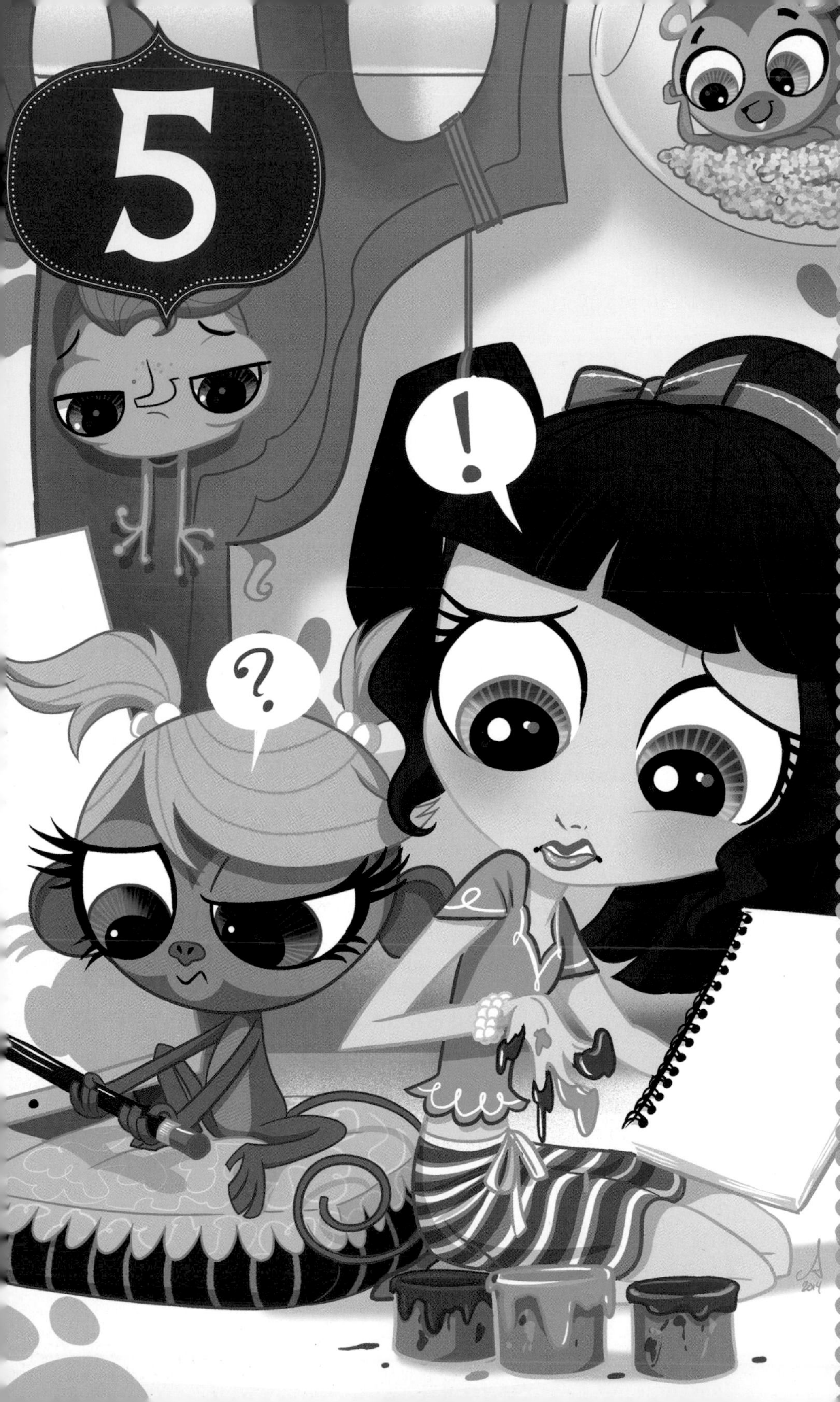
5
!
?

art by: Amy Mebberson

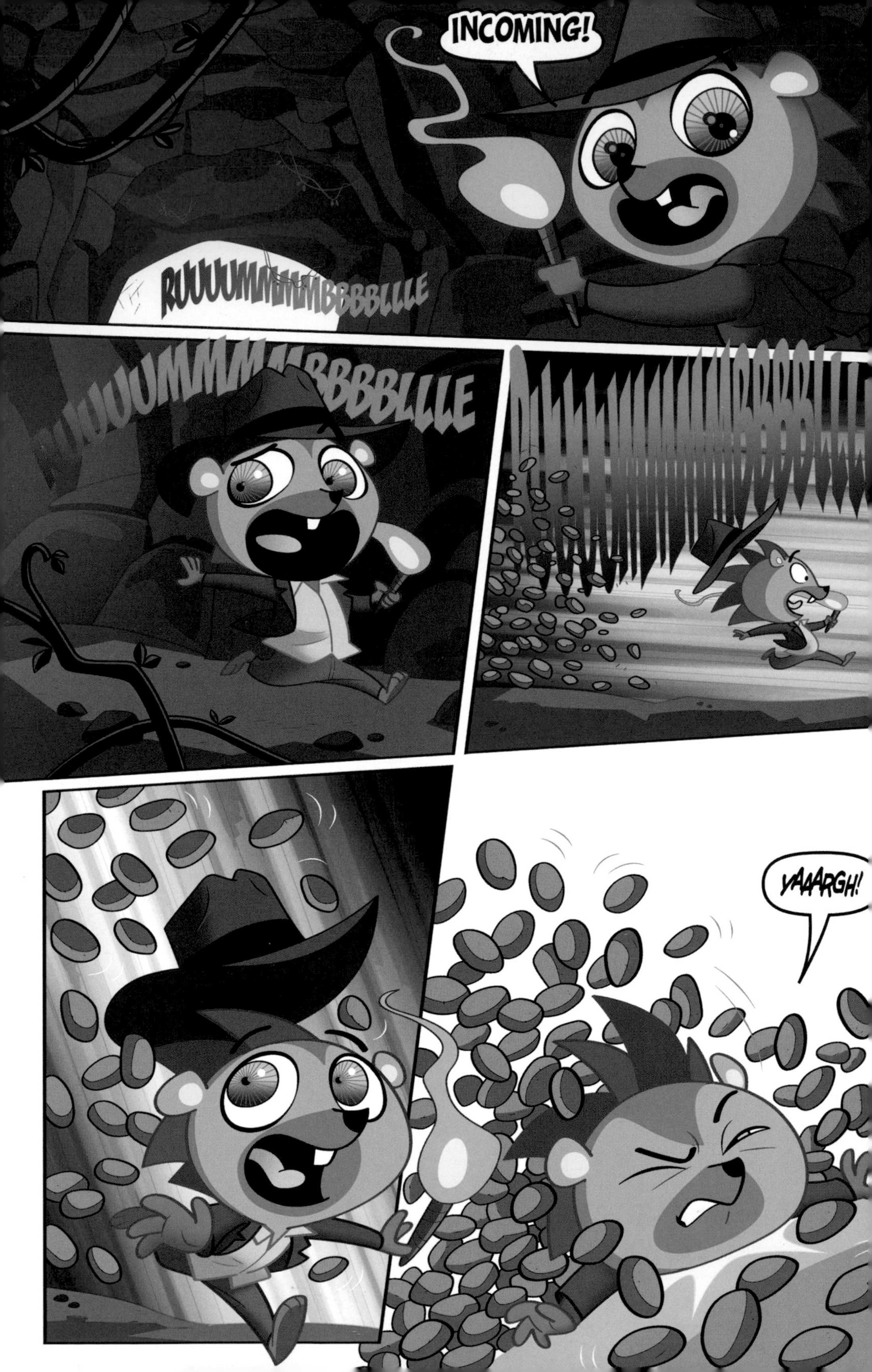
INCOMING!
RUUUUMMMMMBBBBLLLE
YAAARGH!

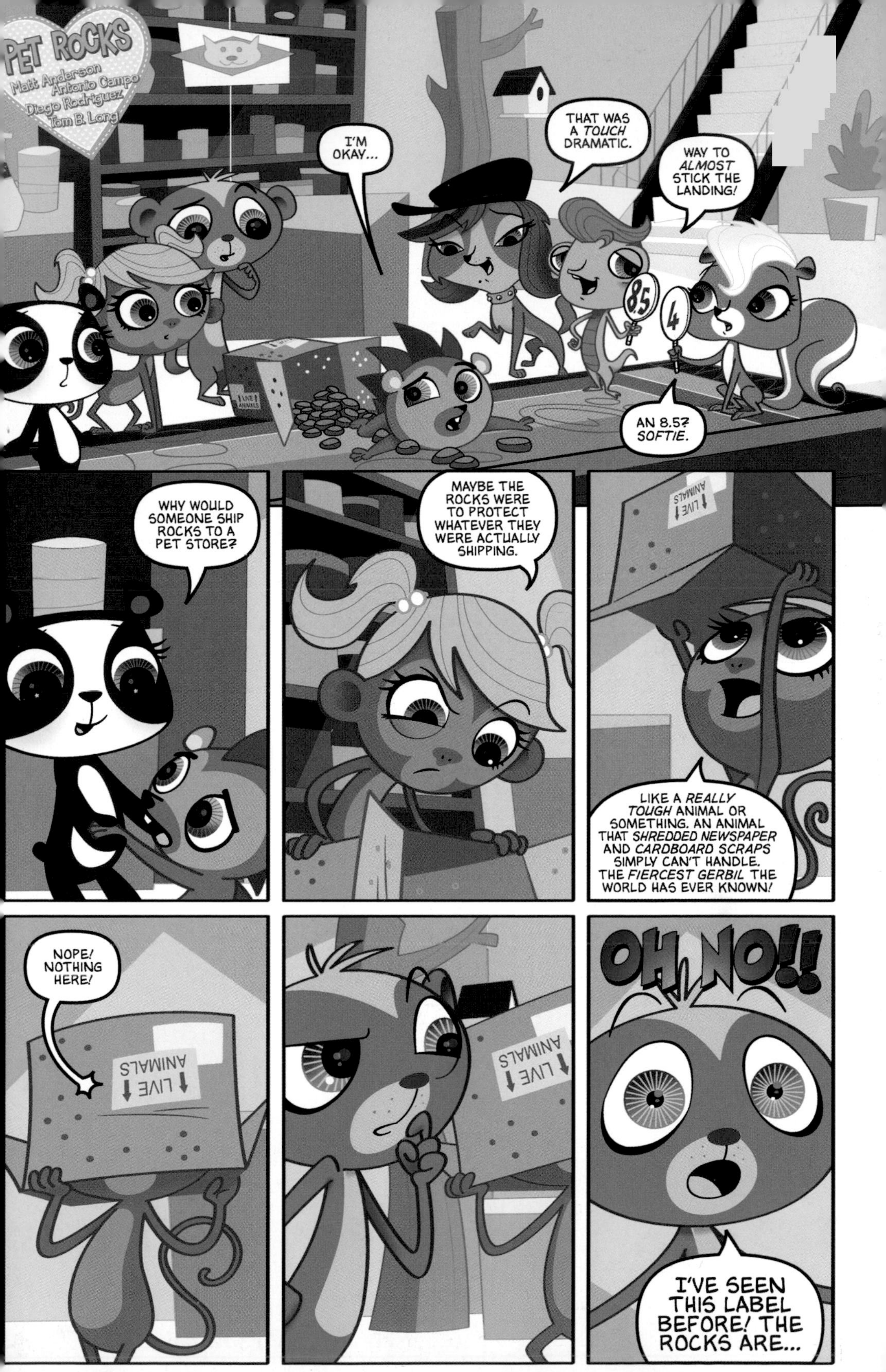
PET ROCKS
Matt Anderson
Antonio Campo
Diego Rodriguez
Tom B. Long
I'M OKAY...
THAT WAS A *TOUCH* DRAMATIC.
WAY TO *ALMOST* STICK THE LANDING!
8.5
4
LIVE ANIMALS
AN 8.5? SOFTIE.
WHY WOULD SOMEONE SHIP ROCKS TO A PET STORE?
MAYBE THE ROCKS WERE TO PROTECT WHATEVER THEY WERE ACTUALLY SHIPPING.
LIVE ANIMALS
LIKE A *REALLY TOUGH* ANIMAL OR SOMETHING. AN ANIMAL THAT *SHREDDED NEWSPAPER* AND *CARDBOARD SCRAPS* SIMPLY CAN'T HANDLE. THE *FIERCEST GERBIL* THE WORLD HAS EVER KNOWN!
NOPE! NOTHING HERE!
LIVE ANIMALS
LIVE ANIMALS
OH NO!!
I'VE SEEN THIS LABEL BEFORE! THE ROCKS ARE...

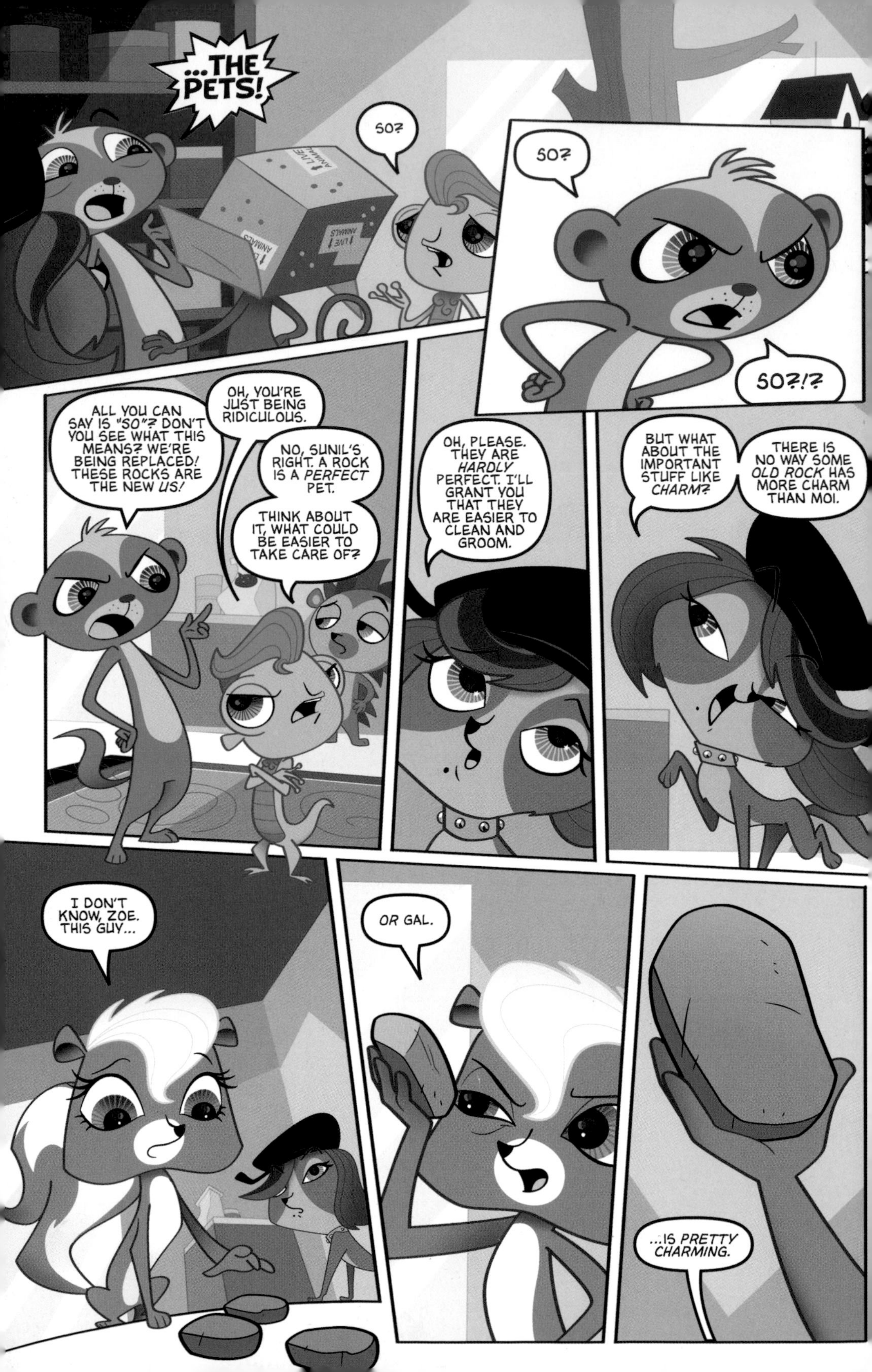
...THE PETS!
LIVE ANIMALS
SO?
SO?
SO?!?
ALL YOU CAN SAY IS "SO"? DON'T YOU SEE WHAT THIS MEANS? WE'RE BEING REPLACED! THESE ROCKS ARE THE NEW US!
OH, YOU'RE JUST BEING RIDICULOUS.
NO, SUNIL'S RIGHT. A ROCK IS A PERFECT PET.
THINK ABOUT IT, WHAT COULD BE EASIER TO TAKE CARE OF?
OH, PLEASE. THEY ARE HARDLY PERFECT. I'LL GRANT YOU THAT THEY ARE EASIER TO CLEAN AND GROOM.
BUT WHAT ABOUT THE IMPORTANT STUFF LIKE CHARM?
THERE IS NO WAY SOME OLD ROCK HAS MORE CHARM THAN MOI.
I DON'T KNOW, ZOE. THIS GUY...
OR GAL.
...IS PRETTY CHARMING.

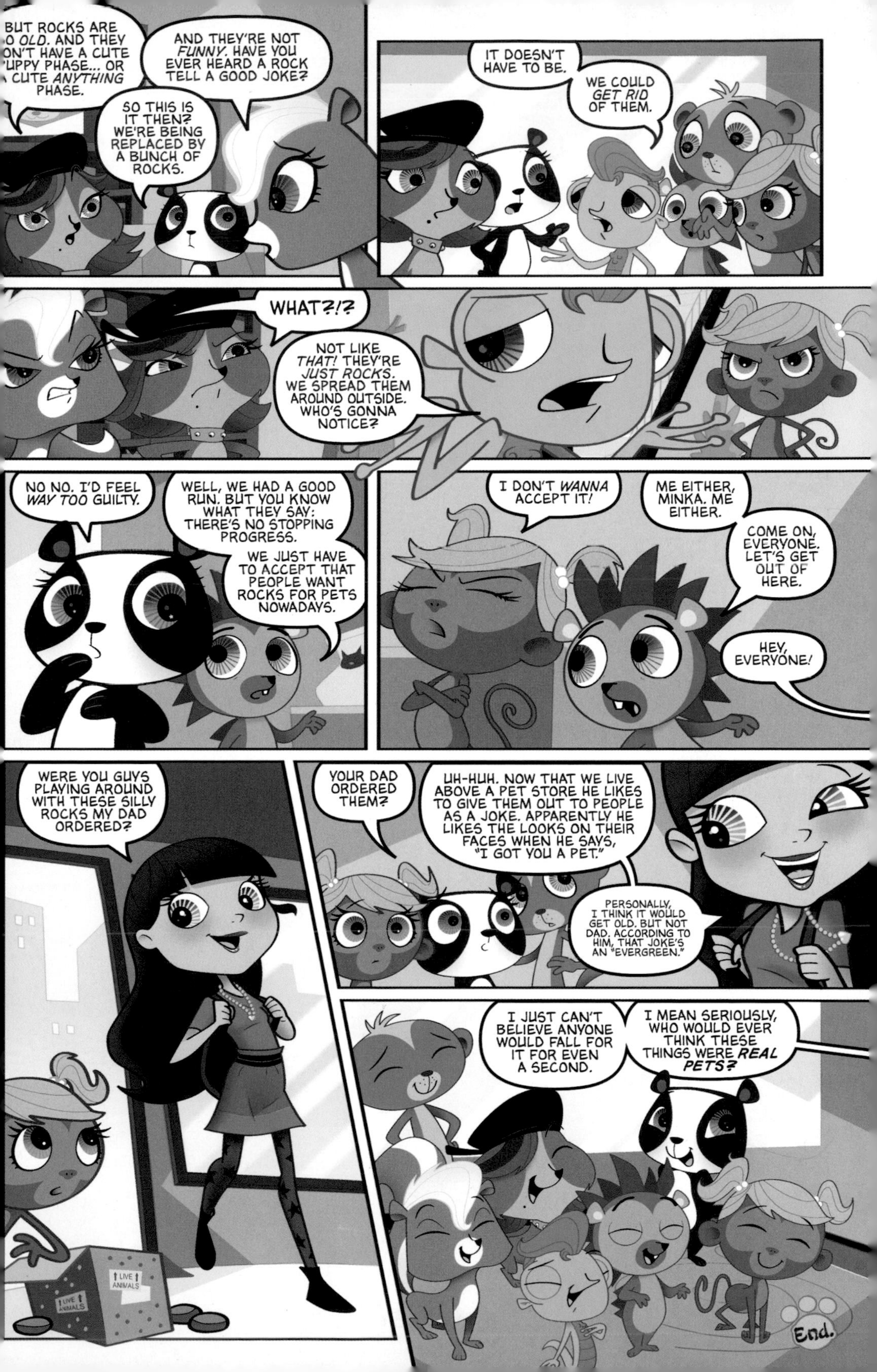

BUT ROCKS ARE SO OLD. AND THEY DON'T HAVE A CUTE PUPPY PHASE... OR A CUTE ANYTHING PHASE.
AND THEY'RE NOT FUNNY. HAVE YOU EVER HEARD A ROCK TELL A GOOD JOKE?
SO THIS IS IT THEN? WE'RE BEING REPLACED BY A BUNCH OF ROCKS.
IT DOESN'T HAVE TO BE.
WE COULD GET RID OF THEM.
WHAT?!?
NOT LIKE THAT! THEY'RE JUST ROCKS. WE SPREAD THEM AROUND OUTSIDE. WHO'S GONNA NOTICE?
NO NO. I'D FEEL WAY TOO GUILTY.
WELL, WE HAD A GOOD RUN. BUT YOU KNOW WHAT THEY SAY: THERE'S NO STOPPING PROGRESS.
WE JUST HAVE TO ACCEPT THAT PEOPLE WANT ROCKS FOR PETS NOWADAYS.
I DON'T WANNA ACCEPT IT!
ME EITHER, MINKA. ME EITHER.
COME ON, EVERYONE. LET'S GET OUT OF HERE.
HEY, EVERYONE!
WERE YOU GUYS PLAYING AROUND WITH THESE SILLY ROCKS MY DAD ORDERED?
LIVE ANIMALS
LIVE ANIMALS
YOUR DAD ORDERED THEM?
UH-HUH. NOW THAT WE LIVE ABOVE A PET STORE HE LIKES TO GIVE THEM OUT TO PEOPLE AS A JOKE. APPARENTLY HE LIKES THE LOOKS ON THEIR FACES WHEN HE SAYS, "I GOT YOU A PET."
PERSONALLY, I THINK IT WOULD GET OLD. BUT NOT DAD. ACCORDING TO HIM, THAT JOKE'S AN "EVERGREEN."
I JUST CAN'T BELIEVE ANYONE WOULD FALL FOR IT FOR EVEN A SECOND.
I MEAN SERIOUSLY, WHO WOULD EVER THINK THESE THINGS WERE REAL PETS?
End.

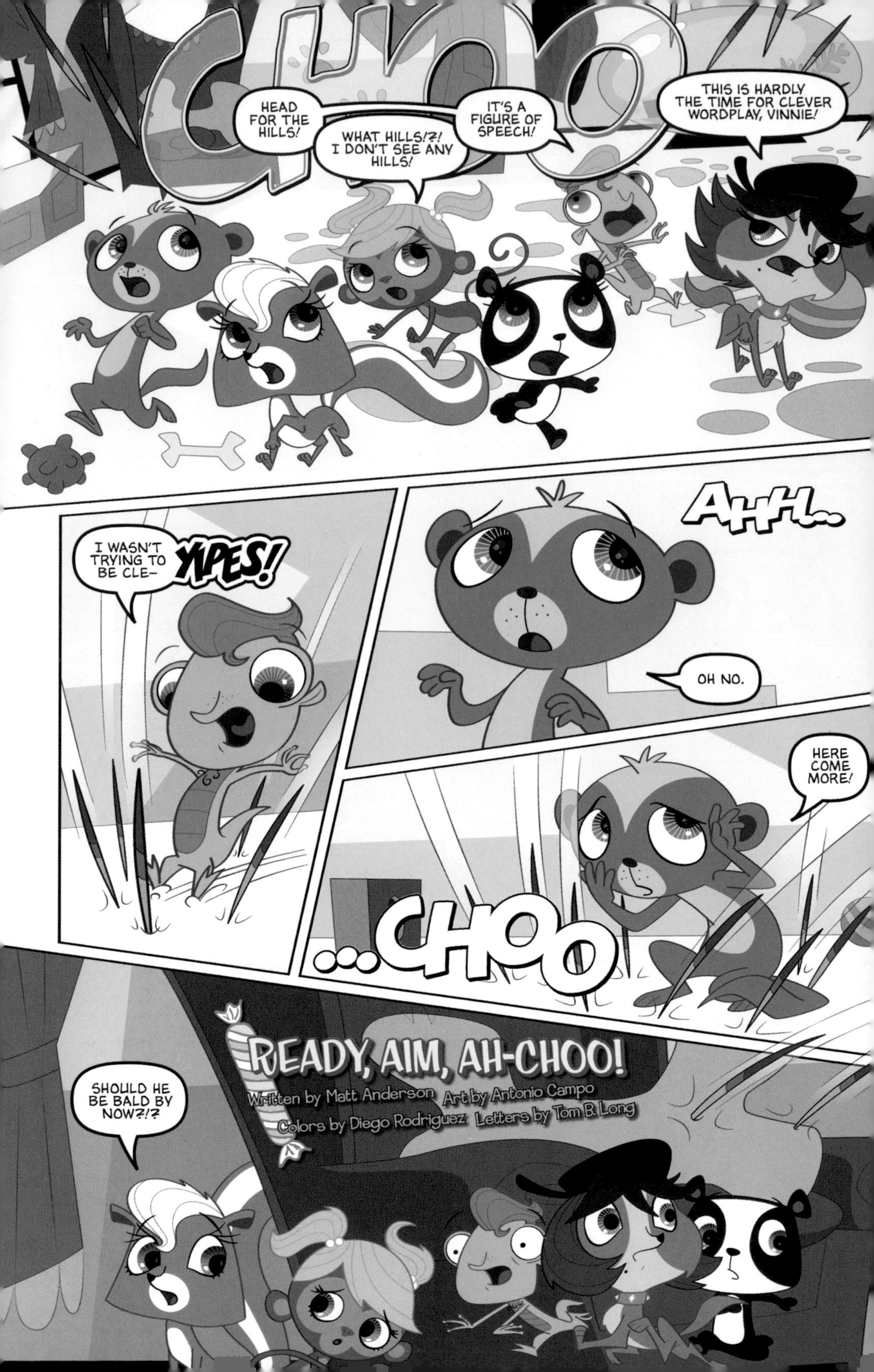
CHOO
HEAD FOR THE HILLS!
WHAT HILLS!?! I DON'T SEE ANY HILLS!
IT'S A FIGURE OF SPEECH!
THIS IS HARDLY THE TIME FOR CLEVER WORDPLAY, VINNIE!
I WASN'T TRYING TO BE CLE–
YIPES!
AHH..
OH NO.
HERE COME MORE!
...CHOO
READY, AIM, AH-CHOO!
Written by Matt Anderson Art by Antonio Campo
Colors by Diego Rodriguez Letters by Tom B. Long
SHOULD HE BE BALD BY NOW?!?

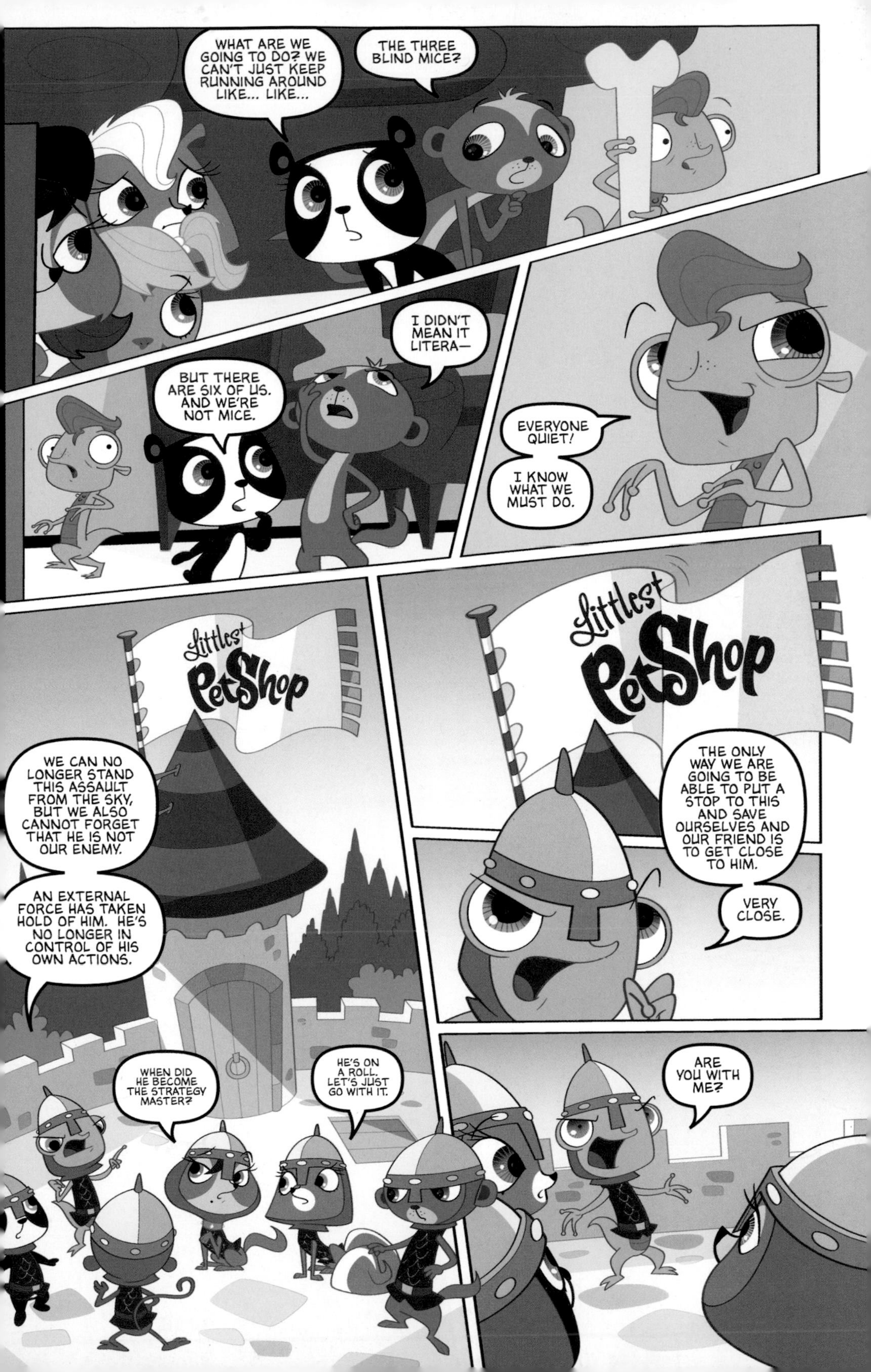
WHAT ARE WE GOING TO DO? WE CAN'T JUST KEEP RUNNING AROUND LIKE... LIKE...
THE THREE BLIND MICE?
BUT THERE ARE SIX OF US. AND WE'RE NOT MICE.
I DIDN'T MEAN IT LITERA—
EVERYONE QUIET!
I KNOW WHAT WE MUST DO.
Littlest PetShop
WE CAN NO LONGER STAND THIS ASSAULT FROM THE SKY, BUT WE ALSO CANNOT FORGET THAT HE IS NOT OUR ENEMY.
AN EXTERNAL FORCE HAS TAKEN HOLD OF HIM. HE'S NO LONGER IN CONTROL OF HIS OWN ACTIONS.
Littlest PetShop
THE ONLY WAY WE ARE GOING TO BE ABLE TO PUT A STOP TO THIS AND SAVE OURSELVES AND OUR FRIEND IS TO GET CLOSE TO HIM.
VERY CLOSE.
WHEN DID HE BECOME THE STRATEGY MASTER?
HE'S ON A ROLL. LET'S JUST GO WITH IT.
ARE YOU WITH ME?

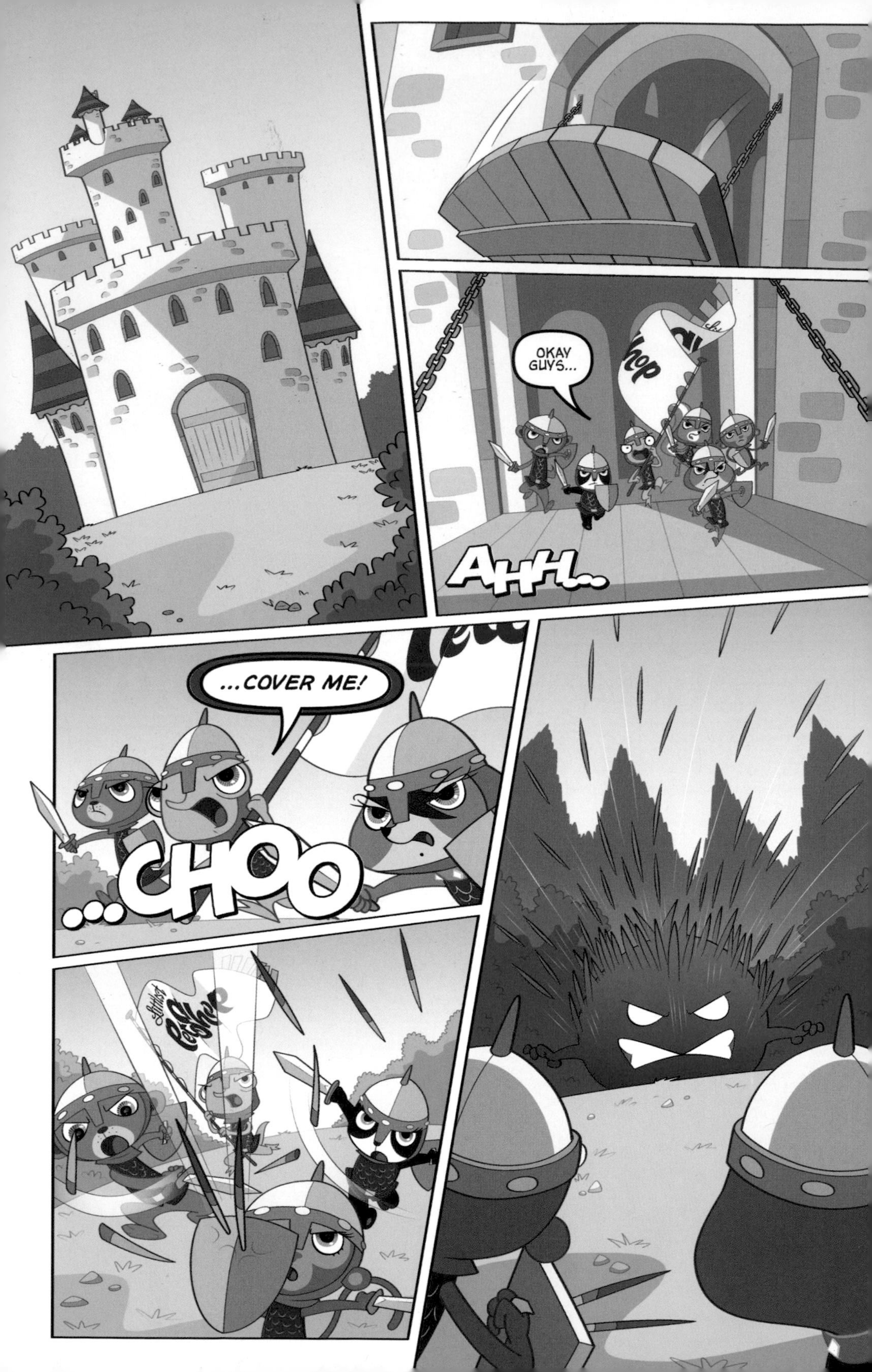
OKAY GUYS...
AHH...
...COVER ME!
...CHOO

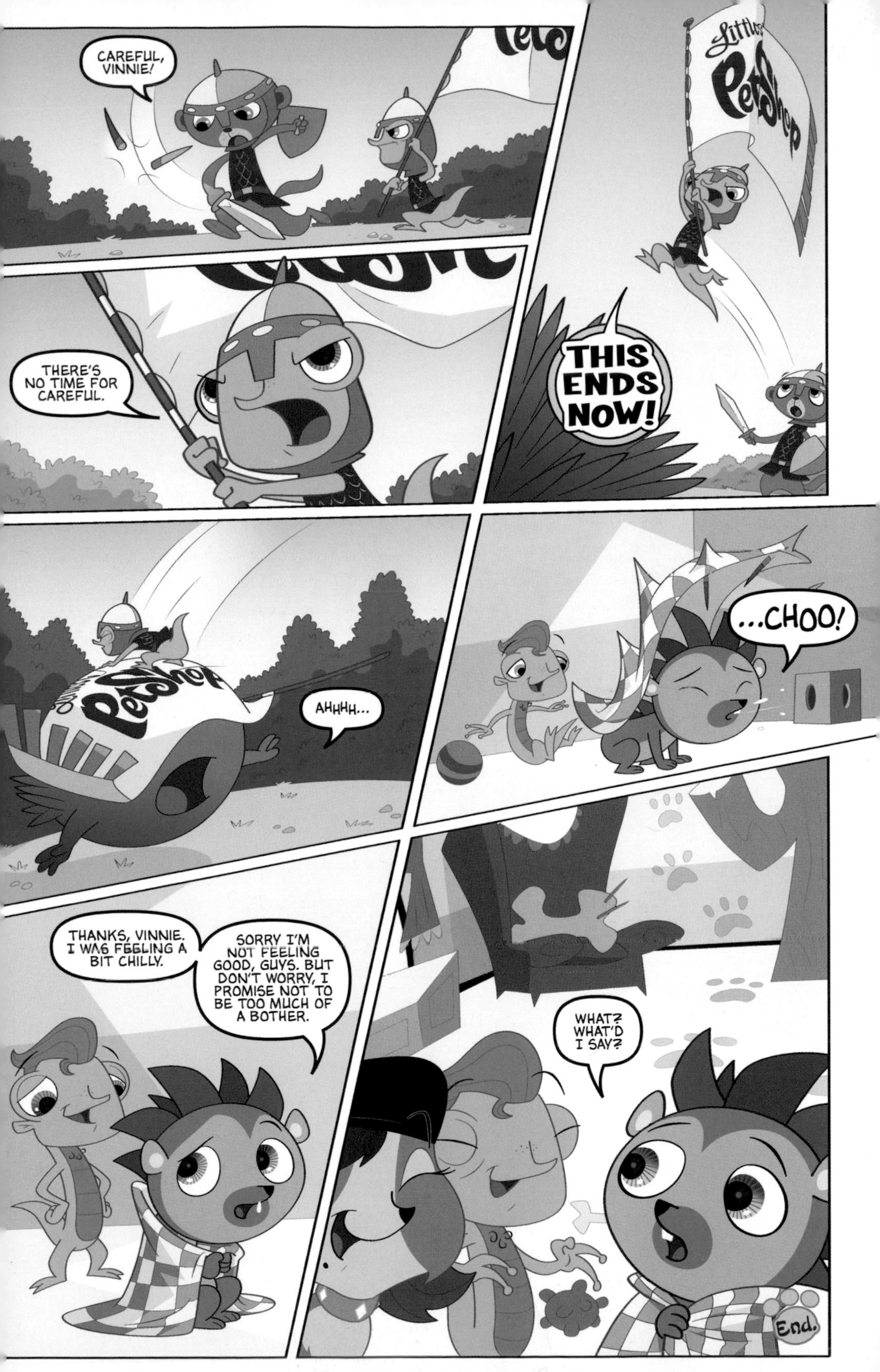
CAREFUL, VINNIE!
THERE'S NO TIME FOR CAREFUL.
Littlest Pet Shop
THIS ENDS NOW!
Pet Shop
AHHHH...
...CHOO!
THANKS, VINNIE. I WAS FEELING A BIT CHILLY.
SORRY I'M NOT FEELING GOOD, GUYS. BUT DON'T WORRY, I PROMISE NOT TO BE TOO MUCH OF A BOTHER.
WHAT? WHAT'D I SAY?
End.

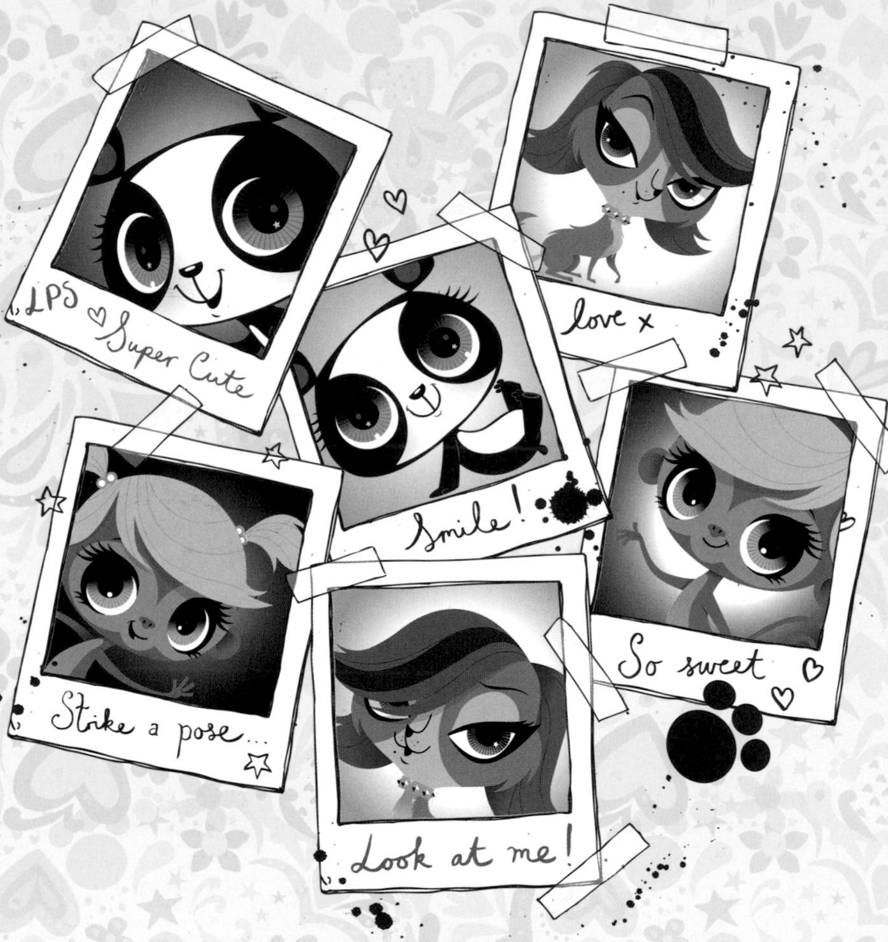
LPS ♡ Super Cute
love x
Smile!
Strike a pose...
So sweet
Look at me!

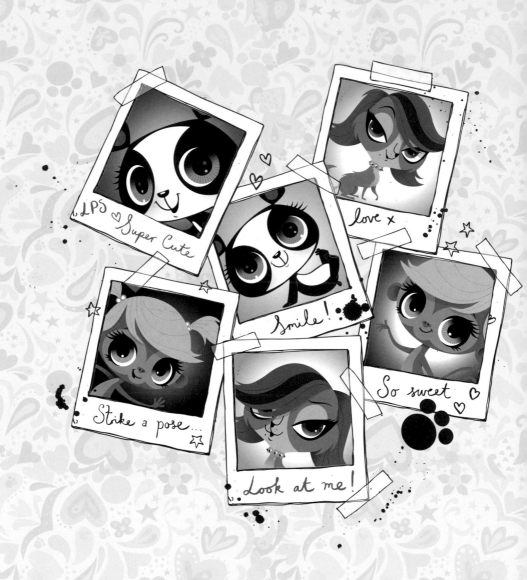